LOVE YOU *a little bit*

KASHA THOMPSON

Cover design by Qamber Designs
Print book interior design by Qamber Designs

Originally published as a print-on-demand edition and ebook in April 2025.

Honey Blossom Press
www.honeyblossompress.com
@honeyblossompress

ISBNs: 9781967565085 (trade paperback), 9781967565092 (ebook)
Printed in the United States of America

HONEY BLOSSOM PRESS

BLACK LOVE NOV·EL

/blak/ /ləv/ /nävə'

noun

1. a novel, with Black main characters that examines the complexity of falling and staying in love.

2. a story centered around Black love with just the right amount of sweet, savory, and spice.

PLAYLIST

Do-Si-Don'tcha – Tanner Adell
My Home – Myles Smith
Hopeless – Kassi Ashton
Half of My Hometown – Kelsea Ballerini
I Hope You're Happy Now – Carly Pearce & Lee Brice
Wild as Her – Corey Kent
Giddy Up Gorgeous – Tanner Adell
Never Met Anyone Like You – Ella Langley & Hardy
All The Cool Girls – Hailey Whitters
Easy Pill – Carter Faith
FU-150 – Tanner Adell
Down For it – Wille Jones
He Gon' Be a Problem – Reyna Roberts
No One Needs to Know – Shania Twain
Let It Burn – Shaboozey
Bless Your Heart – Megan Moroney
The Woman in Me (Needs the Man In You) – Shania Twain
Cry Baby – Clean Bandit, Anne Marie & Tanner Adell
Chasing After You – Ryan Hurd & Maren Morris
Levii's Jeans – Beyonce & Post Malone
I Don't Wanna Dance – Kassi Ashton
Background Music – Maren Morris
Buckle Bunny – Tanner Adell
Love You a Little Bit – Tanner Adell

I've been a rolling stone for far too long.
But no matter how far I traveled,
your heart called me home.

Memories of times we shared, the years
that passed, but I still care.
I wonder if you do … think of me like
I think of you.

TIME TREK – WHISKEY WILD

For anyone who ever thought they outgrew their hometown,
only to find love blooming right where they started.

LOVE YOU A LITTLE BIT
FAMILY TREE

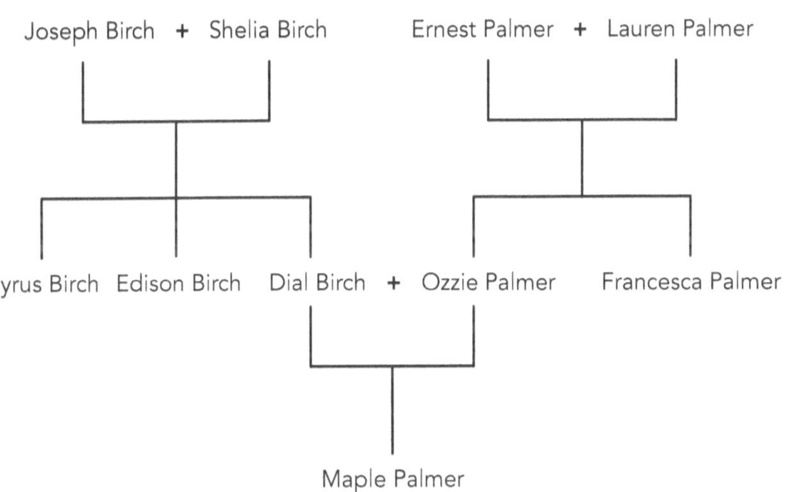

BIRCH FAMILY
PALMER FAMILY
Joseph Birch + Shelia Birch
Ernest Palmer + Lauren Palmer
Cyrus Birch   Edison Birch   Dial Birch + Ozzie Palmer   Francesca Palmer
Maple Palmer

Palmer Ranch
Paper Petals
Hume Post Office
Morton's Hardware Store
The Tipsy Owl
The Crooked Dog

Drunken Zombie
Hot Doodle Dawgs
WELCOME TO HUME, TN
Edison's Farmhouse
Figs & Twine
Mayor Birch's Office
Metcalf Park
Sweet But Sinful
The Gas Guzzle

1

Fancy

I SWUNG MY HIPS IN time with Darla Rooney, the other half of Whiskey Wild. The music break in our popular up-tempo song "Shit Kickin' Boots" always sent the fans wild. Especially when we danced and played our guitars in unison. After the break, we'd sing in melodic harmony about hitting the dusty streets and carousing with our friends on a summer's night.

I'd known Darla since we were in cloth diapers. We'd been best friends forever and every memory I had included Darla by my side. She and I'd been preparing for sold out festivals like the Heritage Fest for years. Pretending the field behind my house was our stage, we'd shake our butts and kick our heels like we'd seen the superstars we idolize on television do. By high school we were no longer singing for fun in the back of my house. We attended farmers' markets and fairs performing on the makeshift stages to crowds that were more interested in who was going to win the chili cook off and not our puppy dog love songs.

But you've heard that saying stay ready, so you don't have to get ready. That was Whiskey Wild's motto. So when we were approached by a music industry cat at one of those fairs where the main event was a pie-eating contest, we were more than prepared.

Now almost ten years later, we were the main event at the Heritage Music Festival in the California desert. Whiskey Wild had come a long way from singing to the horses in my family's stable. As the song faded, we both rolled our bodies like snakes to the music. I kicked up a laugh, it never got old being on stage with my bestie. We fed off one another's energy and it was always a good time with my sister from another mister at my side.

"How y'all doing out there?" I asked the crowd. They responded with rowdy cheers.

"We sure like partying with you all," Darla said. "Don't we, Fancy?"

"Well, we've always been known as good time girls. A little liquor, loud music, and handsome men, and we just go wild." I winked playfully.

"Fancy, shh, that's supposed to be a secret."

"Come on Darla, I suspect we have quite a few good time girls in the audience." There was a smattering of hoots. Jerking my shoulders, I continued, "I don't know, maybe I'm wrong. Where's my good time girls at?" Cheers exploded from the crowd and then the beat dropped to our first ever hit, "Good Time Girls."

Darla flashed me a curled smile before she started the first verse. I accompanied her on the guitar, tapping my foot to the powerful beat. After her verse, I chimed in singing the second verse alone, my voice raspy and deep. At the chorus, Darla's light and ethereal voice kicked in. The combination of our vocal tones brought the signature Whiskey Wild brand to life.

After our set we waved goodbye to hoots and hollers from the delighted crowd. "That was amazing," I said, performing an excited little two-step. Being on stage playing our songs to sold-out crowds was the stuff of dreams for so long and even though we were currently living those dreams, I still had difficulty processing it all.

"Another great show," my assistant, Moniece said.

I scanned the space backstage, searching for Chap. Dylan Chapman was our manager and my boyfriend. I never grew tired of saying those words. Chap was movie-star fine, with sandy blond hair and blue eyes I often got lost in. He also came from a long line of country royalty. The Chapman family had been selling out stadiums and collecting Grammy's and Country Music Awards since before I was born.

"Are you looking for Chap?" Moniece asked in response to my darting eyes.

"Yes." My mouth flashed a bashful smile. I was hooked and everyone knew it. But Chap's personality was just as dreamy as he was.

"He was headed to the bus the last time we spoke," Moniece said.

"Thanks."

"I'll come with you. I have to pee," Darla said.

"There's a porta potty right over there." Moniece pointed.

"Eww, no. I don't use communal toilets." Darla hooked her arm through mine, and we were off.

My cowboy boots were firmly planted on the ground, but having people come up to you requesting an autograph like my signature held life changing properties, was thrilling. Growing up, I envisioned the stage, bright lights, and singing songs penned by me and my best friend. But it was these moments that meant the most; a young woman in a Whiskey Wild shirt, cut-off shorts, and pink cowboy boots telling me how our music saved her life by inspiring her to take the first step toward a new adventure. I can't tell you how many fans mentioned on social media our song "Change of Scenery," about leaving the comfort and security of all you knew and picking up stakes for new horizons, was the push they needed to move to a different city or end a toxic relationship.

Most of the time our music made you want to kick up your heels, but our ballads evoked unexpected emotions. The power of a well-written song could be a catalyst, and we tapped into music that listeners connected with. Maybe because they felt the honesty of childhood friends living our best lives and making our own rules. It also didn't hurt that we were game changers. Two Black women from the south paving our own lane in this industry after discovering most of the roads that lead to Nashville were gated and our access summarily denied.

After signing several autographs and posing for pictures, we continued over the water parched grass. The first time we performed at Heritage a few years ago, Whiskey Wild was an opening act. I remember almost dying of heat stroke as the sun glared down on us. Luckily, we had misters. I don't know how our spattering of fans managed. But today we were one of the main acts. Attendees didn't stumble onto us performing while making their way to better known acts set. Nope, now crowds formed hours before our showtime to get the best possible spot.

"Today has kind of been a movie," I trilled out.

"Yep, we're a long way from Hume, Tennessee. Did you ever think we'd be here?"

"Yes, I always knew we'd be performing in front of screaming crowds one day."

"Liar."

"I swear. I'm not one to brag. But we're talented as hell and we worked hard. We deserve everything we have coming our way. Awards, sold out arenas—"

"Sexy groupies." Darla giggled.

"I'll leave the groupies to you. I already have all I can handle with Chap."

"You're such a cliché," she teased.

"What do you mean by that?"

"The pretty country singer who falls in love with her manager. It's a tale as old as time."

"You know why it's such a popular tale, because it's tried and true."

"You're a hopeless romantic."

I frowned her words away. Truthfully, falling for Chap was the most uncharacteristic thing I'd ever done. Since high school I kept potential love interest at bay because I wasn't going to let my heart get me stuck in Hume Tennessee, a two-stoplight town with a Gas Guzzle Convenient Store and a Farm Basket chicken and ice cream spot. I was destined for bigger things. My future did not include carrying a baby on my hip while I waited for my husband to purchase horse feed.

But Chap wasn't from a small town. He was from the city, and he was showing me things I'd only seen in the magazines I flipped through at Welborn's Grocery Mart while shopping with my momma. Dining at fancy restaurants and hanging out with other celebrities as they trekked from one hot party to the other. You know that feature in *Us Weekly* called "Celebs Are Just Like Us"? I can guarantee you they are not. Most spent insane amounts of money and didn't bat an eye at the thought of chartering a private jet just so they could go swimming in the crystal blue waters of the Seychelles.

Chap would often have to remind me I was a star and I needed to stop with the small-town girl attitude and lean all the way into my big boss energy. So I treated myself to an Aston Martin that often sat idle in the garage of my high-rise, luxury condo because we were always on the road. But when I was in Los Angeles, I would hit the freeway in my convertible roadster.

This festival was packed, Heritage was the biggest country music festival of the year. Every power player in the country music industry was in attendance or performing on stage. And it was a diverse gathering of acts with legacy artists like Rich Nickles, the country group Desdemona and new artists such as Josie Rae and Wyatt Harlow. Heritage was the festival any young country artist would offer up their left arm to attend. After our first appearance, our records sales saw a steady increase and doors we were once told were closed to us started to open. Late night television appearances, big budget videos, and features with country heavy weights.

"Just think in a few weeks we'll start the final leg of our tour and then after that start working on the fourth album." Our future was so bright it made my head spin.

"I still think we should call it Pitching a Fit," Darla said.

"You know how this goes. We write the songs then we name the album."

"Well can you write a song called Pitching a Fit so we can name the album after it?"

"I'll see what I can do." I was the primary songwriter of the group. Darla mostly provided support and catchy ad-libs. Our next album needed to capture our growth as women and artist. My hope was to delve deeper into love and the complexities loving someone entailed. The good sign of an artist was being able to evolve from one project to the next. No one wanted four projects that all felt homogenized. This fourth album should be grown, sexy, and vulnerable.

We'd learned a whole lot in these past few years and there was an interesting story to be told. Plus, the fans and music journalists were all hoping for something big. When we were new there were no expectations, we could do whatever we wanted. I secretly missed that time because we could just riff and take risks. Now those big swings had to be planned and run by everyone at the record label before it was green lit, which stifled the creative process.

It took us several minutes to cross the patchy grass to get to the parking lot reserved for talent. When we finally rounded the corner of the line of trailers and buses that included ours, I was hot and sticky. Even at night the desert temperatures, which had been in the hundreds most of the day, cooled a bit at sunset, but not by much. The tour bus was emblazoned with our faces and group name in cursive. I told Chap I thought it was over the top, but he insisted that's what country music was all about, bluster and big dick energy.

Upon entering the trailer, the cold air chilled my sweaty skin. I released a relieved sigh. Darla pushed past me on her way to the half bathroom. Grabbing a soda pop from the fridge, I headed through the bus toward the back in search of Chap. At the bedroom door, I could make out the faint sound of moans and giggling. You know the moment in the movies when the character's life is about to change irrevocably? I was seconds from my "Oh Shit" moment. The voice in the back of my head told me to run. To get as far away from the bus as my feet could carry me.

I'd never been one to follow instructions. I reached out a shaky arm and when I opened the door, my world came tumbling down. You're probably far smarter than me and can guess Chap was not alone in that room. He was butt-ass naked and balls deep into some pussy that was not attached to me. They didn't even notice the door was open. Chap was just thrusting his pale ass off and telling this woman how good she felt. Words until this moment I'd only heard him utter in my ear.

My stomach turned. I opened my mouth to speak but no words came out.

Darla came up behind me and broke the silence. "What the fuck?"

Chap turned and all the blood drained from his face. The woman underneath him screamed at the presence of an audience. Jumping up, my boyfriend's still erect penis bobbed up and down.

Chap lifted his arms in an attempt to tamp down what I'm sure he suspected was my rising rage. "Fancy, baby. This is not what it looks like."

"It looks like you're fucking around." Darla's expression was one of anger.

Chap climbed into his jeans. "Fancy, let me explain. She came on to me."

So now he thought I was naïve and a bitch he could sneak on? I should have commenced to whooping his ass within an inch of his life. But I was never my best when caught off guard. If I'd had a warning, I would've been prepared to eviscerate him with my words while raining down closed-fist punches that would leave lasting bruises. When confronted with the unexpected, I did the only thing that would allow me to save face and not give Chap and his side chick the satisfaction of witnessing me break down. My feet were already retreating, tears threatening to stream down my face. This fucking bastard. Why do men make you fall in love with them only to do some shit like this?

Chap pursued me hard. I was resistant to mix business with pleasure, but he was charming and handsome and as our manager he was an integral part of making our dreams come true. "If I was your man, I'd let you know every day what you meant to me." His words when he was courting me. Shit sounded good then ... real good. When I got to the bus door, I tossed a glance over my shoulder and witnessed Darla slapping Chap and screaming, "How could you do this?"

He didn't lie. Today at eleven fifty-seven on a Saturday night, Chap showed me I meant nothing to him.

2
Edison

"GUESS WHO I RAN INTO today at the Gas Guzzle?" Dial, my sister said.

This was a dumb question. Living in a small town, if you frequented the town square, you would run into everybody. Your kindergarten teacher, Ms. Noone, the dude you used to buy weed from, or that one person who you didn't click with and was now your unspoken archnemesis. For me his name was Elrod and the sight of him made my trigger finger twitch.

"Who?" I said, humoring my sister.

"Willa."

I rolled my eyes. Maybe I had two archnemeses. Willa Barlowe was the woman I slept with when I needed to forget. Forget about work or my self-imposed loneliness. In between her thighs, I didn't obsess over what ifs or play back conversations as far back as high school. It was obvious she wanted more, but I wasn't looking to build new memories with her. I was hoping to forget old ones.

I sliced open a bag of soil. "Oh yeah."

"She asked after you." I changed out the soil on one of our potted plants which had outgrown its current home. "She's a nice girl." Coming from my sister, this was high praise. Dial Birch didn't like anyone and if that person was dating one of her brothers, she liked them even less. She probably favored Willa for the same reasons I did, she was affable and a true caregiver. If I mentioned having the sniffles, Willa would show up to my door with homemade minestrone soup. When she went to the Shop and Pick, before coming to my house to mess around, she'd purchase two cans of Arizona Iced Tea and a few beef sticks because they were my favorite.

Dial continued, "You should spend a little less time with your hands in the dirt and more time using those digits to play the piccolo." She smirked.

I cringed. "Could you not? I don't even want to guess what piccolo is code for."

"Her pussy, Edison. I'm strongly suggesting you get laid."

"Maybe you should take some of your own advice and stop worrying about me."

Dial was one year older, and she thought that made her the boss over the nursery, the family, and me. I loved my sister dearly, but she was forward and a bully who acted as if she knew everything about everything. She was also better than me at almost every activity … shooting, drinking, and line dancing. Now mind you, I was good at all three, but next to my sister I couldn't compete.

"Don't worry about my piccolo and who's playing it."

"I have the sneaking suspicion it's a one-woman band," I teased.

Dial guffawed, tossing the rag in her back pocket at me, connecting with my face. "You heading to the house after this?"

"We were summoned, so yes I'll be there."

"What do you think that's all about? The last time Daddy called a family meeting he told us granddaddy had gone on to be with the Lord."

"I checked on Gram this morning. She is alive and ornery so you can rest assured it ain't that."

"That woman ain't never gonna die. Neither God nor the devil have the capacity to deal with her."

Our parents requested our presence at dinner tonight. We had family dinners every Sunday, so why they felt the need to expressly invite us was beyond me. When Pops texted me he was short on details, just said we'd talk at dinner tonight. Not knowing made my head spin tall tales. *Had Momma's cancer returned? Was Pops's health failing?* My parents were in their sixties, relatively fit and in overall good health, but people my age lost their parents all the time. My buddy Keni just lost his father two weeks ago. The man just collapsed at work. His heart gave out.

"What do you want to bet Cyrus is a no show?" I asked. Cyrus was the oldest of the Birch siblings.

"He better or I'll rip him a new one."

"I can see it now, he'll call in claiming he couldn't get away from the office."

"He acts like he's the mayor of New York and not Hume. There isn't any crisis that requires him to stay late at the office on a Sunday."

"What about that time Mr. Croft's steer got loose and was meandering down main street?"

"Key word, meandering. That was the laziest steer I ever did see. Just decided to go for a leisurely walk on a Tuesday afternoon."

"That steer broke Mrs. Vicks' flowerpot," I joked. Fortunately, that pot and a pile of shit down main street were the only casualties.

"Ugh, don't remind me. I had to listen to her harrowing tale of coming face to face with a cow and living while trying to help her pick out a new pot."

"You have a heart of gold."

"She was a customer. If it wasn't for that I would have told her to give it a rest. I'm going to call Cy and remind him his presence is required. What if mom and dad finally admit he was dropped off at their doorstep by break dancing nomads because he couldn't catch the beat?"

"That's very specific."

"Have you seen him dance?"

"Fair." For a Black man from the south, Cyrus had no rhythm, and the funny thing was he swore he was dancing on the ones and twos when it was hilariously obvious he was moving his body to the threes and fours. "Like Negro, we can see you."

"Dancing like Frankenstein, just stomping and clapping offbeat. You can't convince me he isn't adopted."

"Maybe that's why he's always a no show. Our presence reminds him that he is not like us."

Dial sang off key, "One of these things is not like the other. One of these things is not the same."

I hoisted my arm in the air pretending to be itching to answer. "Who is Cyrus Birch for one thousand, Alex."

We shared a much-needed laugh. "I'm heading up to the office. Holler at me before you leave," Dial said.

I watered the repotted plant and washed the empty ceramic pot clean. After college, I returned home and joined the family business. Figs and Twine was started by my great, great-grandfather whom I was named after. It had been handed down from one Birch generation to the next. A family business in every sense of the word.

Everyone who worked here was related or so damn close there was no distinction.

Figs and Twine was situated on twenty acres of land. We didn't start out that big but as neighboring businesses went under, we purchased the land and expanded. At one point this place was a small storefront with a plot of land out back. With sweat equity, put in by my ancestors, Figs and Twine was now the first and only stop when in need of flowers, plants, trees, or shrubbery.

We serviced all of Hume and most of the neighboring towns. As a kid I ran down the aisles of the store, mostly getting in the way. By middle school I was helping customers find stock and hauling items to cars. In high school I wasn't allowed to linger around campus because I had to get to the shop and stock shelves and water plants, while Dial shadowed my mom learning to order inventory, and Cy was being taught about budgeting and payroll from our dad.

It was clear our parents intended to pass the family business to us, although they never expressly said it. Cyrus went off to college and when he returned he was no longer interested in the twenty-four-hour, seven days a week commitment running a nursery required. But Dial and I were up for the challenge, working alongside our parents like the Birches before us.

I knocked on the open office door where Dial was now holed up. "I'm going to head home and change. Are you bringing Maple?"

"You know mom would kill me if I didn't." Maple was my niece and our mother's pride and joy. The way my mother doted over Maple made me wonder if she'd been body snatched while no one was looking. Growing up our mother was no nonsense, which is where Dial probably gets her strong personality from. But now Maple got away with murder, and by murder I meant being allowed two servings of dessert or staying up way past her bedtime.

"Meet you at the farm."

"Don't be late."

"I'm never late, always right on time." I smiled before heading to my truck.

Pulling up to my childhood home, my shoulders instinctually relaxed. This place was filled with fond memories and a few sad ones everywhere I turned. My childhood was kind of idyllic, with swimming in the creek, catching tadpoles and fireflies, and barbecues. I loved an evening barbecue with the grill fired up, music playing, and laughter filling the air. While us kids ran in between adults on our way to get into trouble.

When it came to parents, I was luckier than most. Mom and Pops were patient teachers who guided Cyrus, Dial, and me while never pressuring us. They didn't force their expectations on us. Working at Figs and Twine was my choice and not some obligation I felt to the family and its history. Inside the farmhouse, which had been recently renovated, I found Dial and Maple with my mother mixing some specialty drink.

"Why can I always find you two near the alcohol?"

"Uncle Eddy," Maple screamed, jumping down from her stool. She wrapped her arms around me and I gave her a squeeze.

"If we weren't farmers, we would've been in the distillery business," my mother said.

"Birch Brewery has a nice ring to it." I played along.

"Momma you do know Edison is brewing something outback in that garage of his. He won't let me taste it though," Dial said.

"Because it's fermenting. When it's done I'll let you nip a taste." Beer making was one of my pastimes. When you lived in the boondocks you took up a lot of hobbies. I'd tried archery, model cars … the miniature kind, and poetry. Right now, I was working on becoming a brewmaster. All the extracurricular activities kept my mind and hands busy and my dick in my pants.

"I may have to make a trip to your place when you crack that barrel." My mom flashed her warm smile.

"Now what are you cracking open?" Cyrus entered the kitchen and the axis in the room shifted. My mother set down her mixing spoon and crossed the room to give him a hug.

"Nice of you to grace us with your presence," Dial said.

"I promised Momma I'd be here and my word is my bond."

"Well, that must only work with mom because I've been stood up by you more times than I can count," I said.

"Mothers and nieces take precedence over bratty little brothers." Cy kissed the top of Maple's head.

"How is city hall?" our mother asked.

Dial snorted. "It's hardly city hall. It's a store front with a few desks and plants." Our mayor didn't currently have a proper government building. The one that was erected years ago burned down right before Cyrus took office, making it a lost landmark.

"I'm working on fixing that. But it doesn't matter which building I'm in, the power is conveyed to the man, not a structure." Cy winked.

Dial snorted, "Did you wield that power to get yourself reserved parking at the Gas Guzzle?"

"No, Logan decided to do that all on his own."

"The perks of the office I guess." Dial poured a few drops of the mixed drink in the palm of her hand to taste.

Cy turned his attention back to our mother, but his next words were intended for Dial all the same. "I had drinks with Ozzie the other night and he wanted me to tell you hello."

Dial chucked the wooden spoon into the sink. Ozzie was her ex and Maple's father. The two were successfully co-parenting, but the bad blood ran deep between them. Truthfully, the beef was mostly one-sided. Ozzie was a lover and Dial was a fighter. How those two got along long enough to create Maple I'd never know.

"Can we eat now?" My father's booming voice reached the kitchen before he did.

"We were just waiting for you," my mother said, leading us to the wraparound porch out back.

Dinner consisted of steak, potatoes, and grilled veggies and it was a great break from my frozen dinners. I could cook, my mother saw to that, but preparing dinner for one was not a motivator. If I had a family or at the minimum a girlfriend, maybe I'd feel differently. So, for now it was mostly TV dinners and a cold beer. When Willa spent the night, I'd order out, but cooking for a booty call appointment was a strict no no. The last thing I wanted was for her to get any ideas. Or maybe I should say … any more ideas. Willa had designs on a future with me, but I'd made it clear that right now a relationship was not in the cards. All I could offer was my company and this dick.

"So what's the news and why did you soften us up with meat and sweet wine?" Classic Dial jumping right to the point. I loved that about her because she always said the things I was thinking but was never bratty enough to express.

"Well, your mother and I have been talking." My father reached for his wife's hand. "Your momma and I aren't getting any younger and well, this is a lot of property for just she and I."

"And we only have one grandchild," Mom chimed in, eyeing Cyrus and me.

"We've been thinking about selling the farm and maybe even moving to Gainsborough."

Dial's laughter pierced the air. "You can't be serious. This is our home."

"You three are grown. And Pops and I are interested in a change of scenery," my mother said.

"We ain't too grown for our homestead," I protested.

"I'm pregnant," Dial blurted out.

It was my mother's turn to laugh loudly. "You're not."

"You don't know that."

"I'm your mother. I would probably know before you did."

"I could be," Dial insisted.

"No, you couldn't." I brushed her words aside. In the relationship department Dial was worse off than me.

"When are you thinking about doing all this?" Cyrus asked.

"We have some repairs we need to perform around the property but we're thinking this Christmas will be our last here."

"Christmas? That's six months away. Hardly enough time for a change like that," Cy said.

"What about Figs and Twine?" I asked.

"You and your sister are more than capable of running that place on your own."

Dial leaned forward. "Wait … you'd let us do that?"

Sure, Dial and I discussed our ideas on ways to improve the nursery but those conversations always implied implementing the changes years from now when the parental units retired. The thought that we could be months away from being in charge was a bit terrifying for me at least, but I could already see the gears beginning to turn in my sister's head.

Cyrus scrubbed his face with his hand. "Is this something that's still up for debate or is it settled?"

"It's pretty well settled," My father said with a tone of finality that matched his words.

"What about birthdays and holidays? You'll miss all the important stuff." Maple chimed in which shocked me because I thought she was too focused on her cake and ice cream to register the grownups' conversation.

"That's what they have cars and airplanes for sweetheart." My mother reassured her.

"Can I fly to come see you?" Maple asked.

"You can come visit us anytime you want."

"Get your frequent-flier miles up," Cyrus joked.

And just like that my family pivoted to another topic. My father was recounting his run in with my former high school teacher and his new girlfriend who was a student just two years prior. How everyone could pretend like our parents didn't just drop a bomb at the dinner table was beyond me. My chest tightened and I took several deep breaths, which luckily went unnoticed, to stop myself from screaming. I wasn't the best when it came to change. And my parents leaving Hume was a big fucking change. Children were supposed to go off and spread their wings, not parents. Parents were expected to remain a support system and a refuge you could return to when you needed to lick your wounds after the world gave you a swift kick in the nuts.

After the announcement, I wasn't in the mood for jokes and trips down memory lane. I quickly said my goodbyes and headed for the door. Before I could make it to my truck, Cyrus was close on my heels.

"You good?"

Was that a trick question? "No, I'm not."

"Listen I'm just as surprised as you are, but maybe this will be best for everyone."

"What do you care? You hardly see Mom and Dad? And when was the last time you made it to Sunday family dinner?"

"I've been busy."

"Bullshit, you've been selfish." Like most little brothers, I'd looked up to Cyrus growing up. Everyone loved Cy. He was the poster boy for the All-American son. Cy was football captain; I played in the band. Cy was working on the shops books, adding ones and carrying the twos, while I was hauling bags of fertilizer. Try as I might, I couldn't compete with him. Every accomplishment I garnered was measured against achievements Cyrus already received. I was constantly in his shadow, and then there was Dial who was so confident and self-assured. Maybe because she was a girl she didn't feel the pressure to measure up to Cy, but I did. It's hard being a copy and paste son when the original is so impressive.

As an adult he was still the golden child and seeing him was a rarity, which made my parents fawn over him when he did the bare minimum like show up or return a call. For me family was the most important thing a man could possess. Land and money were great, but family was true wealth. It might sound cliché but in the end it will be family gathered at your bedside, not piles of cash. Cy often claimed my recollection of the past was more imagined than facts. When I'd call him out on it, he'd change the subject. Shit, maybe he *was* adopted.

"Tell me how you really feel."

"Okay I will. This move doesn't affect you because you've always been a loner."

"Better a loner than a momma's boy."

"Are you two fighting over who gets the antique serving spoons already?" Dial asked from behind us.

"No because we all know Mom is gifting those to me," I said with a straight face.

"You don't even cook," Cyrus said.

"I would if I had those engraved serving spoons."

Dial placed her hands on both Cyrus and my shoulders. "We need to stick together now more than ever. Mom and Dad's departure—"

I raised up a silencing hand. "Don't call it that. It makes it sound like they're dead."

"With this move we'll need to pool our resources and support each other. That means answering calls." Dial's eyes slammed into Cyrus before landing on me. "And taking each new day as it comes. The good news is we have some time to get used to the idea."

"I have to go home and feed the cat," I said.

"When did you get a cat?" Cyrus asked.

"Read the fucking group chat," Dial and I practically said in unison.

That night I lay in bed searching for sleep that never fully came. My parents announcing they were selling my childhood home and moving to the city to do God knows what was not the news I was expecting. The urge to call Willa even though it was well past midnight was nagging at me. If I did call, she'd answer and invite me over and when I walked across the threshold, she would wrap her arms around me and make it all better. I grabbed the cold pillow on the empty side of the bed and placed it over my head, releasing a haphazard scream.

3

Fancy

WHEN I EXITED NASHVILLE INTERNATIONAL Airport, my brother Ozzie was leaning on his spotless truck. A smile pulled at his lips when he caught sight of me. "Hey Cloud Catcher," he yelled with a wave. Cloud Catcher was one of my many childhood nicknames until Fancy stuck. Oz called me this because I'd always been tall for my age. Like noticeably taller than all the other kids in my fourth-grade class. It wasn't until around junior year when most of the boys surpassed me in height and a few of the girls caught up.

"Oz." I ran to my big brother, hurling myself into his arms, leaving my luggage unattended to roll away into oncoming traffic.

"If shit ever turns sour, you can always come home again," were the last words my mother whispered in my ear before Darla and I headed toward TSA security check. That was close to ten years ago. We were being flown out by a big-time record label. The goal was to sign a contract and start recording our songs. In actuality the process wasn't as easy as all that, but eventually we signed on the dotted line.

After finding my boyfriend fucking another bitch, I hightailed it back to Los Angeles, packed up a few things, because I was also shacking up with the two-timing loser and booked the first flight home. I needed time to think, and I wouldn't be able to do that with Dylan's baby blues pleading for forgiveness. It was safe to say when it came to Dylan, I was sprung and a little bit enamored. His stepmother was Billie Preston, the first African American artist to make a lasting stamp in the world of country music. Billie was the reason I picked up a guitar.

Oz pushed me off him. "Stop with all that mushy stuff. Let me get a look at you." He circled around me like I was a used car he was considering buying. "Well, you're no worse for wear. When Momma said you were coming home unexpected, I thought I might have to make a trip of my own and fuck up the man that hurt you. But I don't see any bruises, so I'm assuming whatever is going on is about your heart and not someone going upside your head."

I swallowed down a dry patch in my throat. If Oz possessed x-ray vision, he would see my heart was torn in two. Maybe I was dumb, or Chap was just a really good liar because I never suspected a thing. I assumed there would be signs of discord in our relationship. Sure we disagreed, but he was always so attentive. Right before I got on stage, he kissed me and told me to knock 'em dead.

How do you go from that to fucking a random woman in the span of two hours? During the flight I'd spent my time recounting all the possible fissures in our whirlwind romance. Fans considered us relationship goals. Chap was a handsome charmer who was the life of the party. I was the beautiful songstress with amazing hair and enviable style. Shallow, yes, but Hollywood wasn't the real world.

Hollywood was about social currency, and together Chap and I were this aspirational power couple. Was he the love of my life? Probably not, but he made me happy. We were happy. At least I was.

I plastered on a brave face. "Why can't I just come visit my family because I missed them?"

"You ain't missed us in years. Too busy rubbing elbows and God knows what else with your rich music friends."

I shrugged off his words. "Thanks for making the drive to pick me up."

"You can thank Momma." He hoisted my luggage into the bed of his truck. Oz was massive and towered over me. Food and beer were his pastimes, and the pooch of his belly showed it. He came off gruff, but he was a big teddy bear who loved cuddles and country music. Opening my door, he stepped aside so I could climb into the cab. He jumped into the driver's seat, and we were off.

The drive from Nashville to the small town of Hume was several hours. There was a part of me excited to come home. Since signing our record deal, Whiskey Wild had been booked and busy. But even with a big label backing us, we still needed to put in the work. That meant singing at the mall to disinterested shoppers and continuing to work the state fair and farmers' market circuit to build word of mouth.

By the time our first single "Good Time Girls" dropped, there was momentum behind us and things took off fast. Sometimes I felt like it was too fast because we didn't have a second to catch our breath. We were on the road as an opening act and making the rounds at radio stations for interviews. Each radio interview was always the same with the DJ announcing their shock we were Black women and not sun tanned, blonde-haired, country gals. A break would do me good.

As he drove, Oz prattled on about the happenings in Hume. Who was shagging who. Who'd gotten divorced. Who was on their fourth baby. I grew up in a small town and even when you tried to be discreet, secrets never remained hidden for long. That's what I hated most about this town. Everyone was in your business before you even had a chance to figure out what all that business entailed.

When he got tired of talking, he turned on the radio and a Whiskey Wild song was playing. Oz flashed me an eye, shaking his head.

"Shut up, Oz," I said.

"I tell you what, that shit never gets old. Hearing my baby sister on the radio."

"They have to fill the airwaves with something."

"No need to be modest. You did your big one with Whiskey Wild."

I wasn't being modest. It just felt silly bragging about shit that was mostly about luck. Darla and I weren't the most talented singing duo to come to Nashville. Our success was based on a series of fortunate events. Like dominos all lined up to perfectly fall into place. Playing at the Gatlin State Fair and piquing the interest of a record label executive who signed us to a deal and then put us in artist development purgatory for months. My job as a hostess in LA at a swanky restaurant and Aurora, the spoiled rich daddy's girl who took a shine to me.

I was her plus one at some of the most exclusive parties in Hollywood. That's where I met Chap. At the time I was unaware of his country connection. We were just two people living in the moment and trying to make ends meet. Later I discovered Chap's form of struggle came with a trust fund. One day he heard me singing in the shower and you could practically see the dollar signs etched in his eyes.

Like I said ... luck.

"You and Darla are real hometown heroes. No one makes it out of Hume."

That wasn't true; plenty of people made it out. Maybe their songs weren't on the radio, but they were off somewhere thriving. At least that's what I liked to believe. For me it was never about making it out of Hume, it was about pursuing my dreams. Ones that couldn't be fully realized in Hume, Tennessee.

"Speaking of Darla, where is she? You two are usually joined at the hip."

"Uhm … we've been on the road hitting it pretty hard. I just needed to press the reset button and take a breath." If I told him I didn't know where Darla was right now that would raise red flags. I was a bad friend for leaving her to cuss Chap out alone, but I needed to be anywhere but there. And when I exited the bus, my next immediate thought was getting the hell out of the desert. I bumped into Moniece, and she just took over. Hiring her was the best decision I'd ever made. She called a car, booked a flight to LA, helped me pack my things between tears and saw me off at LAX. *Note to self, give that woman a raise.*

"So how long are you in town for?"

"I don't know. Long enough to enjoy Momma's home cooking and ride Cotton Candy."

Oz sputtered in laughter. "Cotton Candy. Daddy should not have allowed a twelve-year-old girl to name no damn horse. You got me on the farm yelling, "Hey Cotton Candy come here girl.""

"I named her that because her mane refused to stay tamed. It was all fluffy and soft just like cotton candy."

I was looking forward to pulling up to the ranch, climbing the creaky steps to the second floor and curling under the covers for a few days. When I called my mother from LA, I didn't explain what was going on. But I'm sure she could hear it in between my sniffles as I attempted to bite back tears. If your world is crashing above your head, you need to seek shelter. And Palmer Ranch was my safe place.

Pulling up to the house, two things were clear, the ranch house was smaller than I remembered it, and my mother notified everyone in the family about my return. It was a mini family reunion. I pushed out a long, low breath. "Gotdamnit Momma."

"Is it too much? I told Momma this was going to be too much." Like a true big brother, Oz was protective. He'd read headlines about me online and be ready to burn down the world and the comment section on my behalf.

"I had hoped to ease into my homecoming." I rubbed at my weary eyes.

"Now you know that woman will look for any excuse to entertain."

"I do but I just hoped we could save the pomp and ceremony for a later date."

At one time this house with the blue shutters and the land that stretched for miles was the center of my universe. In some way it still was. Palmer Ranch was like a fixed point on a map and no matter how far I roamed, I could always turn right back around and find my way home. When my feet touched down on the ranch soil, it acted like a reset button. You know when you die in a video game and then respawn at your last saved location? This home was my checkpoint. A chance to soothe my hurt feelings and try again.

Ozzie rounded the truck and leaned close. "Paint on a smile Fancy, and mind your manners."

I did just as my brother instructed. Greeting aunts, uncles, and cousins I hadn't seen in years. Listening as they recounted stories from my childhood. The memories others held of me never quite matched my own. As I moved from family member to family member, the conversations were the same. Everyone wanted to catch me up on what was going on in town like my mother wasn't my resident news reporter of all things Hume.

Granted she rarely had updates about what my friends from high school were up to, but occasionally she'd mention one of their parents and I learned my high school crush got married or Cyrus Birch had been elected mayor. Which was weird because he was Ozzie's best friend. I'd watched as he rapped and danced off beat in our living room.

The highlight of the night was getting to spend time with my niece, Maple. Video chats did not compare to seeing her in real life. At seven she was completely her own little person, and I could see so much of both Ozzie and Dial in her. If she was anything like her mother, this world would have to brace itself. I gave Maple my full attention while she told me all about school and her pet frog, Gorf, which was frog spelled backwards.

After the party began to wind down and there were only a few stragglers, I was able to escape to my old room. Laying across the bed, I took a deep calming breath. While I enjoyed catching up, it was nice to be alone. Even if that meant I had to confront the thoughts swirling around in my head.

My room was just like I left it down to the posters on the wall. When I left Hume, I had no intention of coming back. That statement isn't entirely true, I was okay with coming home for a weekend visit or a few days around Christmas, but I made sure to never stay long. I preferred to have my family visit me in Los Angeles. And Ozzie and Maple had taken me up on that offer more times than I could count.

I loved Hume and growing up in it, but once I saw what the world had to offer, the thought of planting stakes in my hometown became less appealing. But there was something to be said about having a community. Outside of Darla and Chap, I couldn't really claim that in LA. Making friends was a whole lot harder as an adult, and most of my friends were just as busy as I was.

"I know you're not on that bed in your outside clothes." My mother's voice punctured my serenity.

"I'm gonna shower, I just needed to rest for a bit."

"Was it too much inviting everyone over?"

"It was a lot. But I enjoyed seeing everyone again."

"You look tired."

"Well between the flight and the drive, that would make sense."

My mother sat on my bed. "Do you want to tell me why you're here?"

"I missed you and Daddy," I lied.

She rested her hand on my knee and waited silently.

"Chap … I caught him cheating. Like ass to sky cheating."

"And you're surprised?"

I wrinkled my face, giving my mother the side eye. "Yes, I'm surprised. We were talking about marriage."

"With Dylan?" Her voice rose several octaves.

"Yes with Chap."

"I will never understand it. Is it the eyes or the dick that got you thinking like this?"

My mother was never one to mince words. When I hit fourteen, she started talking to me plain about life, love, and sex.

"A little bit of both." I laughed. "Are you not surprised?"

"The first time I met him he reminded me of a snake oil salesman. You know what I mean?"

"Can't say that I do."

"It felt like he was trying to promote himself. He was selling himself as this great boyfriend who would be careful with your heart, but I never fully bought it."

"Why didn't you say something?"

"Would you have listened?"

"I would have taken it under advisement."

"Is Darla going to make an appearance?"

"I kind of left in a hurry. We didn't have a chance to touch bases on next steps." Normally Darla and I moved as a pair. So questions about her presence were expected. But I didn't tell Darla I was leaving because I wanted to be alone, and I didn't want her opinions to determine my verdict. I was mad at Chap now but maybe once we talked, I wouldn't be. It's easier to take your cheating boyfriend back when your best friend isn't next to you calling you a dumb bitch under her breath.

And for the record I never said I was one hundred percent taking him back. But all relationships go through ups and downs. Sure, I didn't think cheating would be one of the lows but maybe with time and therapy we could move past it. I deserved grace after all that transpired over the last forty-eight hours. My feelings for Chap couldn't be turned off like a light switch.

"Can we keep the cheating bit between you, me, and these four walls?"

"I understand you have a decision to make and the less people that know protects Dylan from potential judgement."

When she said it like that I felt stupid. Why should I care about sparing his feelings after he was so cavalier with mine?

"Well, you can stay here as long as you like." She rose from the bed, trying to suppress a smile. Me being home made her happy. And if getting my heart smashed into a million little pieces was the catalyst that drove me back, so be it. It was obvious she was team fuck Chap, a sentiment that would have been nice to know years ago. Perhaps if she or anyone had pointed out the red flags, I was content on missing, my eyes wouldn't be red or my nose raw from excess Kleenex use. "Get some sleep. We're heading into town in the morning."

The trip into town consisted of a stop at the post office to collect the mail and packages in our PO box. Because the ranch was a ways from town, my parents just picked up their mail when they were in the vicinity. We hit up the bakery picking out donuts for Daddy and Oz. Momma returned some library books and allowed me to check out a book I was interested in reading.

At each stop the store clerk, postal worker, or librarian would gush over me. "If it isn't Francesca Palmer. What are you doing back in Hume? I caught you and Darla on *The Tonight Show*, you two did real good. Look at your hair. Are those purple highlights? You are too Hollywood for me." It was a mix of praise and backhanded compliments. I think some Hume residents looked at folks who left as traitors.

Many believed I was too big for my britches and assumed I thought I was better than them because I was on the radio and sold millions of albums. None of that was true. I loved the people in Hume. Hume residents were like my extended family. I was either related to them by blood or connected to them through memories. Hume had a population of just under five thousand people, so no one was ever really a stranger.

Back in the car I mused over the noticeable changes. "I see Morton's finally went through with the expansion."

"He'd been talking about it for years. Most of us were sick of hearing about it. But he finally pulled the trigger. And it's nice inside. You should check it out while you're in town."

"I don't think I'll have a need for a screwdriver or bucket while I'm here."

"You could just stop in and say hello. I'm sure Kendell would appreciate it."

"Maybe."

"Maybe means no."

"Just trying to keep it low key while I'm in town. I'm not looking for a feature in the newspaper like last time."

"People are proud of you Fancy. You can't pour cold water on that."

"I'm not, but it's weird being treated like a celebrity by people I grew up with. I come home to feel normal, not to become a main attraction."

"When you chase fame you tend to become famous."

"I didn't chase fame. I just wanted to sing my songs."

"Well, you got that. Billboards in Times Square, number ones on the country charts, your face on T-shirts."

"That's no different than the shirts Daddy made for the ranch."

"Yeah, but he didn't put his ugly mug on them."

My family trained horses. Palmer Ranch was home to several four-legged superstars. Our horses appeared in films and commercials. That's how I first got the Hollywood bug while accompanying my father to movie sets. Oz had worked on the ranch since he was old enough to walk and now he was alongside my father traveling, training, and running the day-to-day operations.

On our way back home we stopped at Figs and Twine to pick up some seeds and flowers. While my mother chatted up one of the staff members, I wandered deeper into the lush greenery until I reached the greenhouse section, which was kind of like being transported to paradise. The fountains, strategically placed, drowned out any outside noise from the road or nearby customers. I stopped at a pad of sunflowers and inhaled deeply. They should add a few tables and maybe offer coffee. If they did, I would lose hours in this unexpected Zen Garden.

It was impossible to be unhappy in a place like this. Chap who? Nature always had the ability to soothe me. I grew up outside and all I needed to shift my perspective was fresh air and sunshine or a cool breeze with a hint of rain in the air. You couldn't get this in Los Angeles. It was all concrete, traffic and overly landscaped and manicured open spaces. I liked my nature wild and untamed. Tall grass, rich soil and wildflowers leading the way like my own personal yellow brick road.

"Can I help you?" A deep raspy voice with extra Tennessee twang called from behind me.

"I'm just waiting for my momma." I turned to find a tall strapping man standing in front of me. With copper skin from being kissed by the sun. His gray T-shirt was doing the heavy lifting, defining the muscles in his arms and chest. He was wearing jeans, cowboy boots, and a tattered ball cap. The brim of that cap curved, shielding his eyes. When he smiled the sun seemed to shine a little brighter, like it was siphoning some of his energy to power up.

"Fancy?"

"Yeah," I said cautiously.

The man adjusted his ball cap to reveal his eyes. "It's Edison."

"Edison Birch?" Shock was written all over my face. In high school Edison was cute, but he was never this. This man was rugged and grown. Like fuck you on the porch while waiting for the sun brewed iced tea to finish seeping type of grown. Edison's family owned Figs and Twine, but I didn't expect to run into him here. And I certainly didn't expect the butterflies his visage was inducing in my nether regions. I brushed my curls from my face. Why had I opted to sleep late so I only had fifteen minutes to get ready?

My hair was dehydrated, frizzy, and in need of a good wash. My outfit consisted of the first shirt I pulled out of my luggage, I wasn't even sure if it was clean, and a pair of cut-off shorts. I looked a hot mess, and I was standing in front of Edison Birch who'd decided to sprout up at least five inches since I last saw him with biceps for days.

"What are you doing here? Other than waiting for your momma."

"Here at Figs and Twine or here in Hume?"

"The latter."

"Visiting, I've been away for a long time. Too long."

"I know Mrs. Palmer must be tickled pink." He flashed a crooked smile.

Fuck me. They didn't have this brand of male in LA. His muscles were the result of hard work, not hours in the gym. And his flawless skin was the product of fresh air and clean water. Men in LA were often neurotic, maybe because life in a major city required you to be ten steps ahead. Edison's molasses laced speech made it clear he wasn't in a rush. As if standing here chatting with me was the most important part of his day. Everything and everyone else could wait, his attention was trained on me.

"She hasn't stopped talking since I pulled up to the ranch."

"How long are you here for?" His eyes casually tripped down the length of my body and heat whooshed up my neck, ears, and over my cheeks.

That was a good question. I didn't have a plan, people who run away in the middle of the night rarely did. Hopping my shoulders, I replied, "Don't really know. Kinda playing that part by ear." I gave him a long, curious look. "You've grown Edison Birch."

"Have I?" His tone was actually one of surprise as if every single woman in town hadn't told him how fine he was. Hume was small and pickings were slim. If Edison was still single, then I could guarantee there was a long line of women looking to remedy that.

"Before I left you had a bird chest and now … well now you look like a bucking bull." I wish I could claim I was playing it cool, but I was practically drooling.

"Country living will do that to you."

"How's the family … Dial, Cyrus?"

"We're good. Still here."

"I heard Cy's the mayor now. That's … wow."

"We're still getting used to it."

"It's crazy knowing the beer bong champion is now the mayor."

Edison chuckled at the memory. "To be fair he only won the beer bong competition because Ozzie was sick."

"I remember he ate like ten hot dogs, puked, and Dial had to take him home."

"And she's never let him live it down."

Funny enough when my mother delivered her monthly Hume updates, she never mentioned Edison. And I didn't have the balls to inquire. But now, standing just feet apart, I had so many questions.

I gently ran my fingers over the sunflowers. "This place has changed."

"Hopefully for the better." He tugged off his gloves with his teeth.

"You work here?"

"Yep, run the day-to-day with Dial."

"You always did love your plants. Sometimes I thought you preferred this vegetation to actual people."

"Plants don't talk back and their needs are simple. Just water, space, and air." He walked toward me, causing my pits to sweat. Edison always had an intense stare but now his obsidian eyes seemed to be red hot and all consuming. His hand stretched in my direction, and I flinched. "Sorry, you have tinsel in your hair."

Shaking my hair, I attempted to loosen it.

"Let me guess, you went to Paper Petals."

"Yep, I think it's gotten more cluttered than the last time I visited." I continued to shake.

"I keep saying that place is a fire hazard just waiting to happen. And the tinsel hanging from the rafters gets on damn near everything."

"Did I get it?" I looked up at him.

"Nope. Let me." This time I stood pencil straight as he removed several pieces of silver and gold tinsel from my curls, handing them to me. Now that he was closer, the scent of clean overtook my nostrils. His scent was fresh and organic. No overpowering fragrance, just good old-fashioned bar soap and water. "I think I got it all."

"Thank you. Truthfully, the tinsel was probably an improvement."

"I like your hair like this. It's like the just rolled out of bed head. But in the best possible way."

My mother's booming voice broke our gaze. "You ready to head home?" She walked up on us with a big smile. "Edison, you see my baby girl is back in town."

"Yes ma'am, I did peep that. I'm sure it's difficult to contain your excitement."

"We missed you at the ranch yesterday."

"If I'd known it was a homecoming I'd have cleared my calendar."

"It's not so much of a homecoming as it is a pit stop," I corrected him.

"Well, whatever it is. It's nice to have you back in town. Even if it's for a short while."

I knew my mother well enough to know when she was plotting as her eyes darted from me to him and back again. "You two should make time to catch up."

Edison offered my mother what looked like an appreciative smile. "I'd like that. Don't leave Hume without making a little time for me."

My cheeks flushed. Was this man flirting with me? I'd grown numb to people being nice to me because of what they thought I could offer them. But Edison's words seemed genuine and I'd never known him to be a user. So many people had taken advantage of me I'd lost count, but in all the years I'd known Edison he'd always been a straight shooter.

At the car, Edison loaded the items my mother purchased into her trunk. "Drive safe. It was good seeing you again, Fancy." Edison tossed up a wave.

"Uh-huh," I chirped, climbing into the driver's seat.

After my mother fastened her seat belt, she mimicked me, "Uh-huh."

"Shut up old lady," I said, playfully swatting her arm.

4

Edison

WAS FRANCESCA PALMER THE ONE that got away? No. Because I never had her. Don't get me wrong, I tried. But I was a foot shorter and scrawnier back then and she seemed to go for the cowboys. Guys who could rope a steer or ride a bull. I could do neither, so her pretty brown eyes never settled on me.

Seeing her again after all these years caused a twinge of pining to flutter in my stomach. This wasn't the first time Fancy returned to town since leaving. But this was the first time in a long while our paths crossed. Usually by the time I got word she was in Hume, she was already gone. But it sounded like her departure date was up in the air and I was interested in getting an audience with the *superstar*.

We'd grown up together, went to the same schools. It would be nice to catch up. Not that I had much to share. I was in the same spot she'd left me doing the same shit, fucking with the same people. All while she was a top charting country artist who'd met people and gone places I could only imagine. Don't get me wrong, I was happy with the life I created. The nursery, my farm, and family. My life was ordinary by design.

"Were my eyes deceiving me or was that Francesca Palmer?" Dial asked, carrying a pot way too heavy for her.

I ran to where she stood. "I got it."

"I'm good, Eddy."

"Stop insulting me and put the pot down." I was raised to be a good southern gentleman, which meant helping without being asked.

Dial complied; she knew better than to fuss with me about this. "So was it, Francesca?"

"Yeah, she came in with her mom."

"How long's she in town for?"

"She didn't say."

Dial sniffed, "I thought when she and Darla left Hume they had no plans of ever coming back."

"Did she say that?" Dial didn't care for Fancy, which was odd because they were technically family because of Maple.

"Words weren't needed." She wiped her hands on her faded jeans.

"Well looks like she's here now. For a little bit anyways."

Dial eyed me suspiciously. "Edison Birch, don't you dare get entangled with that woman."

"Whoa, wasn't it you who just the other day told me I needed to find a lady friend?"

"I meant someone local and attainable. You've been chasing that girl around in your head since your freshman year."

"In my defense I wasn't the only fourteen-year-old boy with designs on Fancy." Back in high school Francesca Palmer was like the dream girl from every tv show or movie. She had a smile that powered the hearts of all the young, hopeful suitors at Hume High. Fancy would walk the halls in her tattered jeans or floral dresses, her hair fluffy and big like a lion's mane. Back in the day she hadn't quite figured out how to manage her tight curls. She was popular but she never played the mean girl. That role was reserved for Willa.

"Doesn't she have a boyfriend?"

"I don't give a fuck who she dates. You don't have to worry about me. Our momma didn't raise no fool. And my stance on settling down hasn't changed."

"I'm not a fool but you … you are a buffoon," she teased, heading back into the nursery.

I scooped up the pot and set it with the rest on display. Dial was right. When I ran into Fancy inside the greenhouse, my heart kicked like a wild horse. Most times people graduate from high school and in a few years the realities of adulthood in a small town sinks in and weeds start growing around your feet while your hair thins and your midsection expands. But Fancy … she still had the shine on her.

Fancy Palmer was a distraction I didn't need. I already had so much going on with the shop and my parents. In the nine or so years since she'd left Hume, I'd probably seen her in the flesh on one other occasion when she came home for her parents' twenty-fifth anniversary. Damn near everyone in town was invited including me. But since then, we hadn't crossed paths, and a part of me felt like Fancy was deliberately trying to avoid me.

I could be like a dog with a bone when my mind was ruminating on something or someone. It was clear as long as Fancy was in town I'd get no rest. Shit, maybe it was better finding out I'd missed her after the fact. Because knowing she was in town and us not talking didn't sit right with me. I needed to forget, pulling out my phone, I texted the only person I knew could help.

Edison

Are you up for company tonight?

Willa

If it's you, yes.

Edison

I'll bring food. See you at seven.

From the moment I arrived, I knew Willa was the perfect distraction. She was wearing a dress which hugged her curves before flaring out. Her hair was in an effortless ponytail that swung in line with her hips when she walked. She flung her arms around me and her vanilla scent left me a bit lightheaded. *Why had I been avoiding this woman again?*

"Hello stranger."

"Hi. I bought wings. I hope that's good."

"It's perfect." She planted a soft kiss to my lips.

In the living room we enjoyed our food with the tv on mute. And Willa talked my head off. That was another thing I liked about her. She was never at a loss for words while I, on the other hand, was always searching for the right words to say. She'd talk, I'd listen and nod in agreement. If she was happy, then I'd done my job.

"Are you good? Do you need more blue cheese?" I asked.

"I'm great, this is delicious."

"It's just Farm Basket."

"Well maybe it's more the company than the food."

"Oh yeah, you like my company?" I licked my lips.

"I do when you're around."

"What do you mean? I'm always around."

"You don't return my calls, you pretend not to be home when I drop by."

"I work late a lot." That was a lie. I was home, but just not up for company. I'm a call first type of dude. Don't just show up unannounced because it will be a wasted trip.

"I don't mind chasing, Edison, but at some point you have to slow down."

Why was everyone trying to get me to settle?

"You and I both know you haven't had to chase a man a day in your life."

Willa smirked. That woman could be engaged tomorrow if she'd just kick me to the curb. Willa Barlowe was the type of woman any mother would be thrilled to introduce as her daughter-in-law. She was friendly, helpful, and smart. Everyone liked her. In high school she was a bit of a mean girl, but like most teenagers she'd changed. Take me for instance, I used to be considered a nerd in school because I was always reading books about agronomy and plant pathology.

In college I got a degree in horticulture science. Growing up in the nursery, plant propagation, nutrition, and preservation were my passions. I was never much of a people person. I had a robust friend group but my social battery died quicker than others. Which is why, outside of my family, I was known by my friends as the guy who went MIA for weeks at a time, only to pop back up like I'd never left.

"Guess who I saw at the post office today?"

"Who?"

"Guess? You'll never."

I fucking hated guessing games. "Honestly I don't know."

"You're no fun." Willa pouted.

"Okay, Kane?" I hoisted a careless shoulder.

"Eww no. Fancy Palmer."

I diverted my eyes in an attempt to conceal any hint of interest. "Oh yeah."

"Yeah, she was with her momma. Dressed super basic, just a T-shirt and shorts and her hair ..." Willa laughed at a joke inside her head. "I said hi and she acted like she didn't know who I was. She was squinting and looking at me all weird. It took her a minute, but then she was like, "Willa, how are you?"

"I'm sure she didn't mean anything by it."

"Maybe. Not going to lie, it was kind of trippy seeing her in person. Now that her songs are playing on the radio station twenty-four seven, it's almost like her growing up in Hume was a fever dream."

"Our homegrown superstar."

"Shit if I was as famous as her, I'd never step foot in this town again."

My brows twitched toward one another. "Why?"

"Because Hume and its dirt roads can't compete with LA, New York, or London."

"Damn right they can't, if you like a city where no one remembers your name."

"My bad, I forgot the Birch family is pro Hume."

"Why wouldn't we be? Hume is our home. Just because a place has twenty Bean There Done Thats in a ten-mile radius, it doesn't make it better."

She planted her arms across her chest. "And what does Hume have that makes it so special?"

"You …" Willa's jaw slightly dropped at the unexpected compliment. "Me, Mr. Morton, Dial, Keni. The people are what make Hume special. Fuck LA."

"Well Fancy doesn't feel that way."

"Then fuck her too." I didn't mean that but the fact that Los Angeles was blessed with Fancy's presence pissed me off. I knew damn well no one in LA cared a piss about her, not like most people in Hume did. No matter where she traveled, Hume would always be here waiting for her.

"I thought you and Fancy were friends?"

I kissed my teeth, "In high school. We're a long way from that."

"So I shouldn't be worried now that she's in town?"

"Worried about what?"

"You two?"

"Fancy isn't checking for me. She never has, and I've moved on."

"Have you?"

"What's that supposed to mean?"

"Edison …" There was a distinct energy when a woman was about to ask you about your future together. The air got denser, and it became harder to breathe. Willa's smile while still present, was askew. It was flat, no longer sincere. And her eyes were like camera shutters focusing in on every pore and fine line on my face. "Don't you get tired of keeping people at bay?"

"I'm just a private person."

"Bullshit. If you wanted to you would."

She had me there, all I could do was nod in agreement.

Willa cupped my face, rubbing her thumb across my cheek. "Baby, I want to love you, but it seems like you don't want to let me."

My stomach turned. Willa being in love with me was the last thing I wanted. And now that she'd actually verbalized it, I knew this relationship had run its course. She was an amazing woman but beyond the sex, we weren't compatible. We didn't share a single interest. She liked rom-coms. I liked shoot em ups. She hated animals. I had a cat, two goats, some chickens, and a cow named Scout. She wanted a modern country house, and I was comfortably settled on my rustic farm.

Willa continued. "I was thinking, and I don't remember the last time you asked me out on a date that didn't include staying in and watching a movie."

"I don't think that's true. We went for a drive not too long ago." Willa and I weren't a couple. And I never led her to believe our hook ups would transcend sex. But I knew she wanted more. So by not coming around I was trying to end it without having to have the talk and witness the disappointment on her face. "I thought we'd agreed to keep it casual."

"I am keeping it casual. I only see you once or twice a month as it is. I'm starting to think you're interested in keeping it pushing. If you don't want to see me any more just tell me."

Goddamnit, this was not the night I'd envisioned. I'd hoped for a low-stakes evening. My stomach knotted into tight coils. This was the part I hated, which is why I avoided it like the plague. I didn't want to let anyone down. Clearing my throat I said, "I think you're great, Willa. I do."

"But?" Her eyes searched my face for answers.

"I've enjoyed the time we've gotten to spend together. The sleepovers … your delicious quiches in the morning—"

"Ugh Edison, just spit it out. You always talk like someone is feeding you the words through an earpiece."

Ouch. "I just think maybe we'd be better as friends with no benefits." One of the words to best describe me was people pleaser. I was the type who typically went with the flow, only jumping ship when a waterfall was visible. This character trait had me eating food I was allergic to and tolerating others' bad behavior just to keep the peace.

"So you came over to break up with me?"

No, I came over to fuck. But clearly that plan was a complete bust.

"I just want to be honest. I've been stuck on one person before, and I ended up with hurt feelings and lost time. You deserve better than that. Better than me."

"Edison, I get you're scared but I'm not asking for a white wedding and picket fence just yet. I just want you."

Scrubbing my beard, I declared, "You'll get over it. Trust me in a year from now you'll be thanking me."

"So that's it?"

"I'm afraid so. I'll probably wake up tomorrow and regret having this conversation, but I think this is where I exit."

"Edison—"

I stood to leave. "This is all me. You're perfect. I'm just stuck on stupid."

"You don't have to leave."

"I've overstayed my welcome. Thank you for the company."

Willa walked me to the door. The expression on her face was one of shock. Not going to lie, I was surprised too. I didn't come here intending to end things with her. Despite my best efforts, the person I was trying to forget had a way of worming her way into my brain. Obviously, I didn't break up with Willa because Fancy was back in town. That would be stupid seeing how I didn't know if she'd be here for a month or a week. And knowing my luck, I probably wouldn't see her before she left.

Willa and I had run our course. I'd been avoiding her for a reason, but Willa hadn't read the writing on the wall. Maybe because I was practically writing that shit in invisible ink. It was for the best. Neither of us was getting what we needed from the other. She wanted a commitment, and I wanted her to be someone else.

5

Fancy

IT WAS FRIDAY NIGHT IN Hume and despite my protest, I was headed to The Tipsy Owl, a local bar with Oz. The Tipsy Owl was one of four bars in Hume. First you had The Crooked Dog where the older residents of town went to let their hair down with traditional country music and the coldest brews in town. The Drunken Zombie was just that, a place you went when you wanted to disappear. If you frequented that bar you were looking for discretion, which was in short supply in a small town like this. Then you had The Bar, it was hip and edgy. Well as hip and edgy as you could get when you're hours away from the nearest major city.

The Tipsy Owl was the spot the young people in town went. It was the place where I had my first legal bottle of beer. The music was loud, a fusion of country, hip hop, and R&B. And the bartender had a heavy hand. At least he did when I was still a resident. If it was Friday night in Hume, you were liable to turn up at Tipsy.

I'd planned to watch sappy movies while feasting on a smorgasbord of sweet and savory treats. I wasn't looking to make a scene. Coming home was more about hiding out, not showing out for me. Sure, I missed my high school friends and I planned on visiting them real soon, but I'd only been home for a few days. I needed some time to decompress. But Oz wasn't having any of that. When he pulled up to the house and I greeted him in pajamas and a hair scarf, I thought he was going to bust a capillary.

So now we were speeding down the road with the sounds of XYZ Baby playing in the background. My phone dinged, alerting me of an incoming text message. Reaching into my purse, just big enough for my cell, lip gloss, and the key to the front door, I retrieved the phone. It was a text message from Chap. I'd been in Hume for several days and it had been radio silence from him the entire time.

If I'd broken my girlfriend's heart, my fingertips would be bloody from the constant messages I'd be sending. Maybe he was glad I was gone. It gave him a chance to cheat in peace without the nuisance of a nosy girlfriend mucking up his game. The thought made me heated all over again. Was the lady on the bus a one time oopsie? And had he been sneaking around while I was working hard?

Chap

Fancy baby, I know you're thinking the worst of me right now.

Fancy

I don't have to think I saw with my own two eyes.

Chap

That wasn't what it looked like.

Fancy

Oh really cause it looked like you were fucking another woman to me.

Chap

...

Fancy

You're a liar and a cheat.

Chap

Come home.

Fancy

I've already been home.

Chap

Is that why our place looks like it's been ransacked?

Fancy

Lose my number Chap.

Chap

I can't do that. Because I love you too much. My mother didn't raise a quitter and I plan on making things square.

Fancy

For us to be square I'd have to sleep with a random dude and have you walk in on us while he had me spread open like a buffet. THAT WOULD MAKE US EVEN. THAT WOULD BE SQUARE.

Chap

Where are you?

"Everything good over there fire fingers?" Oz asked, interrupting my argument.

I clutched my phone, tempted to chuck it out the window. "Yeah, it's all good." Shit, maybe I should tell Oz about Chap breaking my heart and he'd make a sharp uey and hightail it to Los Angeles. Dylan was strong but no match for Ozzie. Was that what I wanted, for Oz to punch Chap's face a few good times while I egged him on? *"Hit him again for me."*

"Was that Dylan?"

"Uh-huh … he was just checking in."

"Normally when Dylan checks in, your face lights up and you get to twirling your hair."

"Mind your business, Oz."

"You're blood. That makes you my business."

"It's nothing, just a minor hiccup. Dylan and I are fine. Everything's fine."

One thing I've learned in my twenty-nine years on this earth is don't bad-mouth your boyfriend unless you're prepared to make him your ex. Because if you did, when you took him back, everyone would know with one hundred percent confirmation how stupid you are. I was mad at Chap now. But maybe he could explain, maybe it was all an accident. Perhaps he slipped, tripped, and fell into rando pussy which was carelessly hanging around.

Granted it was a long shot, but maybe Chap could come up with a plausible lie I was willing to believe. Starting over was difficult, and our lives were so intermingled. We had a condo, bills, and a fucking dog. Were we going to be one of those couples who break up but co-parent their Cavalier King Charles Spaniel? How would we split the holidays? Knowing Chap he'd probably sue me for full custody.

Cheating was typically a relationship ender, but being an adult was realizing shit wasn't always black and white. Chap was our manager. Could I just fire him? He was a staple in the country music industry, with connections he could use to advance or potentially stifle Whiskey Wild. And what about Darla? I mean I'm sure she'd back me up, but this was her career too.

Oz found a spot in the already packed lot and placed the truck in park.

"Is it always this crowded?" My stomach churned. I was interested in keeping things low key and the minute I walked through that door, it would be anything but.

"This ain't even half as crowded as it's going to get. You just wait, there'll be cars lined up on the side of the road for a mile."

Hopping out of the cab of the truck, we headed to the front door. Music was spilling out and so was the crowd with people drinking and mingling on the porch. The Tipsy Owl used to be a house owned by this sweet old couple who would give me candy. I know it sounds sketchy, but Bert and Erneil were the farthest thing from stranger danger. Even with the creepy similarity in name to stuffed puppets. They passed when I was still in elementary school and their place was gutted and converted into a bar. But the owners maintained some of the sweet touches like the wraparound porch with rocking chairs, the funkiest chandelier I'd ever seen, and a swing set out back framed by trees and an assortment of flowers.

When I crossed the threshold, I didn't know where to look first. The bar was packed, the crowd was loud, and the music had me tapping my feet. I can tell you one thing, Los Angeles didn't have places like this. All the bars and lounges in LA were overpriced and more of a spectacle. People were there to be seen, not for a good time.

At The Tipsy Owl patrons were here to let loose and hook up. The single customers were looking to not be for the night, and the couples were there to grind close while downing cold beers. I'd pick this place over any VIP section. Other than the occasional bar fights, this place was low key. The only designer brands in sight were the Stetson cowboy hats and Tecovas boots.

"You drinking?" Oz asked.

"Dumb question. I'll take a Pilsner if they have it."

While Oz went off to the bar, I slowly circled the outskirts of the room. My eyes pinging from one familiar face to the other. Closest to the door was Mac, we used to be in band class together. He was a beast on the drums. On the dance floor was Nancy. She was moving her hips in a sultry roll, capturing the attention of the man she was dancing with. And in my face was Margie Ford, with a smile as big as Texas.

"Francesca Palmer, are my eyes deceiving me?"

"I sure hope not. How've you been, Margie?"

"I've been busy working at my family's real estate office. I'm an agent now. Can you believe that?"

"You hated real estate. You said no one wanted to sell old, dilapidated farmhouses."

"I did say that, but it turns out I'm a nosy little goose and you can tell a lot about a person based off of their home." Margie had always been a gossip, and it looked like she'd found a profession which enabled her interest in being the town crier. She continued, "I'd ask you how you're doing, but we can't escape you. You and Darla are always on the radio or television making our city proud. How long are you in town for?"

"Not quite sure?" I needed to come up with a good answer to that question. My current response made it sound like I was a drift at sea.

"Well if you're looking to reestablish some roots, take my card." She handed me a business card with succulents framing the bottom.

My eyebrow ticked up. Margie's last name was no longer Ford. "Did you get married Margie?"

"Five years ago. I go by Leftfoot now."

Where the hell had I been? Margie Ford was selling houses and married one of the Leftfoot brothers. "Congratulations"

Oz returned with my drink and I eagerly grabbed it from him, gulping half the bottle before taking a breath. My brain tuned out while Margie and my brother talked in excited tones about a bonfire. In Hume, bonfires, trips to the lake, and the annual parade were a big deal. There wasn't shit to do in this town. We had one movie theater with three screens, a roller rink that was closed for renovations, and the Dairy Queen parking lot.

Oz turned his attention back to me. "I got us a table. Come on."

I followed him closely, holding on to the tail of his shirt so we weren't separated. We passed by the stage where Nancy Sparks was singing bad karaoke to a Tanner Adell song. Sliding into the booth, I took a deep breath. I don't know how he wrangled this table for how packed this place was, but as long as I could remember, people were drawn to Oz and wanted to be in his good graces. Maybe it was because he was as big as a black bear and hit just as hard.

He took a long drag from his Heineken. "So are you going to tell me what's going on?"

"What do you mean?"

"You know exactly what I mean. You, back in Hume holed up in your room. Your frantic text exchange with Dylan."

My eyes were fixed on the table. "We're just going through a transition."

"Meaning?"

I was never good at being nonchalant. If I was bothered, you'd know it. Releasing a big huff, I confessed. "Dylan cheated."

"How do you know?"

"I caught him."

His eyes tightened in the corners. "So you're in Hume for what?"

"To think."

"What's there to think about? If Dylan doesn't appreciate you, he doesn't deserve you."

"People make mistakes."

"Cheating isn't a mistake, it's a choice." Oz was a straight shooter, and he wasn't one to mince words. Which is exactly why I didn't want to share this with him. "Look I can take some time off and we could fly back to LA and pack up your stuff."

I stiffened my gaze. "Why do I have to move?"

"We can pack up his shit if you prefer. I don't really care."

"I don't know if I want to do that. I need to think it through."

"What is there to think about? He lost the privilege of continued access to you."

"I don't know Oz, maybe I love him."

He let out a thunderous belly laugh. "Right … an arrogant, two-timer is just so fucking lovable."

"You don't like Chap?"

"No, he's an asshole."

What was it with everyone disliking my boyfriend? Sure, he could be a bit abrasive, but he got shit done. That sandpaper personality is what secured most of our deals. And Chap wasn't all thorns. He could be soft and sweet when he wanted to.

"Momma agrees with you."

"I know she does. We've talked about it."

"You two were talking about me behind my back?"

"Yes, I don't know why you're surprised. She and I have a standing brunch date once a month where we gossip and drink mimosas."

"During your bitchfest, do you two talk about you and Dial?"

Oz leaned into the booth. "There is no me and Dial."

"But you'd like there to be."

"We all make choices Fancy and Dial made hers."

"I'm just going to say this. I know she's your baby momma, but she's a lot to deal with."

"Dial's always been a lot. That's what I love about her. She's like a cat. One minute she's sweetly purring and the next she's trying to claw your eyes out."

My brows climbed my forehead. "And you like that?"

"Damn skippy." He tipped his cowboy hat.

"So you're not dating anyone right now?"

"Nope, too busy with work and Maple."

"You're never too busy for love."

Oz snapped his finger. "That sounds like a country song."

The music changed to a Teddy Swims' song and a familiar deep voice started singing along. I turned in my seat to witness Edison behind the microphone. This was no surprise. Edison had one of the most harmonious voices in Hume, shit in all of Tennessee. Remember what I said about talent and luck? There were hundreds of regular, everyday citizens that could sing circles around your favorite artist. They were just unlucky or unwilling to take a chance.

Edison's voice was the sexiest thing about him and that was saying a lot because he was so fine, he had good looks to spare. And the patrons in The Tipsy Owl agreed. The loud voices from moments ago were now faint whispers. I could listen to his voice for hours and at one point in time, I did.

"Earth to Fancy?"

"What?" I swung back around to find Ozzie smiling at me. "If you don't wipe that grin off your face."

"I think he's single."

I sputtered, "What … why would I care about something like that?"

"You are an amazing singer, but when it comes to lying, you suck."

"Edison's my friend."

"Oh yeah when's the last time you called, texted, or emailed your friend?"

"It's complicated."

"Edison Birch is the simplest creature on this planet. He loves his momma, plants, and God."

"What am I supposed to call him and discuss the goings on in Hollywood? He doesn't give a shit about that." The crowd cheered as Edison exited the stage and I practically branded him with my eyes only turning away when I lost sight of him.

Ozzie drummed his fingers on the table. "I could go for another round. How about you?"

"That would be great."

Oz made his way to the bar while I tried to disappear in my booth. Hume would always be home, but on nights like this I felt like an outsider. My friends had gone on living and making memories without me. I'd missed weddings, baby showers, and housewarming parties. There were inside jokes I wasn't a part of. They say you can always come home again, but maybe sometimes you can be away for too long. I sorted through the bowl of Chex Mix, selecting only rye crackers and popping them in my mouth.

"One ice cold Pilsner." I looked up to find Edison towering over me. "Oz asked me to run this over to you."

"Thank you. So I see you're still the karaoke king."

He dipped his head. "I don't know about all that." Edison had always been modest, but he had cause to brag. His flawless skin, enviable smile, and his deep raspy voice which was slightly lighter when he sung. And then there were the countless other reasons that made him top contender for God's favorite child.

"You should sit. Catch up." Oz wasn't the smartest tool in the shed, but this move was one of a master wingman. He knew how to set up the play and move out of the way. I would have to buy him a tall stack at the Sunny Side Kitchen.

"You're not in this back corner because you were interested in company."

"You're not company. You're my friend. It's different."

Edison's brown eyes locked with mine and the corners of his mouth kicked into a smile. "Yes ma'am, I can sit for a while."

6

Edison

OZ AND I WENT WAY back so when he suggested I hand deliver Fancy's beer, I eagerly agreed. I did not expect my waiter role to grant me a seat at the table and my heart rate spiked sitting across from her. No one would classify me as a ladies' man. I didn't have quippy pick up lines or the machismo required to land this plane. She was offering up her attention, but before long, I'd say something stupid. Then she'd remember why she never gave me a second glance in high school.

"So, Oz sent you over?"

"Good old, Oz."

"You know you didn't need an invite. You're always welcome."

Let's form a prayer circle and ask the good Lord for a healthy dose of audacity because what I was about to attempt would require balls of steel. Up until this moment, I was content with my life. But sitting across from the woman I still had dreams about at night, I was second guessing all my life choices.

"I'm a gentleman. I always need permission."

She brushed her curls from her line of vision. "Did you want something in particular?"

There were so many ways to answer that question. I wanted Tennessee University to make it to the NCAA Final Four. I wanted the reclaimed wood flooring I'd ordered six months ago to finally get delivered. Most of all, I wanted Francesca Palmer to sing my name soft and low while I rearranged her guts. "Honestly, you were over here all alone deep in thought, and that didn't sit right with me."

"So you came to rescue me."

"I don't save women anymore. I learned my lesson."

"And what's that?"

"That most women are more than capable of saving themselves. If they want my help they'll ask."

"If I grew up with Dial for a sister, I'd probably feel the same."

"Dial definitely doesn't need saving. My sister is a savage. She will break the best of men."

"She broke Oz's heart."

"I have my thoughts on that, but I'm not sharing."

"All I know is they have broken up and got back together more times than I can count."

"Yeah, well I think this time it's going to stick."

"What do you know about breakups? I think every woman you've ever dated dumped you."

"Correction, I've let those women dump me. There's a difference."

"So now you're too much of a gentleman to break a few hearts?" She twirled her hair around her index finger.

"I prefer for the women to think it was their choice. Splits are cleaner that way."

Fancy had always been a shameless flirt. I'd never been on the receiving end of the batting of her long, curled lashes or biting down on her plump lips, so this was uncharted waters for me. But my instinct told me I was in a category five flirting storm. The only thing missing was an unprovoked touch to my person.

"Is that your first?" I asked, gesturing to her glass.

"My second."

I hoisted my beer bottle. "This is my fourth. Which explains the karaoke."

"Shit, I have some catching up to do."

"I got you covered." I licked my lips and stuck my thumb and index finger in my mouth producing a shrill whistle. It was loud enough to catch the attention of one of the bartenders. I mimed pouring a pitcher and Hubbard, the bartender, nodded his head in understanding. In short order, a tall pitcher and two frosty glasses were delivered to our booth.

Fancy's face lit up. "I feel like I'm in VIP," she teased.

"Only the best for our hometown hero."

She wrinkled her nose. "I hate that term."

"I know you do and that's exactly why I said it."

"You're a brat." Fancy finished off her bottle before pouring us both fresh glasses. She looked back at the crowd before turning her attention to me. "Hey, who did Margie get married to?"

"Joshua."

She slapped the table. "Margie married Joshua Leftfoot? Is this the fucking twilight zone?"

"They fell in love. The wedding was nice."

"Wait, you went to the wedding?"

"I did."

"You hate Joshua. He was a bully with an undeserving heaping of bravado."

"Water under the bridge."

Her face sparked in remembrance. "He literally threw you off of Golden Pass bridge."

"Well, this parts going to shock you, I actually consider him a good friend now."

"Joshua Leftfoot?" Her face was a puzzle.

"Yeah, one night he pulled up to my table at The Drunken Zombie and we got to talking. He apologized for the shit he did in high school. You know, saying it was never really about me, it was more about him."

"Pigs are flying. Pigs are sprouting wings and flying across town."

"Stranger things have happened. Look at you … you left town and moved to California with Darla of all people."

"My best friend."

"Your number one hater."

"What?" Her head flinched backward. "Darla's always had my back."

"Yeah to your face."

"You don't know what you're talking about."

"I don't know, maybe she's changed. It's been a minute."

"Darla's my best friend. We are good. Inseparable. So let's just drop it."

Raising my hands, I capitulated. "I'm letting go and stepping away."

I guess some things never change. Darla was the type to preen in your face, but all the while she was tossing daggers in your direction. She needed to be the prettiest, smartest, funniest woman in the room, but if that room included Fancy, it was an impossible feat. Fancy had a way of pulling people in, and Darla and I were not immune.

Shit, I met Fancy when I was five. We were in Mrs. Noone's kindergarten class together. The second week of school I came home and announced I was changing my last name to Pat because seating was assigned by last names and since my last name was Birch and her's Palmer, we were situated on opposite sides of the classroom. At five I didn't have the words to express what love was, but I knew Fancy made me feel good. When she smiled at me or shared her fruit snacks at lunch, it made me feel special and I wanted that feeling to last forever.

"Tell me what you've been up to. You work at Figs and Twine. What else?"

I scratched my chin. "I work at Figs and Twine, I bought the old Castle place a year back."

"Did Mr. Castle die?" She looked distressed.

"No, he's alive, the farm just became too much to maintain on his own, so he moved in with his daughter." I'd looked for a suitable place for a while, going back and forth over whether to buy an existing property or build something new. One thing Hume doesn't have a shortage of is land. On a random Thursday, I was driving home and spotted a for-sale sign outside the Castle Farm. Shit moved pretty fast after that.

Fancy peeled the label off one of the empty bottles. "What about a girlfriend or kids?"

"Nope."

"So you're telling me no woman in all of Hume has swooped up Edison Birch?"

"You make it sound like I have tons of options."

"Sir, looking like that … your options are limitless." My eyes settled on her face, slowly trying to process her words. Before I could respond, she pivoted the conversation.

"What about Dial? Does she have a fella?"

I screwed up my face at the question. "Come on. Dial is hella picky and she is not lowering her standards for a ring. But lots of guys have tried."

"Okay, so you run Figs and Twine, you bought a farm, and you're single. What else?"

"Honestly, that about covers it. My life isn't that interesting. Not like you."

"I think it's interesting. From what I can tell, the nursery is bigger than when I left. And you own the creepy Castle Farm."

"He left all his shit. I'm still sorting through the mess. He said if he needs something important, he'll just swing by."

"See there's another interesting fact: you run a small storage company in your free time," she teased.

She made me smile. She always had. "What about you? How's Los Angeles?"

"Crowded with piss poor air quality."

"Is it everything you thought it would be?" I averted my gaze, not looking forward to her response. The last thing I wanted to hear was how leaving Hume was the best decision she'd ever made. Or how she couldn't imagine building a life in this podunk town. Occasionally people would leave this small town and when they returned for the holidays or a funeral, they'd have nothing but negative things to say about the town and the people who remained.

Her smile faltered. "Sometimes. Mostly no." Fancy's phone rang and she quickly concealed the screen, but not before I spotted a picture of a man with blue eyes and a cowboy hat. Her expression turned sour as she silenced the call. I knew all about unanswered calls. I'd ignored my share of calls from Willa in the past few months.

"Do you need to get that?"

"No, what I need is another drink. I'm still behind by one."

"Two, you're actually behind by two." I pointed to my half-filled glass. "This is my fifth."

"Damn." She poured herself another. "Tell me about your momma and daddy."

While she nursed her glass, I brought her up to speed on the happenings in the Birch clan. Fancy's family and mine were fairly close. I grew up idolizing her big brother, Oz, who to a scrawny kid like me, was a King. He was a few years older and Cy's best friend. I desperately wanted to be a part of their crew, but Cy didn't want his kid brother hanging around. And Dial … Dial adored Oz. Shit, she still did if you're asking my opinion on the matter. But don't tell her I said that.

As I retold the mundane comings and goings in Hume, Fancy's face lit up like I was a master storyteller weaving a tell of times long ago. I don't know how she was capable of making me forget the others in the room. Well past midnight Tipsy was standing room only, but in our booth it was like we were in another universe. The clanking of glasses and boisterous chatter all fading away. Fancy's light, melodic laughter trilled in the air. The soft touch of her hand resting on my arm caused a flood of goosebumps to pebble my flesh. And the overhead lights which helped to conceal imperfections in the decades-old tables and booths seemed to shimmer against her sepia skin. Her breast rising and falling with each intake of air. While her full curls framed her face drawing me to her mink eyes.

Fancy was stalled on her fourth beer while I was five beers in and well past the limit to safely drive home. "I think I need to call it for the night." I slid from our booth and staggered to catch my bearings.

"How are you getting home?"

"Looks like I'm hoofing it. The fresh air will do me good."

Fancy stood and with a tug of my hunter green T-shirt, she pulled me close. Her lips were inches from mine. If I puckered, I could steal a kiss. "Do you want me to drive you home?"

Hume didn't have car services you could call for a ride. I'd practically drunk myself under the table and was more than willing to stretch my legs. "You don't have to do that."

"I know I don't have to, but I'm offering all the same."

"Do you know how to drive stick?"

She flashed a goofy expression. "Do I know how to drive stick? Come on, you're talking to Ernest Palmer's daughter."

"Fair." I smiled, tipping my ball cap. "That would be very kind of you."

7

Fancy

EDISON TOSSED ME HIS KEYS and we were off. I'd nursed my last beer, so I was more than capable of driving us home. In the passenger seat of his truck, Edison was mostly quiet, occasionally reminding me to turn left or right.

"You know I'm from here. I don't need directions to the Castle Farm."

"You've been gone a long time. I don't want you getting us lost."

"I know Hume like the back of my hand. You could drop me off in the boonies and I'd find my way home like the family dog. Remember my dog Yeti Spaghetti? He was lost for weeks. We put up flyers. Daddy went out looking for him, even had some of the guys on the ranch help. But try as they might, they could not find that dog. And then a month later, here comes Yeti all matted and tangled a little worse for wear but no harm no foul."

"And you're just like Yeti?"

"That's what I'm saying. Shit you could blindfold me, spin me around three times and point in the direction of a map and I guarantee you I'd be able to locate Hume every time."

"Bullshit."

"You don't believe me?"

"No because you're full of shit and alcohol."

"Who's driving whom, Miss Daisy? Because I know how to hold my liquor."

"And I don't?"

"Seeing how you are currently a passenger princess the answer would be no."

"I haven't had dinner. So I was drinking on a light stomach."

"No, you're a lightweight."

"Oh you got jokes. Turn right at the stop sign."

Slowing the car to a stop in front of the Castle now Birch Farm, I marveled at the sight. The house was the same but different. A modest two-story farmhouse with a wraparound porch. Stamped concrete replaced the dirt pathway. The façade was now a crisp white, not the dingy, peeling gray paint Mr. Castle preferred. Illuminated porch lights were like a beacon welcoming you home. Back in the day the house would disappear into the night sky and you couldn't see the structure until you were practically right on top of it.

When we were kids, the farmhouse was considered haunted. Back then the vegetation was overgrown and there was a pile of old newspapers next to the front door. Sometimes Mr. Castle would be sitting on the porch, his one-eyed dog lying next to him. If you got too close walking past, he'd yell at you. One time he threw a rock, and it hit me on the arm. Dial turned around and cussed old Mr. Castle out. Claiming she was going to tell her dad and we were all going to come back and kick his ass. Dial didn't snitch, but after that Mr. Castle never threw shit at us again, although he still read us for filth.

"Do you remember daring me to ring the doorbell?" I asked.

"I remember double dog daring you and you marching right up those steps and pressing the bell."

"Yeah and when Mr. Castle answered the door with his pistol on his hip, I tripped down the stairs and you jumped in between us to defend me."

Edison shrugged my praise of valor off. "Mr. Castle was scary to look at, but he was in Figs and Twine all the time. Nicest man you'll ever meet."

"Be that as it may I still thought you were so brave. He could have broken you in two."

"And for you, I'd have let him." Edison climbed out of the truck. He stumbled a bit on initial contact with the ground, but it appeared the air blowing on his face during the ride home had given him a second wind.

"I'm coming in," I announced, slamming the truck door behind me.

"Are you asking or inviting yourself?"

Painting on a saccharine smile, I tried again. "Can I come in?"

"Uh-huh." His gaze rested on me and the undeniable lust in his eyes sent shivers up my spine. Was the liquor the cause of this bold gaze or was this just all him?

Walking toward the house, I felt like that ten-year-old girl psyching myself up to ring the doorbell of the crotchetiest man in town. "Not going to lie, this is still kind of scary."

"It's muscle memory. For most of your life you've associated this place with the stories we spun about dead bodies and captured children. Shit, my first night sleeping here alone …"

"Yeah?"

"Nah, you'll probably just tease me for my confession."

Vigorously shaking my head, I disagreed. "I won't. Cross my heart and hope to expire."

He stopped on the porch, facing me. "My first night here when the lights were off and all you could hear was the wind aggravating the old wooden bones of the house, I couldn't fall asleep. Every creak or howl left me on edge. I'd been in the basement, but had I really checked it thoroughly?"

I leaned in closer, hanging on his every word.

"I could swear I heard someone calling my name. Edison, Edison." His tone was scratchy and hushed. "Not over and over again but frequently enough for me to know it wasn't my imagination."

"What did you do?" I asked breathlessly.

"I headed to the basement with my gun and a flashlight?"

"Why a flashlight?"

"What?"

"Why didn't you just turn the lights on?"

"Uhm, because the power hadn't been cut on yet. Anyway, I went to the basement just to confirm I was alone. Sweeping the area, I didn't find anything. I was at the foot of the steps and then I heard it again. Edison." I grabbed his arm, moving us away from the front door. "I followed the sound, pushing aside boxes and random junk and there it was …"

My eyes splayed wide open. "What?"

"You remember that kid that went missing when we were little?"

"Wait, are you saying Mr. Castle had a dead kid in the basement?" Edison's serious expression broke and a rumbling laugh emerged. "Asshole," I shouted while shoving and not so playfully punching him in the arm. "You've been fucking with me this entire time?"

"I'm sorry Fancy, you're just so damn gullible."

My brows curved upward. "Not cool."

"I see you're still ready to believe any and everything."

Who the hell did he think he was? I wasn't some naive country bumpkin.

"It's not my fault I trust people and take them at their word. Shit words mean things, so when someone says they can't imagine life without you or they love you, why wouldn't you believe them? How the fuck are you supposed to know they're full of shit and are telling every Tonya, Denise, and Harriet the same damn thing? I don't want to live life thinking everyone's running game."

All humor vacated his face. "Hey, I was teasing. I didn't mean to hit a nerve."

"You didn't. My nerves are not that sensitive. Plus, I wasn't talking about myself or any personal events I might be experiencing. I was just generalizing. A man's word should be his bond. Say what you mean and mean what you say because when you say things, people will make life decisions based off of those words. And then next thing you know you have a condo in a city you hate, an overpriced car when all you wanted was a pink Jeep, and a whole fucking dog."

"Hypothetically."

"Of course." I cleared my throat.

Edison leaned in, practically touching his forehead to mine. "Do you want to talk about it?"

"No, open the door."

From the entryway I spied items too old and ornate for a twenty-nine-year-old man's taste level. In the formal dining room, rows of old random trinkets and knickknacks were displayed neatly on the dining table. The room was lined four boxes high so you couldn't see the aging wallpaper. I clutched my purse, eyeballing Edison. Was he an undercover hoarder? His truck was spotless and from the outside this former haunted house gave off quaint family friendly vibes.

"Shit, this is a lot of—"

"Junk, you can say it. I'm going room by room trying to clear all Mr. Castle's shit out."

"If I were you I'd get a dumpster and just get to tossing. You could make a party of it. Invite a few friends, add some drinks and you have a cleaning crew."

"Some of this stuff is sentimental and worth money. I bought the house and the items in it as is." He pointed to a velvet portrait of Jimi Hendrix. "That monstrosity is worth a thousand dollars."

I gasped, pushing him hard. "Shut up."

Edison chuckled while bumping into a nearby doorjamb. "Yep, I've become a bit of an antique roadshow type guy. Initially I was going to hold an estate sale, get rid of all this shit in one shot. But then I found a vintage tea pot and sold it for five thousand dollars."

"And you've been chasing that high ever since." My eyes pinged from one hidden treasure to the other.

"Pretty much. I reached out to his daughter to let her know I thought her father got the raw end of the deal considering what I paid for the place. I offered her the five grand, but she refused." Edison led me to the living room which was less cluttered than the parlor and hallway. "That didn't sit right with me, so we came to an agreement that I'd give her half of the sales price on every item."

"That's very generous of you." I tossed my purse on a high back velvet chair.

"Just seemed fair."

"What are you going to do when it's empty?"

"Renovate, make this place a proper home."

"That sounds like a lot of work."

"Luckily I've never been afraid of hard work and I'm good with my hands."

"Are you going to do all the work yourself?"

"What I can. Anything else I'll hire out."

This house certainly had good bones. I'd watched tons of home renovation shows when Whiskey Wild was on the road. My favorite were the shows that restored older homes that had somehow been forgotten or neglected. The Castle house would make an interesting episode. "Do you know what you want the place to look like in the end?"

His face brightened. "What do you take me for? I have a whole vision board in one of the spare rooms."

"For a few thousand more I bet you could have gotten a place that was move in ready."

"Where's the fun in that? I'm going to curate this home. When it's done it'll have the modern amenities while preserving the vintage charm."

"How long will all that take?"

"I don't have a timeline for it. I find when you rush shit, you end up settling. Sometimes it's best to let shit marinate and develop its richness."

This was also true of relationships. Take Chap and I for instance. He love bombed me. Answering my text and calls in record time. Spoiling me with fancy dinners and gifts from Hermés. When he introduced me to his stepmother, I was so appreciative I sucked his dick on the drive home. I was a fish out of water in LA looking for connection and community, and Chap opened doors to all that.

"Fancy?"

"Yeah."

"Are you good?"

"Uh-huh. Why?"

"You just went away for a minute there."

"Nope I'm right here on this very nice Persian area rug."

"Do you want water or something?"

"Water's good." Edison disappeared into the kitchen, and I continued to admire Mr. Castle's life in his collection of odds and ends. Scanning the room, I landed on crates of records. "Are these your records?" I yelled.

"Nope, old man Castle's," Edison called back.

"Well let's see what he was into." I flipped through the stack, pulling out some gems, smirking when I found Ray Charles. Removing the album from the sleeve, I opened the record player that was as tall and wide as a long dresser. When the needle connected with the vinyl, the room was filled with sharp piano keys as "I Believe To My Soul" began to play. Upon reentering the room, Edison found me swaying my hips back and forth. "You going to make me dance alone?"

He placed the two glasses of water on coasters and crossed the room to meet me. Mirroring my two-step, his eyes were locked on to my face. Edison slipped his arm around my waist, pulling me close. His feet stepped back and then to the side, leading me across the scant empty space on the living room floor. I closed my eyes and leaned into him, turning my brain off.

My skin freckled with goosebumps when his fingers found a patch of bare flesh near my waistband. Opening my eyes, I looked up and immediately met the steady intensity of his cognac gaze. He was waiting for permission. For me to give him the green light to bend me over the couch cushions and fuck me senseless. And I wanted to let him. Maybe I wasn't as sober as I thought. If I just lifted to my tiptoes and dusted his lips with mine, Edison would take care of the rest. Stripping me naked, kissing every inch, and giving me a proper dick lashing.

Get your lick back.

Twisting out of his grasp. I reached for my water, drinking in big gulps. "Let's play a game. You have to guess the artist based on three-word clues."

"Really?"

"Yes, who doesn't love games?" It was one in the morning and my mother's words were haunting me. "Ain't nothing open after midnight in Hume but legs." Was that why I'd invited myself inside so I could let *him* inside?

"I don't."

"We're playing. I'll go first."

"Okay." He dropped to the couch.

"First up … the queen of country."

"That's four words."

"Just guess."

He rubbed his eyes. "The queen of country. Is this some vain attempt to get me to say you?"

I tossed a nearby Beanie Baby at his head.

He caught it and chided me. "Hey, that's worth seventy-five dollars."

"That thing is worth seventy-five dollars?"

"Yep." He tossed the space themed bear in the air. "And Castle has hundreds of them."

"Who in their right mind would want a Beanie Baby in this day and age?"

"You'd be surprised of the amount of people willing to purchase useless shit."

"Stop stalling and answer. We're still playing … queen of country."

"Could it be the great Billie Preston?"

I displayed the record, jumping up and down in delight. "That was an easy one. Are you ready for round two?"

"There's a round two."

"Yes, it's a game and games have rounds, or quarter, halves, sections even." I went to a crate tucked in the corner and flipped through, looking for a hard one. I couldn't help but giggle when I came across this unexpected album. "City of Compton." I did my best not to sing the words because then it would be a dead giveaway.

Edison stood and his gold chain peeked out from the collar of his T-shirt. I can't explain why the sight of the modest gold rope chain around his neck excited me, but it did. My mind flashed to images of his chain dangling in my face while he fucked me.

"I know damn well he doesn't have a Tupac album in that stack." He pulled the record from my hand in surprise.

While Edison examined the back of the record, I examined him. I don't know where all this pent-up sexual energy was coming from, but it was loud and persistent. *Just stick your tongue in his mouth. Or better yet drop to your knees and let him know you're with the shits. I just know it's thick and heavy, I just know it.*

I reached under his T-shirt to tug on the loop of his jeans. "Edison?"

"Yep?" His eyes finally moved from the record to me, pinging across the longing desire in my face.

He dropped the record and in one seamless motion grabbed my right leg, hoisting me into his arms. My thighs tightened around his waist. When his lips found mine, the kisses were frantic and unexpected. Neither of us had planned for this, but we both appeared eager to make this our new reality. We sunk to the couch with me straddling him, never breaking contact. His hands were everywhere, my neck, my breast, my hair.

Edison's kisses slowed as he pulled back to take stock of my reaction. "What the fuck?" he whispered before going in for round two. We laughed between kisses. As my hips floated over his lap, I felt him come to life underneath me. The impressive bulge made the movement of my hips accelerate. Edison pulled off my shirt, plunging his face into my breast. His mouth suckled and teased as his teeth gently clamped down on my nipple.

If I didn't reel this in now, I would devour this man and beg for seconds. "Edison, slow down." I panted, breathless from the kissing and my mind reeling over the possibility of us.

"Yep." He backed off a bit, his hands still roaming.

"You're drunk and I feel like I'm taking advantage of you," I said.

He chuckled, grabbing hold of my ass so I could feel every inch of him. "Shit … use me."

"Okay." Rubbing my finger across his lips, I went in for more kisses. I was tired of thinking and ready for an out-of-body experience. Since commitment meant nothing, I was well with in my rights to fuck whoever I wanted. Chap already was. I was just catching up. But did I want to get up to speed with Edison as my tour guide? He didn't deserve revenge sex. Sex with Edison always seemed like a sacred act. Which is why we'd never done it. Growing up it was clear he liked me, and I didn't want to give him false hope.

"I have a boyfriend, ex-boyfriend … it's complicated," I blurted out.

All movements stalled and Edison's eyes were clear as the night sky. He removed me from his lap, leaning back into the couch cushions.

"I'm sorry. I should've mentioned that sooner."

"Yeah, you should have… it's okay." He rubbed his forehead. I reached for his face, caressing his cheek. He quickly grabbed my hand and returned it to my lap. "Probably best you don't stroke my cheek while my dick is pressing through my jeans."

I nodded in agreement. "Do you want me to help you with that?"

His eyes grew wide.

"Oh my God, I didn't mean it like that. I was just going to change up the imagery. Remember Ms. Applegate with the gold teeth and tangled wig. Think about her and I bet you that hard on will disappear."

"You should probably go. Away from here. Take my truck. I'll swing by in the morning and pick it up."

My face fell, disappointed that he was asking me to leave. But I deserved it. If my senses hadn't kicked in, I would have fucked Edison, which would be wrong. Right? Chap was technically my boyfriend. But if you asked Chap, apparently, we were in an open relationship. Because he fucked another woman behind my back … until it was right in front of my face.

"Yep, that makes sense." I stood collecting my shirt and, heading for the front door.

"I'd walk you out but—"

"It's totally fine. Get well soon." Edison flashed me a crisp middle finger. I mean it was the straightest finger in the history of middle fingers. Scooping up his keys, I headed out.

In his car on the way home. I ran through the turn of events. Why did I have to open my big mouth? Don't get me wrong, I was hoping to open my mouth tonight, but I was looking to have Edison's dick inside it, not my foot. Who were we kidding? This wasn't the first time Chap cheated; this was just his first time getting caught. He didn't deserve me or my loyalty, and he didn't deserve Whiskey Wild.

My phone rang, so I pulled over to the side of the road. Chap had been calling and texting me for most of the night. If he wanted to talk, I'd give him an earful. "Look here you stupid son of a bitch.

You must think I'm an idiot. How long have you been fucking around on me? 'I love you Fancy. You're the only one for me. You make me want to be a better man.' Hmm. The next time I see you I'm kicking you square in the balls. YOU FUCKING ASSWIPE."

"Fancy?" A meek voice broke through on the other end.

"Who is this?"

"It's Moniece."

I facepalmed into my hand. "I'm sorry." I was saying that a lot tonight.

"I totally understand."

"Is everything alright?"

"Yeah, I just wanted to give you a heads up that I'm heading your way. I have some paperwork for you to sign."

"Can't that wait? You don't need to catch a flight to Tennessee just for me."

"No, it can't wait. I also wanted to talk to you about a private matter."

I didn't have the bandwidth to take on much. Between Chap, the pending tour, the implosion of my entire life, and Edison, I was at capacity. "Are you quitting? Because I'd be lost without you. Just name your price."

"I'm not quitting. We can circle back on the salary a little later. But we need to talk."

"About?"

"I'd rather talk in person."

That was fine, I guess. The last time Moniece came to Hume she was overwhelmed by the country of it all. Asking where the coffeehouse and Target were. And pretending to be okay with the smells. "Have you spoken to Darla?"

"Briefly. She's back in LA. Has she not called you?"

"Uhm … no … but I'm sure she's probably just trying to give me some space."

"Maybe. Anyway, I'll see you in a few days."

"Sounds good."

I stuffed the phone into my purse before turning back onto the road. Normally, Darla and I talked via text or in person like twelve times a day. I hadn't heard from her since rushing off the tour bus. Last I saw she was reading Chap the riot act. But not calling to check on me was unusual. Maybe she stayed away to avoid delivering a big fat I told you so. She never liked me getting together with Chap. She warned me about mixing business with pleasure and I was too lovestruck to listen.

When I pulled up to my parents' house, I shot off a message to Darla.

Fancy

Are we okay?

8

Edison

IN THE MORNING, I RELUCTANTLY called Dial, convincing her to drive me to Palmer Ranch so I could pick up my car. Enlisting her help came at a price because as she drove, she peppered me with questions.

"What's your car doing at Palmer Ranch?"

"I let Fancy drive it home?" I took a drink of coffee from my insulated tumbler.

"And why couldn't she drive herself home?"

"Because I was drunk."

"What does you being drunk have to do with her having your car?"

"She drove it home."

Dial smooshed me in the head. "If you don't stop talking in riddles and rhymes I'm going to molly whop you."

"I'm sorry it's early. I didn't get much sleep and I'm slightly hungover." If I was keeping it one hundred I didn't want to answer her questions because that would open me up to her judgement. I should've just hopped on my bicycle and rode to the Palmer Ranch

79

myself. Sure, I'd be sweaty and tired after, but at least I'd avoid the interrogation from Detective Dial.

"Alright I need you to back up. What exactly were you doing keeping company with Francesca anyway?"

"She showed up with Oz at The Tipsy Owl."

Dial's hands tightened over the steering wheel. "Oz was there?"

"Yes ma'am."

"Did you talk to him?"

"We exchanged pleasantries. He briefly mentioned you."

Dial flashed me a look letting me know if I uttered another single, solitary word about Oz Palmer she would drive us into the nearest tree. "What did you and Fancy talk about?"

"Dial it's not even seven in the morning. How do you have the energy for all these inquisitive questions?"

"I just want to understand the circumstances that led me to have to pick up your sorry ass this morning."

Turning the radio up, I reclined my seat, and pulled my ball cap down over my eyes. Hopefully Dial took the hint. I was pleading the fifth. No more questions. From now on, it was no comment from me.

Dial cut the radio off. "I'm doing you a solid and you have the nerve to try to shut me out."

"Not shutting you out. I'm just tired."

"I remember a time when you used to tell me everything."

"When we were kids? I don't have an obligation to tell you what's going on in my life."

"Is that why you didn't tell me about Willa?"

"What are you talking about?"

"You had me over here hyping Willa up. Telling you how great she was and this whole time you've had her on speed dial for booty calls."

"Who the fuck told you that?"

"Cy."

"When did you talk to Cyrus? And why are you two talking about me?"

"What else do we have to talk about but our stupid baby brother?"

"I'm not a baby."

The corners of Dial's mouth turned upward. "But you are stupid." Being the youngest of three had its perks, except when your older siblings teamed up on you. Which Dial and Cyrus often did when we were growing up. They'd say let's play hide and seek and I'd run off looking for the best spot to conceal myself on the farm. One winter I was in the barn for hours wrapped up in a horse blanket, thinking I was a master hide and seek player because they couldn't find me. Come to find out those fuckers were never looking for me.

"Did you sleep with her?"

"Willa?"

"No, Fancy?"

I lurched forward, shaking my fist. "Dial, mind your fucking business."

The tires screeched against the pavement as she abruptly stopped in the middle of the road. "Get out."

"What?"

"Get out of my car."

"Dial you're in the middle of the gotdamn road. This isn't safe."

"Well if you get your ass out I can move."

Inhaling deeply, I hopped out of her car, coffee cup in hand. "You really are a piece of work." I slammed her passenger door and she took off like a bat out of hell, leaving me in a plume of dust and exhaust fumes. "I'm telling Mom," I screamed at the top of my lungs.

Should I have blown up at my sister? No. Nevertheless, driving off and leaving me stranded was childish. Trust me if there was anyone else half as reliable as Dial I'd have called them instead. I just wasn't remotely interested in talking about Fancy with her. My sister acted like I owed her every finite detail of my life. But if I asked one question about hers, she'd knock my block off.

I still didn't understand what happened between her and Ozzie. One minute they were a thing and the next it was over and she was walking around pretending like everything was fine. The last time she allowed herself to be vulnerable with me was a few months after she had Maple. She came into Figs and Twine while on maternity leave and just cried, and I held her while Maple was asleep in her car seat. When the tears dried up, she left and never mentioned it again. Dial liked to pretend she was invulnerable.

Last night was still etched in my memory. Fancy's easy, carefree personality. The way she flitted around my house like her presence was an everyday occurrence. I woke up this morning with a rock-hard dick that was begging to be addressed. In the shower I stroked myself, no longer able to ignore the longing. All I could think about was Fancy's hips grinding against my lap, the softness of her skin, the minty sweet taste of her mouth. I closed my eyes and pretended instead of my rough, calloused hand it was her. That my dick was stroking her cushy, wet, tight pussy. Which was all the motivation I needed to shiver and release, bracing myself against the shower wall, fearful my knees would buckle.

If she hadn't brought up the existence of a boyfriend, we would've fucked. And then what? Fancy had been my religion for years. I'd tried converting to the Temple of Reese, the cathedral of Mari, the church of Willa. But in the end, I'd return to the shrine of Francesca Palmer with offerings and songs of worship. Maybe Dial was right, I was stupid. Fancy was hardwired into my software.

Since she'd been gone, I was dating and making new memories to overwrite the old code. Unfortunately, with her return all my desires and hopes were looking to reboot.

Glancing up the road, I searched for any approaching cars, but no vehicles were in sight. It looked like I was going to have to hoof it the last few miles to the ranch. Last night it seemed like a good idea to give Fancy my car and get her out of my house so she couldn't witness the disappointment all over my face. She had a boyfriend. Possibly ex-boyfriend. *Did she return to Hume to get away from him?* Liking Fancy was one thing, but I had no intentions of getting caught up in her drama.

I purposely stuck to a select group of friends and excluded myself from gossip, which was everywhere you turned around here. You could be shopping for groceries, and an acquaintance would come up to you and just start spilling every intimate detail about themselves and everyone else. Do I look like I cared about Mr. Baxter cheating on his wife or a former classmate getting busted for a DUI? I minded the business that paid me.

The sun was up but not fully awake, which helped to make the walk bearable. Hume cooled off a bit at night, but with first light you were able to predict the weather and today was going to be another hot one. If Dial needed something heavy moved at the nursery today, she would have to get someone else to do it. Okay, that was a lie. I was still going to move it, but I'd grumble under my breath the entire time. That would be my silent protest, letting her know she couldn't just treat me any which way. And at next Sunday's dinner I was going to snitch to our mother and watch with revelry while she chewed Dial out. One of the perks of being the baby of the family.

A familiar black Jeep stopped next to me and the doors unlocked. Dial had circled back and was now staring at me. "Are you getting in or what?" That was the only apology I was getting.

Cautiously approaching the vehicle, I climbed back into the passenger seat. The remainder of our drive was silent. We were both stubborn and didn't want to be the first to say sorry. Entering the Palmer Ranch, Dial stopped in front of the main house and shifted the car into park.

"Thank you for the ride."

"Uh-hmm."

Turning to face her, I said, "Dial?"

"I just don't want you getting hurt Eddy."

"Fancy's never hurt me."

"She ignored you. She kept you close because you were a good friend, and she knew you liked her. And she used it to her advantage. In a pinch, call Edison because he'll wake up in the middle of the night, drive to some party he wasn't invited to and courier her home like a fucking RideX. He'll score her weed, or change her oil, or listen while she laments about the dude who's fucking her dizzy."

"I chose to be there for her. That's not on Fancy, that's on me."

"She's a user. She used you back then and she's probably using you right now."

"Are you done?"

"Are you listening?"

"Dial, I appreciate the concern, but I'm grown."

"Grown people get their hearts broken every day," she warned me.

"Good morning." A cheery voice came from the passenger side of the Jeep, making us both jump.

"Hey you're up?" I said.

"I figured you'd come looking for your truck," Fancy said, leaning into the window. "Hey Dial, how have you been?"

"Fine, yourself?" Dial didn't even bother to meet her eyes.

"No worse for wear, I suppose."

My sister just stared straight ahead, making everything awkward.

I turned to Dial. "See you back at the nursery."

"Yep."

I jumped out and Dial sped off, turning onto the dusty unpaved road.

"Nice to see Dial is still as friendly as ever."

"She's just tired."

"We both know I'm not her favorite person."

I shrugged Fancy's words off. "She hates everybody, really."

Fancy's face drooped. "She hates me? I get I wasn't her cup of tea … but hate?"

"Hates a strong word. She doesn't hate you."

"You just said she did."

"She doesn't wish you any ill will. She just doesn't fuck with you."

"I will never understand what I did to offend her?"

"It's complicated." I wasn't looking to explain that my sister detested her because she labeled Fancy as a selfish bitch. I tagged her arm. "Look, I just wanted to apologize for last night."

"We were both drunk. It's fine. Just a little kissing between friends."

"Good because I thought I'd get here and you'd be all stage five clingy and profess your love or some shit like that," I joked.

"You're a good kisser but you ain't that good." She was dressed in an oversized T-shirt. If she had something on underneath, I couldn't call it. Her purple hair was piled on top of her head with random curls spilling loose from her silk patterned headscarf.

"What do you have planned for the day?"

"Sleep, but knowing my dad, he'll drag me out there with him to water the horses and cows."

"Country living, gotta love it."

She set her hand on her hips. "You know what I miss most?"

"What?"

"The smell."

My face crumpled and I wrinkled my nose.

"I know it's crazy but the smell of hay, wet dirt, and shit. Reminds me of home."

"We might need to get that on a billboard. Hume … hay, dirt, and shit. Ain't nothing like it."

"Maybe I'll write a song about it."

"I'm sure it would be a number one hit."

"The keys are on the dash." She pointed to my truck parked on the side of the house.

"Thanks." I turned to leave before stopping short. "Hey, what are you doing tonight?"

Her shoulders twitched. "Right now, I'm just kind of going where the wind takes me."

"Cool, so let's see where the wind takes us tonight."

"Okay." She smiled and it was like the sun rising.

"I'll pick you up at eight."

"I'll make myself pretty for you."

My dick flexed in my jeans. This was exactly what Dial was concerned about. The subtle tease that kept me dangling on the line until I was out of oxygen.

Figs and Twine was located on the outskirts of town and occasionally we'd have to head to the main square for supplies. I offered to run errands today because I wanted to avoid Dial who was still giving me the cold shoulder even after our talk in the car. After picking up the office supplies, I made a pit stop at the mayor's storefront office.

A bell attached to the door chimed, announcing my entrance. "Hi Presley."

Cyrus's secretary perked up. "Edison, what brings you to this side of town?"

"Errands."

"Did you get anything for me?" She flipped her box braids with a smile.

Hmm? Presley and I went on a handful of dates, never making it out of the talking stage. "No, but next time. Is Cy here?"

"Yeah he is. I'll buzz him."

"You don't have to do that. I can literally see him in his office from here. Cyrus!" I shouted because I loved embarrassing him.

The phone on Presley's desk rang and she answered. "Hello? Yes, I understand."

When she hung up the phone and addressed me, her tone was professional. I was no longer the guy who felt her up in the backseat of my car our junior year. "Mayor Birch will be with you shortly. Please feel free to sit. Do you want a coffee or water?"

I looked toward Cy's office. "Nah, I'm good." Advancing forward, I passed Presley's desk and several others and opened Cyrus's door. "You were going to have me wait in the lobby?"

"Excuse you. This is a government building." Cyrus's words forced me to suppress my laughter. "I could have you trespassed."

"And I could go outside and key your car, but we both know neither of those things are about to happen. What are you doing?" I closed his office door.

"I'm working."

"No, you're not." Taking a seat, I picked through his candy bowl.

"I'm literally working right now." Cy grabbed a stack of papers which were probably all blank.

"Well that can't be true because you're talking to me."

"What the hell are you doing here anyway? Shouldn't you be at the store?"

"I needed to pick up some stuff for the shop. Snacks for the break-room, coffee pods, markers."

"Mom and Dad hand you the keys to the kingdom and you become a glorified errand boy?"

"No, I needed to put some space between me and Dial."

"What did Dial do?"

"You know our sister. She always finds ways to insert herself."

"Did she mention I saw your girl at the Dairy Queen talking close with a fella that was not you?"

If he was talking about Fancy I was going to crash out. "Who's my girl?"

"Don't act like you haven't been spending time with Willa. Worst kept secret in Hume."

"Well if everyone knows I guess it's a good thing we called it quits."

Cyrus's face became twisted. "Damn, she dumped you?"

"No, we mutually agreed to move on."

"Sure you did." He winked at me.

"We wanted different things."

"Are you dumb?"

"What do you mean?"

"You're not going to do better than Willa. Not in Hume anyway."

"I disagree."

"So you just woke up and decided to implode your life." Cy signed some document as if people in this town cared about his approval.

"If you like Willa so much, you date her."

"Shit, she's too much work."

"But it's okay for me to do the heavy lifting?"

"Willa needs a man who's going to let her decorate their home in pink and ribbons and just be happy she knows his name."

"And you think I fill that description?"

"How can I put this delicately? You're a bit of a pushover."

"Me?"

"I didn't stutter motherfucker."

Who needed enemies when you had siblings?

"I'm not a pushover. I just don't like rocking boats."

"You can't make an everything scramble without breaking a few eggs."

"I prefer hash browns and sausage."

Cy shuffled papers into a folder and finally gave me his full attention. "Dial told me you ran into Francesca Palmer at the nursery the other day."

I timidly confirmed his words. "Yeah." I was still raw from Dial cussing me out. I was hoping Cyrus would offer a counter message.

"Eddy, what are you doing?"

"What do you mean?"

"Fancy's a nice girl. I understand why you had a crush on her all through high school."

"But, because your tone is definitely giving a pending but."

"Unrequited crushes are supposed to eventually crumble."

"We're friends.

"Hmm."

"I thought you liked Fancy."

"I do. I just think you get a little loopy when she's around. Her moving was probably the best thing to happen to you. You went to college, you learned what life was like outside of Hume. You had a fucking girlfriend."

"It's funny you and Dial are notorious for doling out relationship advice while not being in a relationship."

"Being mayor, I know all and see all like the great and powerful Oz."

"You do know in that story he was a fake … phony … grifter."

He twirled his pen. "We're all faking it in one way or the other."

"Maybe we're cursed."

"How so?

"You, me, and Dial … perpetually single."

"It's because of Mom and Dad."

My head jerked back. "What the fuck are you talking about?"

"Kiddo, you've got to take off those rose-colored glasses."

"I'm not following."

"Edison, I love that for you. I really do." Cyrus acted like we grew up in different households. I understood the theory of siblings having different experiences and relationships with their parents even when all the kids grew up together, but Cy's reality was so removed from mine. "What's Fancy doing in town?"

"Just visiting."

"For how long? Cause I'd love to get her in some ads for the town. Plaster her face on a billboard that says home of Francesca Palmer of Whiskey Wild. Is Darla here? We need to get her in on this too."

"Funny enough she was pitching me an interesting billboard idea this morning," I joked.

"This morning? Okay, I see you player."

"It's not like that."

"Does that have anything to do with why Dial is mad at you?"

"I'm sure she'll tell you all about it during your sibling chat I'm not included in."

"If you were included, we wouldn't be able to make fun of you."

"Shit I don't even know why I came here because you're never any help."

"You want help, shoot. I'm the mayor of Hume and I'm here to solve my constituent's problems."

"I asked Fancy out. Not a date just a hangout." A twinge of guilt washed over me at my admission.

"You need to keep your expectations low. Like the prices at Bargain Bin low."

"I've mastered that. Low expectations equals minimum disappointment."

"Good and whatever you do, don't sleep with her."

Casting a glance at his décor, I asked, "Did you do something different to your office?"

"I'm serious."

"Never said I was going to do anything. I'm just making conversation."

"You're damn right you're not. Because if you do, she'll still run back to LA at the first opportunity."

"I think you're underestimating the power of my dick, but I hear you."

"Is that why Willa dumped you?"

Rolling my eyes, I shouted, "She didn't dump—"

"An idiot says what?"

"What?" Ugh, why did I always fall for that?

9

Fancy

AFTER EDISON PICKED UP HIS truck, I attempted to get a few extra hours of sleep but failed. All I could think about was Dial's cold reception. I wasn't stupid. There was no love lost between her and me, but I couldn't quite pinpoint when our relationship shifted. Dial was a year older than me and growing up, I was practically her shadow. But in high school she avoided me; eventually, her salutations were nothing but one-word sentences.

Since childhood she'd been protective of Edison and at some point, I think she saw me as a threat because of how close Edison and I were. I know I sounded like a conspiracy theorist, musing over Dial's plot to take me down. Maybe she just didn't like my personality. There were plenty of people I didn't mesh with, but I was at the very least cordial when they came around. If Dial thought her shitty attitude was going to keep me from Edison, she was mistaken. During prior visits, I'd purposefully avoided Edison because of Dial, but you know what … fuck it and fuck her.

Muffled ringing interrupted my thoughts. I reluctantly climbed out of my bed, tripping over a pair of clogs on the way to my phone, which was under a pile of clothes. "Hello." My voice was low and raspy.

"Fancy?"

"Darla?"

"Yeah, how are you?"

I broke down, finding fresh tears. "Crappy. What about you?"

"Oh, babes don't cry. I've missed my best friend."

Gulping down a sob, I attacked, "Well, you haven't been acting like it." When the words left my mouth, I realized how hurt I was that this was the first time I was hearing from her.

"I'm sorry. I wanted to give you some space."

"I don't need space from my best friend." I sniffled.

Darla and I had been to hell and back together. Alongside Edison, she was my closest and oldest friend. She was there when I fell off Cotton Candy, breaking my leg. I was there when her parents divorced. When I lost my virginity, we had a sleepover, and I gave her all the details. We thought we were so grown. And when she got pregnant and needed not to be, I was there too.

"I figured if you needed me, you'd call."

"Frankly, I don't know what I need right now. I'm all topsy-turvy."

"Have you talked to Chap?" Her tone indicated she was walking on eggshells, knowing Chap was a sore and puss riddled subject for me.

"We've texted back and forth a bit."

"He's torn up over you."

"Good."

"You should at least let him try to explain."

My stomach hardened at the hint of Darla coming to his defense. "All of a sudden you're Team Dylan?"

"No, never that. I'm Team Whiskey Wild."

"There's nothing to explain. He cheated and it's probably not the first time."

"You don't know that."

"I don't think I can ever trust him again." I scrubbed my face. "And if I'm being honest, I don't think I care."

"What do you mean?"

"Sure, I care but maybe this is all God doing me a massive favor. Chap and I haven't been in a good place for a while now. I thought it was just the pressure with the tour and getting back in the studio, but he and I have been out of sync for a minute."

"Why didn't you tell me?"

"How do you say your relationship is failing?"

"Are you done with him?"

"I'm not saying that. Shit, I don't know what I'm saying. But if I stay, some things will have to change."

"Like what?"

"Like the way he treats me for starters."

"Fancy, I'm so sorry." The line was silent except for Darla's muffled cries.

"Don't you start boo-hooing because I'm going to start and then we'll just be on the line in a pool of tears."

"I just … Fancy … I don't like to see you hurt. Fuck."

I didn't want to think about my current situation, deciding instead to change the subject. "What else is going on?"

"Uhm … give me a sec." Darla blew her nose to stop the sniffles. "Did you get my email?"

"What email?"

"The label is asking questions about the remaining tour dates. We put out a statement."

A sudden coldness hit me at my core. "What kind of statement?"

"I emailed it to you."

"Hold on." I pulled up my inbox and scrolled until I found Darla's message. My eyes frantically scanned the one-page attachment.

To our fans,

Due to unforeseen circumstances, Whiskey Wild missed day two of the Heritage Festival. We apologize to our fans who purchased tickets and incurred expenses to attend this event. If you've purchased tickets for Whiskey Wild's Girls Behaving Badly tour we are determined to make every effort to resume the tour, with little to no missed dates after a brief hiatus.

Whiskey Wild loves our fans and looks forward to getting back on a stage near you in the coming weeks. Until then drink CHEAP WHISKEY and make some QUESTIONABLE CHOICES.

Fancy & Darla

Whiskey Wild

Turning my attention back to Darla, I asked, "Who greenlit this statement?"

"Well Chap and I—"

"Chap," I shouted. "He does not speak for me."

"He kind of does, he's our manager."

Fuck him. Whiskey Wild was my baby. Mine and Darla's. Chap didn't get to make unauthorized decisions about my career. "I never agreed to canceling tour dates."

"Fancy you've been MIA, decisions had to be made."

"And so you and Chap are just making all the decisions now?"

"Don't do that. Don't you dare do that. I've had your back since day one."

I was directing my anger at the wrong person. This wasn't Darla's fault it was Chap. If it wasn't for Chap and his wandering eye, I'd be in Los Angeles rehearsing for the second leg of our tour. "I'm sorry. You're right. I didn't mean to imply otherwise."

"It's okay, I know this is a lot."

"Look Darla. I fucked up. I just up and left and didn't stop to think about the group or the tour. I did the one thing we promised never to do … fuck up our money."

"This is all just a minor hiccup. We'll get back on track … you, me, and Chap." I flinched at her inclusion of the bastard who broke my heart, but remained silent. "Where are you?"

"I'm in Hume."

"You went home?"

"I didn't exactly have many options." I guess I could have booked a room at the Omni Hotel, but what I wanted was to escape, not hide. "Hey, do you know why Moniece is coming all the way to Hume?"

"What?"

"She said she had to speak to me about something important."

"No, I haven't got a clue. Maybe she wanted to tell you about the potential canceled tour dates face to face."

"Maybe, well I'll worry about it when she gets here." I released a long sigh. The sound of vehicles drew me to my window. Outside, Ozzie and my dad were fussing over something or other. My father could be a real hard ass when it came to work, but I guess that's why Palmer horses were the best in the business because my father was a perfectionist. Oz was the opposite, but he was dedicated and one of the best horse trainers in the game. "Guess who I ran into last night at The Tipsy Owl?"

"Who?"

"Okay you're no fun. Edison."

"Edison Birch? How's he doing?"

"He's been drinking his milk, chopping piles of wood, and baling hay."

"Edison Birch?"

"Edison Fucking Birch." I bit my lip at the thought of him.

"Remember you have a boyfriend."

"No, I don't. Chap and I are on a break. He broke my heart and I'm considering letting Edison break my spine."

"Fancy." Darla was the most immodest person I knew, so why she was over there clutching pearls I'd never know.

"Okay not really, but I can flirt a little."

"I thought you went to Hume for clarity?"

"No, you're right and I don't plan on doing anything reckless."

I decided not to share I'd already been a little reckless by making out with Edison last night. Darla would judge me. I didn't want to hear any of her rational thinking right now. I was mad. Mad at Chap. Mad at myself. I knew better. Everyone said he was a ladies' man, but I ignored the red flags because I wanted the fairy tale. Girl from a small town moves to LA, becomes a huge star, and she starts dating the handsome well connected guy.

What I hadn't told Darla is for months now, I'd been questioning whether this fairy tale was one I wanted. Mostly the relationship part, not the celebrity part. Dylan's expectations of me and our relationship were ones I didn't quite agree with. It was as if he was slowly trying to change me. He said I was a country music outsider and people knew it. After each concert or interview, he'd have a list of notes on things I could change or ways I could improve. Funny thing is he never gave Darla similar notes.

I wasn't interested in changing my personality. Not saying I was perfect, but I didn't need a bullet point list of all the things I needed to tweak. If you loved someone, why would you want them to change? Dylan could be selfish and didn't recognize his immense privilege, but I accepted all of him, even the parts that weren't polished.

"Are you still there?" Darla asked.

"Yeah."

"If you need me just say the word and I'll come running."

"Thanks. I love you."

"Love you too."

When the doorbell rang, I gave myself one quick pass before heading for the stairs. I'd opted for a yellow sun dress that showed off my legs and cowboy boots. My hair was loose in big, deep curls which showcased the mulberry purple highlights I'd gotten a few months back. Downstairs, I found my dad and Edison on the porch talking about roofs.

"Hey, sorry to keep you waiting." Edison was in his uniform of choice, jeans, a sage green T-shirt and rustic brown boots. He'd ditched the ball cap and I was treated to a freshly tapered cut. In LA, men spent thousands on designer clothes and none could touch the sexy simplicity Edison was giving.

"It's fine." Edison's eyes tripped down the length of my frame before he remembered we were in mixed company. "I was just telling your dad about my tin roof."

"He's thinking about replacing it. I think he should keep it," my dad said.

Edison frowned. "When it rains it can get kind of loud."

"Best sleep I ever had was your momma and mine's first place. Good food, a fine woman, and a tin roof, that's all you need."

"Rain on a tin roof is like a lullaby. I agree with Daddy, you should keep it."

"Noted." Edison licked his bottom lip and my pussy constricted. I could sense the seat of my panties moisten.

"I watch a ton of home improvement shows. If you ever need expert advice, I got you."

"Are you supposed to be the expert?" my father asked.

"With the hours of screen time I've clocked, I could gut a room and restore it if I had a mind to." Turing to Edison, I asked, "Are you ready to go?" I kissed my father on the cheek. The last thing I wanted to do was stand on the porch talking about roofing materials.

"Nice seeing you again Mr. Palmer." You have to love a good southern gentleman. Chap grew up in California and referred to my father by his first name. I hated it.

As we descended the stairs, my father called after us. "Have my daughter back home at a respectable hour."

Edison placed his hand over his heart. "Of course, I would never dream of disrespecting your home by bringing her back too late."

My father erupted into a fit of laughter. "I'm joshing. It's been a long time since my baby girl's been home and I could play the scary father role. You two are grown and I trust you to keep her safe."

"Thank you, sir." Edison shut the car door behind me before making his way to the driver's seat.

When he drove off, I teased him. "No sir, I would never do anything to defile your beautiful daughter."

"Shut up."

"You know you guys from the south get away with murder. A little country twang and you have people agreeing to just about anything. Abscond with their daughters to do God knows what. Late night hang outs, driving down dark back roads, promises of just the tip and nothing more."

Edison's eyes grew wide. "Which dude from high school was telling you he was only going to put in the tip?"

"I fell for it every time. Next thing you know we're both acting shocked like 'Oh no how'd that whole dick slide inside.'"

"Fancy, we haven't been in the car for a full minute. Can we save the dick talk for later?"

"Okay, note to self, Edison would like to talk about his dick later."

I couldn't tell for sure, but I liked to believe his face was flushed. "Fancy Palmer."

My naughty giggle filled the cab. Making him blush was one of my favorite activities. Edison wasn't a prude, at least I don't think he was, but he didn't like talking about S.E.X in mixed company. A girl knew if she kissed Edison, he wasn't going to tell. "Where are you taking me?"

"Does it matter?"

"No, I'd go anywhere with you."

Edison's head swiveled and his eyes slammed into mine. He had kind eyes, always had. Edison was the guy you called when you were in a jam. When I drove my car into a ditch driving back home after a non-sober high school party, I called Edison. When Ricky Moore assaulted me at a band performance after I said no to his advances, I told Edison. And the next day before first bell, Edison beat the piss out of Ricky.

"Eyes on the road, mister." I can't believe how many years passed since we'd last seen one another. You expected time to make things muddy and awkward, but being with Edison after all this time felt natural. The test of true friendship was the ability to pick up where you left off. Even after years apart, the bond hadn't deteriorated.

As we approached the main part of town, Edison offered some clues. "I was thinking you've been gone for a minute. So why not show you the sights you've been missing?"

"The sights in Hume?"

"Yeah, we've made some improvements since you left."

"Really?"

"The movie theater got new seats. They recline. The Gas Guzzle finally fixed their sign, unfortunately it burned out a few months ago. And they painted the high school."

"Wow, it's just a hub of activity here in Hume."

"We are the epicenter of nothing. But we did recently acquire …"

"What?" Edison turned left onto Monroe Way the corner was illuminated by a orange and white neon sign. "Hot Doodle Dawgs?"

"You're not saying it right. The Doodle's got a little hop to it. Hot *Doodle* Dawgs."

"Wow the name is—"

"It wasn't well thought out, I'll give you that."

"Hot Doodle Dawgs"

"*Doodle*." He corrected me by adding a singsongy note to the word doodle.

"Ahh yes, my bad. Hot *Doodle* Dawgs."

"Best hot dogs ever."

"Better than Gas Guzzle?"

"The Gas Guzzle, where if food drops on the floor they hold it to the sky and ask the Lord to bless it before putting it back on display."

"Yes, but the dirt and germs from Gas Guzzle is kind of the secret sauce."

Edison parked his truck in the lot Hot Doodle Dawgs shared with the bank. Inside we ordered and found an empty booth. I got an onion ring and bacon hot dog, and while it wasn't the best hot dog ever, it was the best hot dog in Hume.

Edison bit into his dog topped with potato chips and sauces, exaggerating his enjoyment with moans. "Admit it, this is pretty good," he said around a mouthful of food.

"It's not bad."

"You see what you're missing?"

"Is Hot *Doodle* Dawg a big tourist attraction for Hume?"

"I mean it gets customers from the adjacent towns every now and then."

"Never in my life have I seen a man ride so hard for a hot dog joint."

"I go hard for everything Hume related."

"And I'm sure your ancestors are very proud."

"Shit not a lot of towns like Hume survived. People didn't appreciate groups of Black folks building their own shit. Creating their own wealth. When we rolled up, this was the town no one wanted. Dirt that wouldn't grow, threats of flooding of the creek and the river. But our families made Hume home and so much blood was shed to keep it that way."

Hume was founded by three Black families, the Birch family among them. In the middle of town there is this huge plaque in honor of the founders, and you couldn't go into many buildings without seeing the now famous photo of the group standing together on Birch Street for the first anniversary celebration.

"You're like our resident Hume historian."

"I don't know about that, but I do find the story of this town very interesting. I blame Dial. She is obsessed with that shit." He waved the conversation away. "Nobody wants to talk about this town's history. Tell me about your boyfriend."

My hope was that my having a boyfriend wouldn't come up, but Edison was owed an explanation. "Kind of, sort of boyfriend."

Edison looked at me with his gentle eyes and I just spilled my guts.

"His name is Dylan, but everyone calls him Chap. He was a fixture in the young Hollywood club circuit. His dad's a big-time music producer and his stepmother is Bille Preston."

"Wow, legend."

"Yeah, she really is. We started dating casually at first and then I was always at his place, or he was at mine. At the time Whiskey Wild was still struggling to make a name for ourselves. Anyway, Chap had all these great ideas and connections and before long he became our manager and my boyfriend."

"Business and pleasure often get messy."

"Yeah, that's the thing, I didn't think so at the time. I should have, but I wasn't really thinking with my head."

"What were you using your kit kat instead?"

"No, I was thinking with my heart …" We stared at each other in momentary silence. "And maybe my kitty just a little bit."

"It happens to the best of us."

"When's the last time you led with your dick?"

"I plead the fifth."

"We will be circling back to that. Anyway, Chap and I have been together for several years. And four days ago, I found out he was cheating. Like I walked in during the act."

"Ouch, I'm sorry."

"The thing is, after the initial shock, all I kept thinking is maybe it's for the best."

"Why do you think that?"

"Chap and I are two very different people, and I was kind of all wrapped up in him. Have you ever done that? You meet someone and then you slowly start to lose yourself. Their likes become your likes, so instead of hot dogs on a stick, you're asking for tuna tartare."

"What's tuna tartare? Is that the raw stuff?"

"Yes, it's the raw stuff. And it's disgusting." I tossed my arm in the air. "I just think I was starting to lose sense of who I was. And I needed to come home to try and figure out what was real and my next steps."

"And you don't think your next move includes Chap?"

"Have you heard that saying the thought of being with someone is often better than the reality of being with that person?"

"Yeah."

"That's what I think this is. With Dylan. Listen, I'm hurt by his cheating. I'm not gonna pretend I haven't cried an ocean of tears, but maybe that asshole did me a favor."

"You have to know any man who would cheat on you is an idiot, right?"

"I know. You might be surprised to hear this, but in LA I feel like a fish outta water. Every day, just struggling to breathe. And Dylan gave me legitimacy."

"Why do you feel out of place?"

"I'm just waiting for people to figure out I'm a fraud and I don't know what I'm doing and I never have."

"You've written, what, five number one records?"

"Seven."

"Seven number one records, gold and platinum albums. Sold-out concerts and headlining tours. That sounds real official to me."

"Well Dylan doesn't think so."

"I thought we already established Dylan is missing a few brain cells. What he thinks doesn't matter."

Fuck Chap, I wasn't going to let him ruin my time with Edison. "What about you? Give me your sappy love story."

"There isn't much to tell."

"Don't lie."

Edison cracked his knuckles. "I was kind of seeing Willa for a bit."

My eyes grew wide. "How did you pull Willa? She was the prettiest girl in school."

"She wasn't … you were. But she and I just kept bumping into each other."

"And one day the bumping turned to grinding." I gasped. "How was it?"

"I'm not telling you that. But I'm not complaining."

"So what happened?"

"Hmm … you walked into Figs and Twine with your rumpled up shirt and ashy elbows."

My face, neck and ears grew hot. "You noticed the elbows?"

"Yes, I did."

Growing up I always felt loved and appreciated. My father wasn't perfect, but he set the bar for how I should be treated. Chap lowered the bar to the floor and casually walked across, expecting a six-gun salute for doing the bare minimum. Why was I settling when I was the prize and the talent? Chap was a people person, but he didn't have a musical bone in his body.

In my conversations with Edison, he actively listened and cared, something Chap never did. Talking to Chap was always a competition in which I'd speak, and he'd be chomping at the bit to interject, refute, or call me out right dense. The past few days were intense, but the fog was lifting. Searching Edison's familiar face, I knew what I had to do. I pulled my phone from my purse, typed out a text message, and pressed send with no hesitation. Handing Edison my phone, I let him read my final message to Chap.

Fancy

IT'S OVER.

10

Edison

AFTER DINNER, THE TOUR OF Hume continued with a stop at the post office. Not your typical first date destination but … *Wait was this a first date? Fancy literally dumped her boyfriend in front of me and I still wasn't sure.* We all know what happens with assumptions. You end up going in for a kiss at the end of the night and someone laughs in your face.

When we jumped out of my truck, Fancy scanned the building. The office was closed, so I'm sure she was wondering why I brought her here. "It's the post office. Looks exactly the same," she said.

"Yes, it hasn't changed much."

Fancy shimmied the skirt of her dress in place. This may not be a date, but Fancy had taken her time on the finer details. Her nails were red with cherries on them, which meant she hit up Arnelle shop for this occasion. Francesca's curly hair was fluffy and made her look like a true rockstar. The body was tea with her dress hugging curves I'd long admired.

"So what are you about to show me, the new mailboxes?"

"No." I held my hand out to her and my heart jerked against its reins in anticipation. Fancy's eyes flickered from my face to my outstretched arm, sizing me up. When she slipped her hand in mine, my stomach fluttered like someone was inside, unspooling ribbon. We walked to the back of the building, and I pointed to an adjacent wall.

Fancy slowed in her tracks, dropping my hand, which I didn't like, but it was worth it to see the look on her face. "Is this for real?"

"Yes."

She spun around, shock etched across her face. "Edison, that's a mural of Darla and me on the back of the hardware store."

"I see it." The lot behind the hardware store was home to a community garden. Figs and Twine partnered with the elementary and junior high schools, donating seeds and tools for the students to use to grow their own vegetables and plants. Dial and I took turns leading the classes. I had nothing to do with the mural, but I did think it was cool Fancy and Darla were kind of overseeing the garden and inspiring the kids who volunteered.

The mural was colorful and captured the vibrant spirit of Whiskey Wild. The two women were painted with guitars in hand. Fancy's hair looked like it was in motion and her torso was bent back as her fingers played a riff. Underneath Fancy and Darla the name of the group was emblazoned in bold font.

"How long has that been here?"

"A few years."

"Years? My mother has all the tea on what's going on in Hume, but she forgot to mention this mural." She pulled out her phone to snap some quick pictures. "This is unreal. Who made this?"

"Some kids from the high school."

"High school, are you shitting me?"

"Almost as impressive as the billboard in Times Square."

Fancy shook her head in denial. "How'd you hear about that?"

"You know your momma likes to brag."

"She is president of our fan club. But seeing how she never mentioned this mural, I may have to strip her of that title," she joked.

"Listen you and Darla are global superstars, but some of us in Hume remember the humble beginnings and we are so proud."

"I remember you were our security guard when we'd sneak into some sketchy bar a town over to perform. For a scrawny fella, you had one hell of a right hook."

"When you're skinny like I was, you have to be able to protect yourself. Plus, I grew up with Cyrus, Dial, and Ozzie picking fights all the time. I had no choice but to hold my own."

"I know. I always felt safe when you were around."

"That's because you didn't have any sense. We were three baby faced kids frequenting bars and taverns we had no business in."

"True, but we got free beer after."

"That was the least they could do since they weren't paying you."

"They paid us in beer and cheeseburgers. And they ignored our obviously fake ID's."

"Yeah, and I never got to drink because I was always the designated driver."

"Well you couldn't expect the talent to drive. We had to rest our vocal cords and guitar fingers." She pressed her lips together to stifle a smile.

"Chauffeur, security guard, water boy."

Fancy invaded my personal space, reaching for my hand with a squeeze. "Friend. You were a good friend."

"Yeah." And that's what it boiled down to, Fancy always saw me as a friend and nothing more. The guy who'd lugged their guitars and equipment to the truck. The guy who held her hair back when she barfed. The shoulder to lean on when some dude that didn't deserve her fucked up. And I was happy to fill the role. Because being Fancy's friend was still important to me. I wasn't her friend because I was in love with her. Love may be too strong a word. I admired her passion and perseverance. Francesca made me curious about a world beyond my backyard. She owed me nothing, and I learned to keep my expectations low. Fancy was my friend before anything else. And the fact that she still saw me as a friend after all this time meant what we shared was just as special to her as it was to me.

I wasn't a pick me trying to get chosen. I genuinely wanted her to be happy. Sure, I thought I had the ability to make her happy. But the minute she got stars in her eyes, I knew I'd never be enough. She was too big for Hume and it was impossible and unfair of me to expect her to dim her light or make herself microscopic for me.

"Do you still play the guitar?" she asked.

"I don't know if you can call what I do playing."

"You're being modest. I used to love to sing while you accompanied me on guitar."

"You sang like an angel while I missed every other note."

"You never missed a note. You never overpowered my voice. It's like I was made to sing to your melody. You were so good without even trying. I wanted people to hear my music. Sing my lyrics so bad I could barely stand it. And you could take it or leave it."

Instruments came easy to me. I'd been playing since I was seven, guitar, piano, and the trumpet. I was in band alongside Fancy and Darla. Music allowed me to feel things I couldn't articulate. "I just wasn't as passionate about it as you were."

Studying my features, she asked, "What are you passionate about, Edison?"

Just because I was reserved didn't mean there weren't things that fired me up.

"I'm passionate about beautiful sunsets, summer lemonade, my goats, who hop around when I come to feed them in the morning. I like to think they're excited to see me and not the bucket of food. I get a kick out of guitar solos, and that first cup of coffee in the morning. I have a basin in the barn out back and sometimes I'll fill it with piping hot water and just soak, listen to the whistle of the wind through the trees or the birds chirping hello. I lost my shit when my cow had her calf. How she got pregnant is a story for another time. When I come into town, I'll get taffy from Sweet But Sinful and I can't have a piece until I'm headed home. That first chewy sweet bite is always the best."

Fancy's chest heaved and her words were low and breathy. "You are a rarity, Edison Birch. And it seems wrong that I'm just now figuring that out."

Ducking my head, I said, "You can just call me simple it's fine."

"I didn't mean simple, I meant rare, unique, one of one. Like no one I've ever met and I've met a shit ton of people. Take the fucking compliment."

"Okay, thank you. Are we ready to move on?"

"Yeah."

Back in the truck, we drove for a few minutes to MetCalf Park. It was lush and green, with walking trails and ponds. I'd racked up hundreds of hours at the park on a lazy weekend eating homemade PB&J sandwiches with Doritos stuffed in between just people watching while Fancy wrote songs.

I pointed to the massive jungle gym and Fancy offered an enthusiastic nod. She lowered herself into one of the swings and I settled in beside her. The night was clear and the sky was like a map with limitless possibilities. I thought about Fancy in some shape or fashion every single day since she left. Usually it wasn't obvious, just a whisper of a memory from our childhood. Swimming at the lake, skinned knees, and timeouts to catch our breath. She'd been part of my life for so long it was hard to find a memory she wasn't a part of.

"I had my first kiss in this park," she said, lazily swinging back and forth.

"With who?"

Her eyes grew wide. "With you."

"Me?"

"You don't remember our first kiss?"

"I remember kissing you, but it wasn't *my* first kiss."

"Wait a second, we were twelve. Who else were you kissing?"

"Ma'am sometimes my business ain't your business."

"I thought I was your first."

"Just because you weren't my first doesn't mean it was any less special."

"I was so nervous. And you were looking at me funny. My palms were sweaty, kind of like they are right now."

"I remember thinking you were going to push me away and say 'Eww Edison, gross.' But you never did."

"I leaned into it."

"You leaned all the way into it, even slipped in a little tongue."

"I just figured if you're going to kiss, you should make it a good one."

"It was a good one. Best kiss I ever had."

Fancy rolled her eyes. "I seriously doubt that."

"No it was because it was sweet, and there were no expectations for anything more. The kiss, our kiss wasn't building up to a bigger moment … it was the moment."

The swing she was gliding on came to a stop and Francesca examined my features. All night her eyes were acutely affixed to my face as if she was looking for deeper meaning or a sign. "I remember thinking after, so that's what the love songs are all talking about." She tucked her hair behind her ears. "Life was so simple back then. Hanging out in the park, feeding the ducks, catching fireflies. When puberty hit, all that shit changed. The boys were now young men and they had mischief in their eyes. When did it all get so complicated?"

"When you're younger, you can't wait to be grown. I remember thinking in high school once I graduate can't nobody tell me what to do. But the joke was on us because adulthood comes with responsibilities and expectations, and you can't blame your fuck ups on youth. I spend more time worrying about the farm, the shop, and my parents then anything else. Still, it doesn't have to be … complicated. I mean some things you can't avoid. We all have choices, and some choices lead to more treacherous paths."

"Do you regret staying in Hume?"

"No, I've never regretted that." When Fancy and Darla decided to leave Hume for California, they asked me to come with them. We were best friends, practically inseparable. They said I could be their stage manager, and we'd get a place and be roomies. But California was never my dream, so I passed. "Do you regret leaving?"

"No, I can't say that I do."

And that's where we stood. I wanted to milk my goats and sell eggs at the farmers' market, and she wanted to perform on stage and travel the world. In so many ways she and I were similar. We loved the tranquility of country living, our families were paramount to us. Trust if her parents or Ozzie needed her, it didn't matter where she was in the world, she'd make the trek back home to support them. Despite that, when it mattered the most, our views on life were starkly different. All I needed was the love of a good woman and maybe a dog and Fancy … well she wanted shit I couldn't provide. But I was willing to pretend none of that existed if she was.

Taking a deep breath I surveyed the sky. You'd think I'd be able to identify the consolations for all the nights I stood in the yard with my head upward. The world was vast, but at the end of the day we all looked to the same stars with hope. I found the biggest star in the sky and made a wish. People claimed you could only wish on shooting stars, but that was bullshit. The luminaries were magical and filled with inspiration. After casting my deepest desire to the heavens, I spoke it into existence. "Would you like to come back to my place?" I asked.

There she was looking at me again. Probably plotting on the nicest way to let me down. Sometimes wishes didn't come true and that was fine. Fancy's eyes brightened and an easy smile took over her face. "Yes, I would like that."

Warmth radiated throughout my body as a surge of energy invigorated my muscles. I dragged my feet back and swung high. Fancy giggled and mimicked my moves, inertia pushing her forward as she swung her long legs back and forth trying to gain momentum. Our timid, excited laughter peppered the air just like when we were kids. All our adult struggles washed away, and it was just me, her, and the power of what could be.

Back at my place, we both knew what was about to happen, but we went through the motions of acting surprised when my lips found hers in the entryway of my farmhouse. Fancy wrapped her arm around my shoulders, pressing her supple body against mine. We tumbled back and forth, knocking tacky artwork askew on the walls as we made our way to my bedroom on the second floor. I kicked my door open, never letting go of her lips.

The sixteen-year-old inside of me was freaking out. Francesca Palmer was in my bedroom, kissing me with an urgency I could never have anticipated. You know the saying good things are worth the wait. Well Fancy was a good thing and I'd waited a lifetime for her.

She giggled between kisses and I pulled away slightly to make sure she wasn't having second thoughts. "What?"

"I just can't believe I'm kissing little Eddy Birch." I grabbed her hand and placed it on my dick, which had expanded substantially in my jeans. Fancy's jaw dropped into a slack smile. "I stand corrected. Little isn't the correct adjective."

I gently pushed her onto my bed and bending down, I removed her boots and socks, massaging her feet.

"Edison, you are not about to suck my toes. They've been in those boots for hours you can't—"

"I don't care, Fancy. I don't care. I'm going to savor every part of you because I've been wanting this forever." When I put her big toe in my mouth, she crashed to the bed. It didn't even taste bad, it was just salty. If this was my one opportunity to fuck Fancy Palmer, I was going to fuck her good and proper. After giving my attention to both feet, I worked my way up her frame. Skipping her sweet center, I placed strategic kisses across her stomach, leading to her neck.

Nuzzling into her collarbone, I kissed and licked as her hands slipped under my T-shirt, exploring my muscles. "Take that dress off for me," I asked, rolling back on my heels.

Fancy stood unzipping the side of her dress and pulled it over her head. She was perfection and I needed a moment of silence to take her all in. Her long legs and curve of her waist that rounded at the hips. Her breasts, which were a little less than a handful and exposed because she never wore a bra, the slope of her long neck. Her plump lips that were swollen from our endless kissing.

I leaned in, kissing her side until I landed at the space between her leg and hip joint. She dissolved into laughter. "That tickles."

"Right there?" I pointed to the spot I'd just finished kissing.

"Yes."

I made a second attempt to kiss her sensitive spot, and her giggles quickly turned into a long moan. When I looked up at her, her eyes were hooded and clouded with lust.

"Lay back on the bed." When she complied, I planted kisses on the inside of her thighs slowly and deliberately. I wanted her to know what was about to happen next. Anticipation would upend her breathing, as her bodice heaved with longing. The warmth of my breath hovering over her pussy would cause her legs to twitch. When I opened her wide, I would feast on her from the rooter to the tooter.

Pressing my lips to her clit through her cotton panties, I got the reaction I was looking for.

"Oh, fuck me," she groaned.

"I'm gonna get to that part," I promised her.

The moonlight casting shadows made everything feel surreal even though her pussy was inches from my mouth. Hooking my fingers into the sides of her underwear, I removed them with an assist from Fancy who lifted her hips. I resumed kissing her thighs and every area around her pussy without ever making contact. Fancy squirmed underneath me. Her breathing pattern was erratic as she groped at the duvet.

She grabbed my face and said, "Please don't tease me."

I offered an apologetic smile. But between you and me I wasn't sorry. I wanted her to need it, need me. I wanted her to beg for it, so when I gave her what she asked for, she had no choice but to rejoice. Sliding my tongue across her slit, she seeped in air. With the second pass, she tugged at my shirt. When I plunged deep on the third lick she melted in my mouth, her juices coating my tongue.

I moaned against her clit as her hips worked in tandem with me. Fancy sat up, folding her body over mine. She kissed the back of my head while my face was submerged in her. Finding my ear, she groaned, kissing the side of my face.

"You're gonna make me come," she whispered. Grabbing hold of her waist, I worked hard to make that a reality for her. Brushing my fingers over her slickness, I inserted a finger or two. Fancy fell back to the bed, her voice crisp and clear as she called for me. "Edison, you're making me see stars."

I didn't let up fucking her with my fingers while practically French kissing her clit. When her left leg wouldn't stop shaking, I knew I had her. Fancy's screams filled the room as she shivered. She tried to run away from my tongue, but I wouldn't allow it, laying claim to that pussy with suckles, slurps, and messy kisses until her juices were dripping down my throat.

Pulling away, I climbed onto the bed next to her. Brushing the hair from her face, I asked. "Are you okay?"

"Actually, I've never been better."

11

Fancy

MY BEING COMPLETELY NAKED WHILE Edison was still fully dressed didn't sit right with me and needed to be rectified immediately. He lay there smiling sheepishly like he hadn't just blown my mind with the flick of his tongue.

Edison reached out, tugging on a strand of my hair. "I like the purple."

"Yeah? Darla said it was crazy to dye it anything other than my signature red, but I needed a change."

"With the softer color, I can make out your eyes better and the light flecks of gold at the edge of your pupils."

"Strip," I commanded. "You are not going to sit there and sweet talk me all night. I need to feel you on top of me."

Edison moved like molasses. He always had since childhood. He was never in a rush, he was always observing the world around him. While Darla and I had our faces aglow in UV lights from our phones, he was just out there raw dogging life. Like he didn't want to miss something important. Back then I didn't get it, but now I understood he was the one really living because he experienced each moment distraction free.

When he finally stepped out of his boxers, my face lit up with delight. It blew my mind that men could walk around unassuming and then drop trou and you realize this whole time they were concealing a third leg.

His toes curled into the carpet. "You're embarrassing me," he said.

"Don't act like I'm the first woman who lit up like a Christmas tree at the sight of you." I couldn't resist. Reaching out, I took the weight of him in my hand, stroking his member, lightly applying pressure to the tip. Edison stood rod straight as I smiled up at him. All I wanted was to witness him come undone. For calm and collected Edison to grab me tight and call me dirty names. I wanted to suck him off sloppy and wet while telling him he was a good boy. But the throbbing in between my legs was deafening. With his dick inches from my lips I said, "I need you to fuck me right now." Making sure to talk slow and extra airy, so he felt my breath on the tip of his dick, my mouth just out of reach.

Edison backed off and rummaged in the pockets of his jeans looking for a condom. My eager eyes were as big as saucers as he rolled the rubber over his member. I grabbed him by the neck and pressed his lips against mine. Playfully nipping at his bottom lip, he moaned, sweeping his tongue into my mouth to dance next to mine. We were like teenagers exploring each other for the first time, languishing in that long kiss like we both weren't naked and able to do so much more. I just couldn't get over the way his tongue tasted like a combination of both of us, it was sweet and savory at the same time.

When he finally climbed on top, he offered a crooked smile, teasing me with the tip before leisurely slipping inside. I held my breath until all of him met all of me. He stroked my cheek and I could tell I was in trouble. His deep-set eyes consumed me, blocking out every other thought. The first strokes were nice and easy. What you'd expect from someone who was laid back and chill like a three-day weekend with no particular plans. His large hand rubbed my legs and he buried his head into my chest. Selecting a tit, he teased my nipple with his tongue before swiping it over my areola, practically inhaling my entire breast.

I moaned and writhed underneath him. Tossing my hand to the back of his head, I rubbed his tapered fade. This wasn't fucking, this was grown and sexy. Edison was making love to every part of me. His lips brushed my chin before nestling next to my ear. I thought he was going to tell me how good I felt or how long he'd waited for this, but he did none of that. The sound of his breath against my ear as it went from steady to more labored the deeper the thrust was sending me.

The perfect song is a culmination of several factors: words, melody, and voice. Sex with Edison was like the perfect song. Every thrust expertly timed. The tap of his fingers against my waist silently urging me forward. Our breath syncopated, when I exhaled air he'd breathe it in. I called out his name like it was the chorus in a number one record.

When he increased the pace it was like we'd been singing a cappella and the beat finally kicked in. It was heady and aggressive. His body was in urgent need of mine as he drove deeper, taking away my ability to speak. I clawed at his back as his teeth bit down on my shoulder. All of a sudden, I was a contortionist as I opened myself wider for him, my back arched.

Edison grabbed my waist, flipping us over so I was on top. He was letting me sing lead and I decided to dip into the bridge. Rocking back and forth then up and down, wanting to experience him from every angle. His hands coasted over my frame. Sometimes he'd guide my hips, making it a duet, and other times I was performing solo while he reaped the benefits.

We barely spoke any words, but there was no need when our bodies were doing the talking for us. My face flushed as heat slid over my body. I dropped low so our noses touched, letting him know with just my eyes I was about to come. He grabbed my ass and worked me over his shaft again and again until I unraveled like a loose thread, one final tug making the garment pull apart. When Edison grunted deep and started to shake I lost the last bit of my composure. His orgasm made me come harder knowing we were feeling the exact same feeling at this unique moment in time.

It took me a minute to slow my hips. I honestly didn't want to let him go. We would never have this moment again. When he pulled out, it would only ever live in our memories. As if he was thinking the same damn thing, Edison kissed me hard and long like he wanted to sear this occasion in our brains forever.

When we finally released one another, I collapsed to the mattress next to him. "Well, that was—"

"Yeah," he said, agreeing with words I hadn't yet spoken.

"That was the worst sex I've ever had."

We shared a chuckle.

"Well, I guess we'll just have to keep trying til we get it right."

"You have shitty reception out here," I said as I entered the kitchen with various forms of roosters all around. Rooster artwork, rooster cookie jar, rooster tea kettle. I do not understand how Edison lived in a home so opposite his style.

"I know it."

"What do you do in case of emergencies?"

"I got my landline and my rifle."

I tossed my phone on the counter since at Edison's place it was the equivalent of an expensive paperweight. If anyone was looking for me, I wouldn't know because my phone had no bars and this man had no internet. "No cell service. No Wi-Fi. What do you do for fun?"

"I invite wayward country stars to my place for a quick lay." It was a little past midnight, and he was scrambling up some eggs.

I made myself comfortable on the rooster shaped stool. "Seriously."

"This place keeps me plenty busy. Between the animals and the shit in the house, I'm never bored."

"I don't know how you do it. I would lose my mind. It's so fucking quiet."

Edison flashed an eye in my direction. There was something behind it, but I couldn't rest my finger on it. "You used to like quiet."

"No I didn't. I never did. I was always looking for something to get into. I didn't like being alone for too long with my thoughts."

"Yeah, why was that?" He stirred sugar into his tea, licking the spoon.

"Because all my thoughts ever told me was I wasn't enough. Pretty enough, smart enough, talented enough."

"They're lying to you Fancy. The thoughts in your head. You are so much better than you know."

"You don't ever doubt yourself?"

"All the time. Late at night I lay in my bed wondering if I'm going to die alone in a farmhouse that smells like cheese surrounded by kitschy shit."

Slamming my hand on the kitchen island, I agreed. "It does smell like cheese. Why is that?"

"I don't know? I keep thinking one day I'll move a box and find a big wheel of gouda"

"Despite the house being made of Manchego, you could probably have any woman you wanted."

He scooped eggs on two plates. "You and I both know that's not true."

"Maybe back in high school. But I saw the way the ladies were looking at you at The Tipsy Owl."

"No one was looking at me."

"Them bitches were following your every move. I should know I was one of them."

"Do you want bacon?"

"Have we met? Of course I want bacon."

"I mean eventually I'll find someone and settle down. That's what you do in Hume."

"Well don't settle. Never that. It needs to feel like a Shania song. I thought I had it once or twice, but the melody was always slightly off."

"Hmm, I fear settling is in my future." He placed a plate in front of me before taking a seat.

"I still believe in love and so should you."

"I believe but that doesn't mean we're all going to find it. What are there like eight billion people on this planet?"

"That's a lot of opportunity."

"You know that saying there's someone for everyone? I used to believe that, but now not so much."

"What changed?"

"The math ain't mathing. What if my soulmate is in Peru? Now what?"

"I think your person is right here in Hume." There it was again. Edison shot me a look I couldn't quite identify, but it was giving hints of uncertainty and frustration.

"Love comes with too many variables. That person needs to feel the same thing I'm feeling at the exact same time. It's a gamble."

"When did you become the love sucks guy?"

"I never said love sucks. It's amazing when you can find it. But finding it is like sifting through a haystack for a needle. Honestly, and I know this might sound weird, but I think the Birch siblings are cursed."

"Explain."

"Cyrus, Dial, me all single for years now. Maybe that's just our fate."

"Hey, look at me." Claiming his chin, I continued, "You deserve all the love you can hold. Now you may be on to something with Dial because she is like a cat in a bag. But not Cy and certainly not you."

"Oh, so Dial's just catching strays."

"Yeah, cause she was mean to me yesterday."

Edison was the easy choice and until this minute, that never interested me. But in his rooster themed kitchen, with his shirt off and his easy, humble demeanor, it sort of made sense. I'd traveled the world searching for meaning and acceptance, and Edison embodied that without even trying. I appreciated him in this moment the same way he appreciated me. Same feeling at the exact same time.

Turning my attention to my plate, I shoveled food into my mouth like Edison wasn't sitting next to me. A forkful of egg, a tear of bacon, a bit of toast.

"You know in some cultures people chew their food," he teased.

"I'm chewing," I said around a mouthful of toast and tea. A black and white cat rubbed up against my leg with a meow. "Well hello pretty kitty. How'd you get in here?" I scratched the top of her head and was celebrated in a wash of purrs.

"That's Katt with two T's."

"You have a cat?"

"She's not mine. I mean I didn't adopt her. One day she just showed up and I offered her a bowl of milk. Next day she showed up again, I give her some milk and scraps of food. The third day … you guessed it, she shows up. But this time the milk and food are waiting for her. She let me pet her and we've been friends ever since."

"And you named her Katt?"

"It didn't feel right picking a name for her. She likes to roam. Sometimes she's gone days at a time and sometimes she'll cop a squat for a while."

"She's just so beautiful. Yes, you are." Katt meowed one last time before taking a bit of deli meat from Edison's outstretched hand.

"My mom told me your parents are talking about retirement." I continued to clear my plate.

"They're looking for a new adventure. My mom's in remission so I guess it's as good a time as any for a pivot."

My face dropped as I recalled a few years back my mother telling me Mrs. Birch had been diagnosed with cancer. "I meant to call. I just didn't know what to say." Resting my hand on his knee, I offered up a lame excuse.

"Nah it's okay. No one knows what to say when shit like that happens. But it would have been nice to hear your voice."

"It's not okay. But thank you for not thinking less of me." Not calling was selfish of me. If the shoe were on the other foot, Edison would've dropped everything to show his support. I was a bad friend. I'd been a bad friend to him for quite some time now. When Darla and I left I tried to keep in contact. Every Thursday night we had a standing agreement to call each other even if we could only chat for a few minutes. But life got so busy I'd have plans with my new friends, or he'd need to study for an exam. The calls became less frequent and eventually stopped all together.

"They're thinking about moving to Gainsborough ."

"How would that work with running Figs and Twine?"

"They say Dial and I can handle it." He laced his finger with mine.

"That's pretty major. Do you want all that responsibility?"

"I'm torn. Of course, I don't want my folks to sell the house and leave, but I'd be lying if I said I didn't have ideas I was itching to implement."

"Like?"

He slowly circled the pad of his thumb over my palm. "Like gardening classes on the weekends."

"Gardening classes?"

"Yeah, people think just because you live in the country, you're born with a green thumb. But that shit isn't ingrained in our DNA. You have to learn somehow. We could teach the basics and new innovative gardening techniques."

"That's actually brilliant. Parents are always looking for something to do with their kids. Mom circles interested in a day to themselves, or individuals looking to learn some new tricks from professionals."

"I'm not a professional."

"You have a degree and the greenest thumb I've ever seen."

"I also thought about opening a cozy coffee shop—"

"With some tables so people can sit in the garden and enjoy a latte with a friend or a good book."

Edison laughed. "Yeah, exactly that. People wouldn't have to go all the way into town if they wanted a good cup of Joe." His hand rested on my bare thigh. I was wearing one of his T-shirts and nothing more.

"You should do it. Both. I don't think you've failed at a single thing you've ever tried."

"I don't know about that."

"I do. I have faith enough for the both of us."

He smiled wistfully, his voice soft yet deep. "You have faith in me?" His hand slipped under my shirt, finding my clit.

I gripped the edge of the stool, only able to manage a weak, "Uh-huh."

"Do you have faith I can make you come a few more times tonight?"

"Yes," I moaned.

Edison jumped up and pushed away the items on the kitchen counter. A bowl with roosters painted along the edge shattered when it accidentally hit the floor spilling bananas and apples to the hardwood. Undeterred Edison grabbed me, setting me on the counter. He pulled off his boxers and fucked me in the cozy kitchen of his creepy old man house.

His dick was substantial and while I couldn't prove it, I believe it was reaching my belly button. Big dick was a dime a dozen. Most men thought aggressive pumping was enough. Edison had the tools and understood how to use them. Each stroke was calculated for my pleasure. Pulling out, he used the tip to tease my pearl and I sat up and paid attention. Occasionally he'd dip into my honey pot before swiping it across my slit once more.

"Hey, can you be a good girl for me?"

My face lit up. "Yes."

He lifted me off the counter and moved us to the hallway. "I want you to lay face down and not move a finger."

"Okay." I complied, removing my T-shirt before taking to all fours.

"Face down, Fancy." Edison's voice grew closer as he shifted from standing to kneeling. "Are you good? Do you need a pillow?"

"No, I'm good." Edison slapped my ass and I knew I was in trouble. "What's about to happen to me?" I meekly asked.

"Oh, I'm about to fuck you within an inch of your life." I could have come off the strength of those words alone. "Arch that back, darling."

Edison massaged my clit while sliding inside and I cried out. "Just take my money."

I started rocking back and forth and was chastised. "Did I tell you to move?"

"No."

"Tonight, you have to follow my rules."

"Done. Can I beg because I feel like I want to beg a little?"

"Uhm … that's fine."

"I really need all of it right now." Edison claimed hold of my waist and went to town. When I tell you he demolished my pussy. The strokes were long and methodical. He hit every nerve as he slid in and out over and over again. "Oh God punish this pussy, baby."

He switched his position, and I went into a fugue state. Edison had me pinned and there was nothing I could do but get fucked. Each pump inching me closer to the upper rooms. The clapping of my cheeks laced with my uncontrollable moans was a fucking bop. "Edison, you fuck me so good."

His massive hand encircled my neck, and he pulled my torso upward. "You like that."

"God, yes. Choke me harder."

The pressure around my neck tightened. "Whose pussy is this?"

"It's yours for the taking. Get it baby." While Edison was deep in my guts, I realized I would cut a bitch over this man. Was he fucking everybody like this? I would let him ruin my life. Tank my credit score, burn down my house, slap my momma. Shambles, I was in shambles over this dick. "I think I'm about to cry."

A heavy weight settled in my stomach. Edison was in too deep, and I wasn't talking about his dick. He was in my head and tugging at my heart. This was more than sex. He was uploading malware that was rewriting my code and corrupting the possibilities for any other suitor.

Edison switched me on to my back and reentered, his eyes laser focused on me. I tried to hold back the tears, but each stroke made it harder to deny him. "Ed -i- son …" My words were punctured by moans and my voice was thick with emotion. Tears slid down the sides of my face. "What the fuck are you doing to me?"

"Do you want me to stop?" All his boldness was gone as he wiped away a tear that was quickly followed by others.

"No, don't stop. Don't ever stop." Edison softly kissed my lips, his arm cradling my head as his strokes slowed to an attentive pace, which while still life wrecking, allowed me to better process my big feelings. He wasn't fucking me any longer. We were making love.

"You are so beautiful, and I feel safe when I'm inside you."

"I can't … I can't talk or I'm going to say some crazy shit."

"No judgement." He followed with strokes that dismantled my lifelong beliefs.

"You make me want to do dirty, such dirty things. Like cook dinner, wash clothes, raise a family, and suck your dick every night, every fucking night."

"I'ma need you to come for me now." Edison leaned into my ear, talking me through it. "Show me how much you love this dick. I want you to mark your territory and cream all over this motherfucker." And I did, I creamed all over his dick and then licked it clean for good measure.

12

Edison

WHEN YOU LIVE ON A farm, you don't get to sleep in. It was Sunday and I wanted to lie next to Fancy a little while longer, but duty called. After fifteen minutes of me trying to untangle myself without waking up Fancy, I headed downstairs and was shocked to see the dishes and fruit all over the floor. What possessed me to do that shit, I'll never know. Circling the kitchen island, I cleaned up before pulling out a broom to sweep any remaining pieces of glass.

If she wasn't still in my bed, I would have sworn last night was a vivid hallucination. Sure, I'd imagined sex with Fancy hundreds of times. Saying it now sounded pathetic, but for me, Fancy was always the one. Everyone else was a place filler for the real thing. I'm not saying there weren't women who made me forget about Fancy. My last real girlfriend Mari and I were happy until we weren't.

Pouring myself a thermos of coffee—the programmable coffee pot was the best birthday gift ever—I headed out. In the barn I loaded up on feed and water and drove off in my UTV. I could perform this loop in my sleep. First, I visited Scout, I pulled up a stool and milked her as we talked. She let me do most of the talking.

After changing out her water and food, I headed over to see my goats. They came with the purchase of the farm. When I walked near their stall, they acted so excited to see me and it gave my tired ass a boost of energy.

Last was the chicken coop. I checked on the hens and collected the eggs. And before walking away, I thanked them for their sustenance. The whole circle of life thing was in full effect. Eggs and milk my animals produced would be used as fuel for my body and that connection and reliance on nature and the earth wasn't lost on me.

When I made it back to the house, Fancy was on the porch steps with a cup of coffee.

"Morning." Her gaze didn't meet my eyes.

The muscles in my jaw ruminated. "Good morning." After sex clarity was a motherfucker. I already knew sleeping with Fancy was a mistake because she'd effectively ruined me for everyone else. When I told her I'd probably end up settling, I meant it because if it wasn't her, I didn't really want it. Maybe after fucking me, she'd realized she needed to head back home and fix her relationship with old boy.

A rush of air escaped her lungs. "Can I just say … that … last night I said some things … and you said things. We both made statements in the heat of the moment and maybe we said things we meant … or not. But we definitely said some things."

The corners of my eyes tightened. "Did you practice that?"

"I did not."

"So when you told me I could put it anywhere was that just a thing you said?"

Her eyes finally met mine and there was longing behind them. "No, I fucking meant that shit."

"Then what are you saying?"

Fancy surrendered her hands in the air. "The crying Edison … I don't want to talk about it."

"I'm not going to hold you to your excited utterances or tears."

"Do you have a lot of women boohooing over your dick?"

"I mean maybe one or two."

Her head drew back quickly. "Hmm, okay pussy whisperer."

"Your secret is safe with me."

Cradling her mug, she announced, "I think this is the best coffee I've ever had."

"Thanks, it's a mixture of different beans. I grind them fresh." I took a seat next to her and stole her mug, taking a sip.

"Where'd you go?"

"To feed and water the animals."

"You should have woken me up. I would have helped."

"Woman, I know you. You would not have helped. You would have complained. You would have made jokes. You might've even broken a nail, but you would not have helped."

"I wasn't built for physical labor. I mean look at my arms. Like chicken wings. I'm more of a bring lemonade to the crew type of girl. For a while there, Daddy tried to make me into a horse trainer, like Oz, but he gave up. He told me I was an unserious person. And thinking back on it now, that was a fair assessment."

"Sometimes our parents know us better than we know ourselves."

"I think that's true when we're younger, but as an adult I don't think my father has a clue about what motivates me."

Her words unlocked a core memory for me. The last time I'd had a semi real conversation with my father was right before I went off to college. My mother encouraged him to check in with me. Our stilted discussion included him reminding me to always use a condom, don't fall to peer pressure, and whatever I did to not sully the family name. That was years ago. Today our conversations focused on three topics—sports, the nursery, and food. My father would probably forget my birthday if my mom wasn't around to remind him.

Fancy cast her eyes in front of her, looking off into the distance. "This is a nice view."

"I bought the house because of that view."

Fancy leaned her head on my shoulder and started to hum low. Not going to lie, I almost creamed my pants. This was perfect. She was perfect and in the short time she was here, she made this house feel more like a home, despite the frilly drapes and dog-shaped umbrella stand.

When she started to sing, I just closed my eyes and listened. Singing was like sharing a piece of your soul, oftentimes telling the listener more about a person than just words alone could. Anytime Fancy sang a cappella you could sense her vulnerability in each note. She was the reason Whiskey Wild was so successful, because from the first guitar string she hooked you.

"Sing with me," she requested.

I grimaced with a slight shake of my head. "You're doing fine." We used to sing together all the time, but nowadays I only sang after several glasses of liquid courage.

"Please." Her big mink eyes pleaded.

It was nearly impossible to say no to that pouty face. Humoring her, I sang along with the familiar words. I could carry a tune, but my skills were no match for Fancy's. She was a powerhouse and when her deep raspy voice sang a song, you felt it in your bones. Fancy just came alive when she sang. Tapping my foot on the steps, we fell into familiar cadence.

She swayed from side to side, beaming up at me as my bass harmonized with her soprano. Fancy couldn't help but perform, shimming her shoulders and rocking her hips. We didn't need an audience, she would entertain the trees, and they'd pendulate in appreciation. Fancy jumped up, dancing barefoot in the dirt while I slapped my knee to keep the beat. Our melodies drifted into the soft morning breeze. She was the fire, and I was the match. Without her flame, I was useless.

Fancy fell into my arms as the last refrains died on our lips. *"It doesn't make sense but love rarely does."* She kissed me and my heart was set ablaze. The way her mouth moved was deliberate, like she was giving me time to grasp the unspoken words behind our lip lock. Her fingers fumbled over my belt buckle and I was ready to fuck her in front of God and Katt who stopped for a lazy stretch before continuing on her way. The landline in the house rang, interrupting the action.

"Ignore it," she begged.

Pushing her hair from her face, I objected. "Can't, it could be important." I wanted to. I really did, but not many people called the house number, so when it rang I picked up. Standing, I carried Fancy inside, depositing her on the couch.

"Hello?" I said.

"Good morning, Edison, sorry to call so early on a Sunday." It was Fancy's mother, and I felt like a kid who'd got caught with his hand in the cookie jar.

"No need to apologize ma'am."

Fancy rolled her eyes mouthing the word "Ma'am?"

"Is Fancy with you?"

"Yes Mrs. Palmer, I'm looking at her right now. Do you want to speak to her?" I hit the speakerphone and Fancy's back straightened.

"Oh no need to bother. I just wanted to make sure she was safe. Didn't want to assume."

"I apologize. We should've called. I feel awful about making you worry." I noticed my belt was still undone and cringed like this was a video chat and I'd been caught red-handed trying to diddle the rancher's daughter.

Fancy chimed in. "I'll be back Monday morning Momma."

"Is that okay with you Mrs. Palmer?" I asked respectfully.

"You don't have to clear anything with me. I'm not keeping tabs."

"I totally understand."

"Well, I better run. I have meat to season and a pie to make."

"Bye Momma," Fancy yelled from across the room.

When I hung up the receiver, Fancy's eyes grew wide. "You know what this means right?"

"What?"

"She knows you fucked me."

"She doesn't know that."

"I slept over at your place." Her voice was incredulous.

"You could have just fallen asleep. She doesn't know."

"Oh, she knows your penis has been in my vagina … and my mouth."

What was it about parents having confirmation of your sexual activities that made shit weird? I remember back in high school when my mom walked in on me and my then girlfriend having sex. Mortified wasn't a strong enough word. We never talked about it. But one day before dropping me off at school she asked, "Are you being safe?" and I answered, "Yes ma'am."

"Wait until I give her the play-by-play," she teased.

Fancy and her mother's relationship was open door policy, and they shared information most mothers and daughters didn't, which I always thought a bit weird.

"You better not."

Her breathing pattern shifted as she clutched her chest. "I'm going to tell her about the funny noises you make when you come."

Grabbing a floral pillow from a nearby chair, I hurled it at her. "I don't make funny noises."

"It's the combination of noises and faces that I like the most."

"You are such a fucking brat. If you tell your momma about this dick, you ain't getting no more."

Fancy shut her mouth, turned an imaginary key and threw it away before dissolving into a laughing fit. When she wiped the tears from her eyes, she asked, "What do you want to do now?"

"Let's take a shower and make some funny noises," I said, chasing her up the stairs.

After lazing around the house most of the morning, we made a quick run into town for groceries. Fancy was wearing one of my T-shirts and a pair of jeans I found that might've belonged to Willa. My property didn't have internet service, not because I was choosing to live off the grid, but because it wasn't a priority to me. I wasn't a big TV watcher, and I preferred music or silence over anything else.

Anytime Dial or Cyrus visited, they'd complain because they were forced to talk to me and couldn't disappear into their phones. Annoying my siblings was reason enough to never get Wi-Fi. When we took to the road, Fancy's phone popped out as she searched for a signal. She even went as far as to stick her phone out the window in hopes a bar would appear.

"These back roads are essentially dead space," I informed her.

Rolling up the window, she turned her phone over in her hand as if she was scheming a way to MacGyver cell service with paper clips and gum wrappers. "How do you doom scroll at night?"

"I don't."

"What do you do before bedtime?"

"I read, listen to music, play solitaire."

"On your phone?"

"No actual cards."

Her eyebrows folded inward as she crinkled her nose. "I mean, I guess. But why? The world moves so fast I've already missed several news cycles."

"News is the worst. Everything is breaking, urgent, must-see TV. Come to find out it's just a mundane story about a world leader making threats. Shit that's a Tuesday in America."

"Your house is like a horror story. Secluded farmhouse, no neighbors for miles, and no Wi-Fi. All you're missing is the maniacal killer."

"Gee thanks."

"I'm not saying your place is a death trap … but—"

"Sometimes disconnecting is a good thing. You discover what's truly important and what's just noise."

"How am I supposed to keep abreast on the newest lip shimmer, nail trend, or whozeewhatzit without internet?" she teased. "I don't know I like something until the internet tells me I should."

"I know you're joking, but for a lot of people that's their reality. They need validation from faceless masses to confirm their next move."

"So you're anti social media and the world wide web?"

"Nope. I just think that shit is nuanced. And while it can keep us connected, it can also pull us apart."

Fancy scanned her phone again. "I just need the serotonin boost staying connected provides. I haven't even done my WordBop of the day."

"What's that?"

"You'd know if you had fucking internet."

"You want the internet? Here's the internet … check out my outfit of the day. Someone asks complete strangers if he's the asshole for doing XYZ. Spoiler alert, he is indeed the asshole. A video tries to convince you to buy this amazing chair, cheese shredder, or pair of butt lifting jeans. An influencer with over a million views gets ousted as racist. And people are going back and forth about who should pay for the first date."

"So you *are* on the internet." She crossed her arms over her chest.

Once we hit the edge of town, the bars went up and Fancy's interest in me went down. The cab was flooded with dings, chimes, and whistles to signify all the calls, messages, and alerts she'd missed in less than twenty-four hours. She quietly scanned through emails and texts, her face neutral. If the world was burning down, I couldn't tell. Parking, I exited the truck and made my way to the passenger side to let her out.

"Is it okay if we hit up the hardware store first, I have to get a few things?"

"Uh-huh." At Morton's she stopped short. "I'm just going to hang back and reply to some messages."

"Okay."

"Could you tell Mr. Morton I said hello?"

"You could just come inside and tell him yourself."

"These replies aren't going to send themselves. But I'll stand by the window and wave."

"Yeah, that's just as good." I went inside, not waiting for a response. Let's start with the obvious, Francesca owed me nothing. We weren't a couple, we'd had a one-night stand. It's not like I was shopping for tuxedos or making plans. I knew what the fuck this was when I invited her home. Now that being said, I was pissed. Was I the asshole for wanting my attention to be reciprocated? Probably. Shit, was spending time with me so unbearable she needed to virtually be anywhere but here? For a brief second, I allowed myself to wonder if she was hoping for a message from her ex begging her to take him back.

Outside the hardware store, I was treated to a big smile. "All done?"

"Are you all done?"

"Yes?" She lifted a bag with a smile. "While you were in Morton's I dipped into Sweet But Sinful and got us some taffy."

Damn, I am the asshole. "You didn't have to do that."

"I wasn't sure which flavors you like so I just got a little bit of everything." Pulling her in, I kissed the top of her head. "Hmm, you do know this is how rumors start."

"You're right, I probably shouldn't have—" Fancy's phone ringing cut me off.

"I need to take this." She shook her cellphone. "I'll meet you at the market." Fancy called over her shoulder while walking away.

I was relieved when we were back on the road on our way home. After a few miles, service became shoddy and she tossed her phone into her purse.

"It's going to be a nice night to grill," she said, her arm halfway out the window.

"Uh-huh."

"I can't wait until you taste the grilled pineapple. You're going to love it, just add a little cinnamon or honey."

"Yep."

Fancy side eyed me. "Is everything okay?"

"Uh-huh."

My voice was saying unbothered, but my body language was giving anything but, with my tight jaw and bobbing Adam's apple. It was clear that everything was not okay. My knuckles gripped the steering wheel tightly as I just stared forward into the empty road. Fancy allowed me to stew, focusing on the vast nothingness that passed us by.

When I pulled up to the house and cut off the ignition. Fancy turned to me and said, "Did I do something wrong?"

"How could the perfect Fancy Palmer ever do anything wrong?" I climbed out of the truck and headed to the flatbed to collect the bags.

She followed me, her hands settling on her hips. "What's that supposed to mean?"

There was a tightness in my chest as my body temperature increased. "Let's just forget it."

"No, your attitude is kind of hard to ignore."

"My attitude?" I had to laugh to stop myself from going feral.

"Yeah, you're being rude."

"I'm not being rude. Rude, is complaining about the lack of Wi-Fi. Rude, is incessantly checking your phone for bars or signs of life. Rude, is steadily focusing on your phone while I was just hoping for a chill afternoon."

"Excuse the fuck out of me for having a life that consist of more than just a cat and a few goats."

Words like quaint and cozy were just code words for ugly and boring. One minute she's gushing over how cute my house is and complimenting me on the beautiful views and then in the next breath my animals were unremarkable and my life meaningless. "Oh, so now you hate the farm."

She lowered her chin to her chest while slowly shaking her head. "I never said that. Edison can we just take a beat?"

This was me hurt. I was never her first choice, not back then and not now. "Did your boyfriend call you? Did your message last night fire him up? Is he finally ready to fight for you?"

"Where is this coming from?"

My shoulders slumped and the tightness in my chest became almost unbearable. "I don't like being used, Fancy." Being upset came with unavoidable discomfort because it almost always meant my feelings had been hurt. Which is why I probably stuck to myself. Because letting people in also invited an uneasiness that was difficult to shake.

"Used? I'm not—"

My voice was shaky, and my tone was harsher than I'd intended. "You couldn't wait to get to town so you could check your messages to see if he'd called or texted you. I was right fucking there. You could've at least waited until I went into the hardware store."

"Okay … okay I've hurt you." She looked toward the sky in search of the right words. "Whiskey Wild is my baby and right now everything is sort of up in the air. The record label is asking about the tour. People are talking and there's all these rumors and I just needed to get ahead of that. Was there a part of me hoping for a response from Chap? Yes. I want a heartfelt apology. Or some sign he was suffering with the fact he fucked up and lost me for good. He hurt me and I wanted to hurt him back. And I know that sounds crazy and I shouldn't care, but the wounds are still fresh."

"Listen to me. You know how much I care for you. So while this may be brief it's not a game to me. My very real emotions are all tangled up in you like creeping vines. When you head back to LA, I want to be left with fond memories, not regret. If you can't promise that, then I don't want this." I shoved the keys to the truck in her hand. "If you can't offer me that, then take my truck and go home." I grabbed the bags and headed for the house.

In the kitchen, I silently berated myself for losing my cool. We both knew eventually Fancy would return to her normal life. But if we were going to spend time together while she was here, that time had to be the best time of our lives to compensate for the heartbreak that would follow. I wasn't asking her to give up her life in LA any more than she was asking me to leave Hume. But it couldn't feel like I was a void filler. It had to be real.

I stood staring out the kitchen window, for what felt like an eternity, waiting for the whining of the motor, the rumble of the engine catching, and the wheels turning over the pavement as she drove away. I'd asked for too much. She was looking to have fun, take her mind off her life back home and I was over here, a bleeding wound begging her to consider me.

When the front door squeaked open and Fancy entered the kitchen, I was finally able to breathe unfettered. She dropped my keys on the counter and wrapped her arms around me from behind. "Edison—"

"It's okay." I turned to face her. "We're okay."

"Do you mean that? I need you to know there is no place I'd rather be than on this farm with you."

"Even if we get terrorized in the middle of the night by masked assailants?"

"Shit, just call me Kevin McCallister cause we would boobie trap this place like *Home Alone.*"

I chuckled.

Fancy brushed her finger across my bottom lip. "Listen, I'm crazy about you, Eddy. I don't know what that means. But I know what I feel."

Nodding, I soaked up her affirming words like a parched philodendron. "We should probably marinate the meat first to give it a chance to sop up all that good flavor."

"While you do that, I'll start boiling the potatoes for the potato salad."

Fancy selected a bluegrass record and turned it up loud as we got to work. Prepping the food, we danced around the kitchen sneaking kisses. It was like the quarrel out front never happened. I felt like the only one. Like I was her choice and not just the nearest option, and I loved that for me.

13

Fancy

AFTER DINNER EDISON SAID HE had a surprise for me and left me on the porch alone for over thirty minutes. More than enough time to obsess over what transpired this afternoon. Coming home was about a reset, not a rehashing of the past. I was already dealing with my own hurt feelings, the last thing I wanted to do was hurt Edison. Should we have slept together? Probably not. Was I counting the minutes until we did again? One hundred percent.

My life was all sixes and sevens. I'd dumped my cheating ex. Fans were sending thoughts and prayers based on the cryptic Whiskey Wild statement. I couldn't turn to my manager for advice because he was my cheating ex. Darla was in Los Angeles on pause, waiting for me to figure my shit out. The record label was emailing me with questions. And God knows what Chap was telling them. He was probably torching my reputation as we speak.

Why was I so fucking impulsive? Fleeing LA, fucking Edison. I was always reactive, never proactive. I'd been in Hume for a week and didn't have a game plan. What was my next move? Fuck all if I know. I was in Tennessee dicking around while the world burned down around me. And by sleeping with Edison, I was just adding more bodies to the fire.

I surveyed the sky, spying as the stars came into focus and the last of the sun was chased away by the moon. A cool breeze rumbled through the trees as insects buzzed about, their only worries being who they were going to sting tonight. The scent of the grill still lingered in the air and made my stomach grumble for one more bite of tri tip. Somehow the tranquility of the farm forced me to turn my brain off and just be still. *I could get used to this.*

A shrill whistle pierced my ears, and I turned to the direction of the barn and spotted Edison waving his hands like a madman. I grabbed my glass of wine and headed in his direction. The grass on the property was the richest shade of green. Should I expect anything less from the man who ran the nursery?

"Did you just whistle at me like I was an animal?"

"I didn't want to walk all the way back over."

"I'll have you know I'm a refined lady," I said, obnoxiously slurping from my wine glass. "There should really be more pomp and circumstance when my presence is requested."

"Like a member of the royal family?"

"Exactly, I'm talking bending at the waist, an old nasty, cunty curtsy, and a sharp salute."

"And they could all shout Queen Fancy for good measure."

"I like how you think. But when it comes to country music right now, I feel more like the ugly stepsister than queen."

"Maybe they were so mean because everyone was commenting on their looks."

"Shit I'd be a bitch if everyone in town was referring to me and my sister as ugly. I'd have burned that motherfucker down."

"Just fuck the royal ball and everyone in attendance?"

"Fuck the ball and my weird ass stepsister who talks to mice." We shared a laugh before my curiosity got the better of me and I shifted the subject. "So why are we at the barn?"

"Because I have a surprise for you."

"Does this surprise include wine? Cause I could really use a top off."

Edison pulled back the barn doors to reveal a spa-like experience. It was a barn, there was no mistaking that, but he'd transformed it into an oasis with ginormous potted plants and trees, several large area rugs and jazz music playing through the speakers. In the middle of the barn was an extra-large circular tin tub, steam visible on the surface of the water.

"What did you do?" I squealed.

"I thought we could have a soak. Drink some champagne."

Edison put some thought into this. There was a bench with fluffy towels and two robes. Underneath the bench were slippers and next to the tub was a short stool with a bottle of champagne and glasses with strawberries in them. Right now, my internal dialogue was telling me to hate all men. But Edison's thoughtfulness left a soft spot in my heart and a wet spot in my panties.

I pulled off my T-shirt, tits on display and said, "Giddy up."

After stripping down to our skivvies, we both climbed in. He wrapped his strong arms around me and it was like I was transported to heaven. The temperature of the water was perfect, hot but not scolding, and there were tiny jets distributing the water like a jacuzzi tub. A soft warm breeze traveled through the open barn doors, setting the tone. I could stay out here forever in his arms, surrounded by nature.

"Who has a tub in their barn?" I asked.

"You know I've always been a tinkerer. Jack-of-all-trades, master of none."

"I can think of a few things you do very well." I smirked.

He raised a single eyebrow.

The last thing I wanted to do was hurt this man. I told you Darla was my best friend but so was Edison. We met in kindergarten, and I remember I liked having him around. Even at five years old I sensed he was special, and I was lucky to have him in my life. During our freshman year of high school, people tried to sort us into separate queues. I was considered part of the popular clique, Darla was artsy, Edison was a bit of everything tech, band, track.

Despite the drama that comes with high school, we remained close. However, after our kiss in the park at twelve, we went our separate ways romantically. I was more experimental, and Edison was more of a true-blue monogamous man. He almost always had a girlfriend because he was sweet, charming, and loyal. Me, on the other hand I entertained several suitors at once and gained a bit of a reputation as a good time gal. I wrote a song by the same title, and it became one of Whiskey Wild's biggest hits.

"You mentioned shit was going sideways with your label. Is it fixable?"

"I don't want to bore you with that."

"If it's important to you, it's important to me."

"I guess anything can be fixed if you make them enough money."

"Well, Whiskey Wild has to be pulling in bank."

"We are, but it's a balancing act. You're only as good as your last project, single, tour. And the label's got a lot riding on us fulfilling our dates."

"It sounds like you're in between a rock and a hard place."

"And now my assistant is coming to town, and she probably has a message from the label. I just ghosted everyone and everything and there will be repercussions for that."

"What are you going to do?" Edison reached for my hand under the water, giving it a squeeze.

"I don't know. So much goes into these tours. Booking arenas a year or more in advance. Hiring crew. And the fans spent their hard-earned money to see us and I've jeopardized all that. I think I fucked up."

"Do you want me to be honest or empathetic?"

"Can't I get a little of both?" I bit the inside of my cheek.

"My dad always said, 'When you make a commitment, you build hope. And when you keep it, you build trust.'"

"Wow, Papa Birch just made me feel ten times worse."

"I wasn't trying to make you feel bad, but I do think you need to do everything in your power to make your tour dates. I'm not saying you can't take the time you need, but Whiskey Wild is still a business. How many tour dates have you missed?"

I took a long, silent swig of champagne. "Technically, I've only missed night two of the Heritage Fest. The second half of our tour doesn't start for another three weeks."

"So why are you so upset?"

"There was a statement. Whiskey Wild put out a statement. And the blogs are gossiping. Saying all kinds of stuff about me and Darla battling it out for the spotlight. They said I left the desert in tears. Which is true, but I was upset about Chap. Everyone is spinning it like there's trouble in paradise with Whiskey Wild. There're breakup rumors and the fans have gotten a hold of it and some of them are picking sides. Can you believe that?"

Edison looked around the barn as if he was searching for answers. "If you haven't missed any tour dates, why put out a statement about missing tour dates?"

"I don't know, that was all Chap and Darla."

Edison's eyes screamed disapproval.

"Don't look at me like that."

"I'm just saying for someone who claims Whiskey Wild is their baby, you sure are pawning it off to others to burp and swaddle."

"Okay I'm impulsive, next. And just so we're clear. I left my baby with my partner, Darla. I didn't just lock it in a room with Cheez-Its and juice boxes."

His eyebrows rose in a slow arch. "Umm, same difference."

"Bullshit, Bullshit, Bull-fucking-shit."

"I wouldn't let Darla watch the time, let alone the future of Whiskey Wild."

"Are you finished? Are you done?"

"I'm just saying Darla isn't someone I'd call responsible. I let her borrow my truck and she drove it into a lake."

"Okay that's fair. But let's not act like I'm the textbook example of responsibility. I'm really just out here with my dick out trying to figure my next move. I'm knocking on thirty and I haven't got a fucking clue. Not about our next album, where I'm going to live, if I'm ever going to see my dog again."

"You have a dog?"

"Yeah, Yeti Spaghetti II. But Chap calls him Zeus."

"Okay two things. One, if you want your dog back, we'll get your dog back. And two, you need to reach out to the label and make things right. Whatever that means in the music industry. And then I fear you and Darla need to have a serious conversation about your management and whether you can separate business and personal."

Edison made it all sound so simple. And maybe it was. If I'm being honest, I'd been consumed with how Chap's actions affected me and hadn't considered much else beyond that. It was time to put my big girl jeans on and solve this shit. Chap was out, Darla and I could resume the tour, and after, we'd start writing our next album. And I'd sue Chap for full custody of our dog.

"That's one way to skin a squirrel," I said.

"Problems and conflict make me anxious, so I like to solve them as quickly as possible."

Leaning closer, I caressed his cheek. "I appreciate you listening."

"Of course." Edison kissed the top of my head.

We both retreated into our thoughts. Was he thinking the same thing I was? That our time together now had a clear endpoint. I'd go on tour and then nights in the tin tub would be a fond memory. I couldn't ask him to wait for me. Because I didn't know when I'd be coming back or if I even wanted to. Hume was my hometown, but it was no longer my home.

But LA didn't feel like home either. I was just going through the motions in LA. Hikes on trails that paled in comparison to Hume. Fighting to get a spot in a reformer class at Helix Fitness. Eighteen dollars for a smoothie. Going to a club just to sit in VIP and not dance because VIP was for the rich cool kids and the dance floor was for losers who couldn't get into VIP.

All my life, I wanted to be known for my music. But being famous and followed by paparazzi wasn't ever part of that dream. I never wanted to lose my privacy and ability to navigate freely in the world. Everywhere I went, I was recognized and the reality that my life was no longer mine and mine alone was sinking in. Fans had expectations of the group and me. Expectations about who I should date. How I should dress. About the length of my bangs. Over a year ago, after a fight with Chap in which he picked apart my appearance, I got a little scissor happy and cut my own bangs. It looked hideous, but I chose to rock them until they grew out, my form of a silent rebellion.

The fans roasted me. There were think pieces about my bangs. Videos of people just laughing at a picture of me and my fucked up bangs in the background. My hairstylist received death threats over my chopped bangs. That moment made me hyper aware that the parasocial relationships fans were creating were unhealthy. Don't get me wrong, I loved our fans, but sometimes they'd cross the line, and it was hurtful and occasionally scary.

Edison cleared his throat. "Hey, I was thinking, why don't you just stay with me until you get ready to leave?"

"With you?" I thought he'd be looking to put some distance between us, not pull me closer.

"Yeah, it would give us time to catch up."

"I feel like we've already caught up and now we're working on new material," I teased.

He splashed the warm water over his face. "No pressure, it was just a thought."

I tilted his chin, so he was looking at me. "I like the way you think. An extended sleepover sounds fun."

I had three weeks to get my shit together. After that the already frustrated label would be pissed. Hiding out in Hume forever was not a viable option. People depended on the Whiskey Wild machine to keep churning. The band, the stage crew, security, craft services, if we didn't perform, no one made money. I was tempted to text Darla and ask her to fly out. Edison's advice was appreciated, but I really needed to talk things through with my bandmate. My choices affected her more than anyone else and her advice was always delivered plain with no sugar coating on top.

"Whiskey Wild has a show in three weeks." I wanted to make sure Edison knew how much time he had. How much time was left before the carriage turned back into a pumpkin. Three weeks didn't allow for making plans or figuring things out. I didn't know what I was doing and now I'd dragged him into it.

My head was resting on his shoulder and I could sense him nodding thoughtfully. "Edison?"

"Yep."

Floating, I positioned myself so I was straddling his lap. "I would never use you. You said you felt like I was using you. And I just need you to know you're too important to me to do something like that."

"Okay."

My head jerked back slightly. "Not okay. I need you to comprehend."

"Fancy you've always had options. For you, life is a smorgasbord. Maybe *use* wasn't the right word. Perhaps I should have said consumed or depleted."

"You make me sound like a vulture."

"You just take Fancy. You make me want to give you everything, even if that means I have nothing left for myself. And I'm not saying you don't offer value in return. Your smile alone is worth a million dollars. Being near you is like summer rain, light and refreshing. I'm just saying it's not easy to recover after you've moved on."

I'd be the first to admit that in my youth I was flighty. But I wasn't a taker. "How is that my fault? I never asked people to get all caught up in me."

"Your presence practically demands it. It's not something you purposely do, it's just in you. A trigger that makes people want to please you. Your parents, Oz, every guy in high school."

I opened my mouth ready to disagree.

Edison flashed me a warning glare. "I don't want to fight."

"We're not fighting, we're just having a conversation."

"Well maybe I don't *want* to have this particular conversation."

I moved to the other side of the tub, sizing him up. "You know you're not perfect either."

"I know it."

"You can be possessive, you only see things in black and white, and you're afraid of change."

"Guilty. I'm fiercely protective of the people I care about. Nuance is fine but most people hide behind that concept, so they don't have to pick a fucking side. And I am keenly aware of who I am and what makes me happy."

"Good, just want to be clear I'm not the only one with flaws."

"When did I say you had flaws?"

"You compared me to a succubus."

Edison chuckled.

"What's so damn funny?"

"Fancy, we have three weeks. Do you want to spend that time fighting or fucking?" He floated forward, pulling me back onto his lap. His dick was erect and ready, and I lost all my righteous indignation. Edison's kisses had the ability to fold time. My nipples brushed against his chest and a ribbon of desire fluttered in the base of my stomach. My heartbeat was so loud it drowned out all the doubt. Our kisses were deep and rapid like a raging river. The night breeze chilled my wet, naked skin.

I grabbed his face and said, "I need you right now." You'd think I was a cat in heat the way my chest was heaving. All that was missing was the plaintive wails.

Edison released an audible gasp as he entered me. When he finally slid into place, my body was awash with relief and excitement. His hands landed on my thighs and he gave them a quick rub before gently guiding me up and down. He leaned forward to kiss my neck and chest before slapping my ass hard. The splash of water and his heavy hand caught me by surprise, causing me to moan low and long.

Edison collected my damp curls which were a bit tangled and frizzy from neglect after all this carefree country living. His thrust became harder and more urgent as if my body was the cure to every last one of his problems. All my other senses seemed to dim as my sense of touch became heightened. The gentle tugging at my hair. Edison's free hand cupping my breast while the pad of his thumb teased my nipple. My ass slamming into him and the shiver that connection produced. We were sweaty, and something about fucking in the barn with the doors wide open for any passerby to witness felt primal and raw. Just two horny people looking to satisfy our need to experience the heady high of pleasure.

When his hand found my clit my body felt electric, the sensation pulsing through my veins, the harshness of the impending wave was almost painful and my body tried to scurry away in fear. Fear of this man who knew my body like his own, even though he'd only been granted access a day ago. Fear of the quicken of my heart at the nearness of him and my longing for this to never end. Fear of the unknown and what this all meant.

Edison chastised me, his voice rough and no louder than a grumble. "Stop running from it and take this dick."

His words were like a whistle, and I complied, opening myself wide so he could go deeper. Which caused me to scream as loud as my lungs would allow. The benefit of living in the country was there weren't neighbors around for miles. So when I yelled, "Fucking take this pussy. Take it all," there was no one to eavesdrop.

"Are you ready for me to make you come or do you want to play a little longer?"

I didn't know this was a choose your own adventure. I'll take orgasms for one thousand Alex. "Please fucking make me come," I said out of breath, throat dry, sweat running down my ass crack.

The water acted as a conduit to our gratification. His next thrust left me thunderstruck. All I could make out were random shapes as my eyes crossed. Circles and swirls floating all around me. The last stroke stole my very soul like Ursula hijacking the Mermaid's voice. I shivered and convulsed and thanked the gods for my good fortune. I would do anything for this man. Swat down a wasp nest. Streak naked down Birch Street. Read the mean comments on my social media post. There was no rhyme or reason to it. That dick and the very fine man attached to it was my kryptonite.

14

Fancy

IN THE MORNING EDISON DROPPED me off at my parents' house before heading to work. The plan was for me to pack a bag, and he'd pick me up at the end of the day. When I walked into the kitchen, in the dress I'd left in on Saturday night, my mother took one look at me and said, "You look like yesterday."

"Good morning to you too." I curtsied.

She surveyed my messy hair and ashy legs. "So, your date with Edison went well?"

"Not a date, Momma. It was just two friends making up for lost time."

"I'm sure you two spent a lot of time making up." She wriggled her eyebrows.

Grabbing a sausage link, I shoved it into my mouth. I was exhausted and famished, but in a good way. You know when your body is sore and tight after a hard day of work on the ranch? That was me. My body ached, I had a crook in my neck, and with each step I took my pussy reminded me it had been fucked and sucked multiple times over the past two days. If I was a taker, then Edison was a

154

giver. And he gave me every inch of himself at every conceivable opportunity.

Having a man who adored my body and was intent on showing me was new. When Chap and I had sex, it was every man for themselves. Because Chap was going to nut in under ten minutes and if my ticket wasn't punched in time, I'd just miss the ride. No foreplay, no naughty talk except for occasionally calling me a whore. He was good at other things. If you asked me what, I wouldn't be able to tell you now. But I stayed for a reason.

"I've always liked Edison; he's a fine young man. He was raised right."

"I agree." A smile tickled the corners of my mouth as I remembered the fine way he'd woken me up this morning. He pulled me from the bed and hoisted me onto his dick, supporting both our weight while fucking us into morning nirvana. The sun was barely up and the house was still just the creaking of the floorboards and my pleas for him to go deeper.

"Did you hear me?" my mother asked.

"What?" I shook the thoughts from my head.

"I tried texting your cell phone several times."

I guzzled down an unattended glass of juice. "Edison lives in the Stone Age, he doesn't have Wi-Fi."

Her brows smashed together. "What did you do to entertain yourself all that time?"

I flashed her a glance. "Edison kept me plenty entertained. Why were you texting?"

"Your assistant, Moniece, showed up last night."

My lashes flipped wide open. I totally forgot Moniece was coming to town.

"I put her up in Oz's old room."

I hugged my mother and rushed up the stairs. At Oz's bedroom door, I knocked softly. "Come in."

Opening the door, I dipped my head inside to find Moniece performing a lotus yoga pose. "Moniece, I'm so sorry. I completely spaced."

She waved me off. "It's fine, your folks were really nice. Did you know they traveled the country one summer following New Edition from city to city?"

"No, I didn't. They told you that?"

"Apparently your mother is a huge fan. They also gave me a story time while flipping through your old baby pictures."

"Once again … I'm sorry." Moniece stood and I wrapped my arms around her. It was surprisingly nice to see her face. Moniece was my right-hand woman. Nothing moved without her. She helped to make my life easier, and I loved her for it. Moniece anticipated my needs before I could speak them. She'd gotten me tampons, Plan B pills and scoured eight stores in search of my favorite ginger ale brand. "What do you say, I hit the shower and then we go for a walk before it gets too hot?"

"Sounds good."

After a quick shower which included detangling my hair, Moniece and I were off. We took the well-worn path to the stables. In the summer, this was the perfect time of day because it was still cool enough to get chores done without sweating your balls off.

"I forgot how peaceful it is at night," Moniece said.

I wrinkled my nose. "Did you hate it? I get country nights can be eerily still. With the silence amplifying your thoughts."

"It was a nice change of pace from always being on the go."

"You didn't have to come all the way to Hume. We could've caught up when I returned to LA." I opened the half fence to the stable.

"So, you do plan on coming back to LA," Moniece said.

"Of course I do."

"Good … that's good. The gossip blogs are going wild with made up stories. You, Chap, Darla, cheating, and drugs."

"What do you mean drugs?" I retrieved an apple from the pail I was holding and fed Candy girl.

"Some blogs are saying that you went MIA because you're in rehab."

"Rehab?"

"You know how they are, anything for clicks and engagement?" Moniece's steps were deliberate as she tried to navigate the dirt and hay.

"And who said I was MIA? It's been a week."

Moniece shrugged. "I don't know. Chap's been spearheading the messaging."

I cocked a half eye. "Is he suggesting to people I'm on drugs?"

"He's not really looping me in. But he's talking to Darla."

Circling the stable, I offered apples to all the horses. "Well, he can stop speaking on my behalf. I have a plan. I'm going to call the label, come up with some lame but plausible excuse and let them know Whiskey Wild is better than ever."

"That's a good idea. I think they just need assurances Whiskey Wild is still on track."

"Were they really pissed about me missing the second night of Heritage Fest?" I stopped at Cotton Candy's stall, and she ambled over, looking for love.

"I think Chap told them you were sick. Claimed you'd caught a bug at the festival."

"As long as he's mitigating damage and not tossing me under buses, I'm good."

I pointed to a bench just outside the stables under a large tree and we took a seat. "When you called you said you had something important you wanted to discuss with me. What's up?"

Since starting our trek, Moniece hadn't stopped fidgeting with her hands and clothes. "First let me start by saying I really enjoy working with you." My stomach dropped. I was already down pretty bad. The thought of her quitting would send me over the edge. "I believe in discretion and confidentiality. I'm here to make things run smoothly for you, not mess things up."

"And I love you for it. I know this past week placed extra work on your plate. I'd be stuck in place without you." I gave her shoulder a reassuring squeeze.

"I appreciate that."

"But?"

"It's about Chap."

My eyes slammed into her. "Oh my God, was he inappropriate with you?"

"No, nothing like that."

Placing my hand over my heart, I released a sigh of relief. The last thing Whiskey Wild needed was a sexual harassment lawsuit on top of a cheating scandal. "Thank goodness." Sometimes Chap told off-color jokes and when people complained he'd say Hollywood had gotten too sensitive and PC. Because he was a nepo baby, he was often given a pass to be an entitled asshole. *I know what you're thinking. "Fancy, he sounds like a horrible person." And he makes it hard for me to defend him. But trust me, it wasn't always bad. I think I clung to the good times hoping the Chap I fell in love with would make a return.*

"It's just that the Heritage Festival wasn't the first time Chap was unfaithful."

I blinked owlishly for several seconds. I figured that much. You don't go from a loving, faithful boyfriend to buck naked and balls deep in another woman's honey pot. "Go on."

"Right before we headed out on the first leg of our tour, I was dropping off some dry cleaning and I walked in on Chap in bed with a woman."

"In our bed?" My voice cracked.

"Yeah. At first, I thought it was you but when I gasped they turned to face me and Chap was … with Darla."

"Darla who?" I only knew one Darla … Darla Rooney and she was my best friend and bandmate, so Moniece must be referring to another Darla I wasn't familiar with.

Her features were crumpled, pain written all over her face. "Darla, Darla."

My eyes stung with tears. "Moniece, that's a cruel thing to say."

"And I wish I didn't have to say it but it's true. When they realized it was me, they went into damage control, claiming it was a one time mistake and they were drunk. But it was three in the afternoon. They begged me not to tell you. Promised it would never happen again. They said there was no need to upset you over nothing."

"They both said that." I swallowed hard, hoping to gain control of my emotions, which at this moment were a mixture of confusion, sadness, and searing hot rage.

"Yes. I know I should have told you sooner, but I didn't want to get caught up in a he said, she said."

"And you're sure it was Darla. My Darla?"

"Yes."

My gaze grew hazy as I stared off into the distance. There had to be some mistake. Darla was my best friend. She was the shoulder I cried on when Chap was being distant or mean. She'd offer advice and listen while I vented. There was no way she'd do something like that and not confess. No, uh-uh, nope. This wasn't possible. She taught me how to slick back my edges. I looked over the field behind the house. The same field where she and I performed our first concerts for Edison. I futilely wiped the tears from my face.

"There's more."

My tear-filled eyes landed on Moniece. I didn't think I could stomach much more.

"During the tour, I noticed them standing too close, sneaking kisses, or a quick hug."

"So you don't think it was a one off?"

"I don't think so."

My thoughts flashed back to the tour bus and how angry Darla became. At the time I thought she was defending me, but now it appears Chap was cheating on both of us. Hindsight being twenty-twenty, I could recall several moments which left me scratching my head between the two of them. Our trip to the beach in Greece when Chap playfully carried Darla into the sea. Darla's high-pitched giggles trailing after them. Or the time I arrived a few minutes late for a business meeting and found Chap and Darla sitting close with their heads together as if they were in a conspiratorial discussion.

"I kind of want to dig a hole and just lay in it. Why would she do that?"

"I don't know."

"She doesn't even like Chap. She's always telling me to break up with him." I swallowed hard. Looking back on it now, maybe that was for her own benefit. "So how long?"

"What?"

"You caught them right before our international tour started. That was months ago. So quick math tells me they've been messing around for at least six months." SIX FUCKING MONTHS! You know the saying about the rug being pulled out from under you? I was experiencing that right now and surprise, surprise underneath the rug was an endless pit, and I was falling deeper and deeper.

All I could do was blink sheepishly as tears streamed down my face. I couldn't fix this. Moniece rubbed my back silently as my shoulders rounded into a pathetic heap. When I caught Chap cheating, I was shocked but not surprised. But Darla? So, this has all just been some open secret and they've been smiling in my face while fucking in the bed I lay in at night. *If this isn't my villain origin story, I don't know what is. Fuck Chap, fuck Darla, and fuck Whiskey Wild.*

15

Edison

I SPENT MOST OF MY day avoiding Dial's questions about my weekend. If she knew I spent the time with Fancy, she would throw a fit, and I didn't want to deal with that. Normally, I showed up at Figs and Twine at least once during the weekend, even though Saturday and Sunday were my days off. Since I deviated from my routine, my sister was bound to have questions.

Plus, all day I felt like I was floating on a cloud, and I didn't want Dial ruining that. Fancy had that effect on people. When her big lips twisted into a delicious smile, I knew I was in trouble. And over the past few days I'd been graced with the smile time and again. Waking up to her face all serene with a bit of drool in the corner of her mouth was a dream come true. Yep, I dug everything about her, even the saliva stains she left on my pillowcases.

"We need to talk." Dial entered my office, which was a converted shed in the back of the greenhouse.

The contents of my stomach dropped to my toes. I didn't have the energy to go back and forth about all the ways Francesca was bad for me at three in the afternoon. "Hello to you too."

"No time for pleasantries. I've been thinking." She moved a stack of my Good Organic Gardening magazines and took a seat in the only other chair in the room.

"No, not that. Anything but that."

"If Mom and Dad are serious about moving, then we should get serious too."

"Serious about what?"

"About our plans, Eddy." She shook her head like I deserved to wear a dunce hat. "This place is going to be ours. That means no more running major decisions by the parentals. The buck stops with you and me."

"And Cyrus." If we were speaking about the future, Cy should be included.

"Fuck Cyrus. The nursery is our baby and Cy doesn't care about watering schedules or the best way to trim butterfly bushes. He's too busy kissing babies and cutting ribbons at the renovated library."

"Wow, I thought it would be a few months before the knives came out."

"Knives out? Don't be ridiculous. Cyrus left the family business and never looked back."

"Maybe, but things are different now and we still own the nursery equally."

Dial snapped her fingers. "Great point. Let's start there. I think we should buy Cyrus out."

I closed my laptop, realizing I was going to give this conversation more attention than I initially expected. "Excuse me?" This topic was too heavy for a Monday afternoon. My only concern was spending the night wrapped in Fancy's arms. I was not prepared for cutthroat succession planning.

"Don't start clutching your pocketbook now."

"Do you understand what you're asking?"

"Yes, I spent the weekend crunching the numbers. The shop is worth approximately ten million. That doesn't include all the land. Ten split three ways is a little over three million. So, we'd each have to come up with one point five mill."

"Oh, great, I'll just pull my half out of the shoebox in my attic."

Dial's face brightened. "We could take out a business loan."

"Or we could do nothing and not incur unnecessary debt. You're acting like Cy is our enemy."

"After we start implementing our changes, revenue is bound to increase. We'll be sitting on a substantial nest egg. And Cyrus won't be the mayor of Hume forever."

I hopped my shoulders. "It's Hume so he could be. Mayor Hathaway ran undefeated for twenty years."

"Let's be realistic. Cy's a one term politician, maybe two."

"And you think when his reign is over, he'll come slinking back to the nursery. Cyrus hates dirt so much, he gets manicures every two weeks."

"He wouldn't be coming to do manual labor. He'd want in on the business side, not the hauling manure side."

My sister's angle finally took shape. "And you're afraid he'll come for your position." Dial and I both had our strengths; I was the plant guy. I knew everything about gardening, landscaping, and vegetation. All the nursery orders were made by me with a detailed monthly supply schedule that couldn't be easily replicated. My stake in the business was solid.

"He could try but I'd crush him. I know more than anyone when it comes to the business behind Figs and Twine. Our supplies, our budget, or team members. And, that's why you and I make such a great team. I tend to the books and you tend to the begonias."

"Do you have some kind of acquisition proposal I could review?"

Dial sputtered a laugh. "What do I look like a newbie? Of course I do." She tossed a folder on my desk.

"I'll look over your proposal and get back to you."

"Okay, great doing business with you." Dial headed for the door.

I tipped my ball cap.

Stopping short, she said, "For now let's keep this between you and me. No Cyrus and no Fancy." When she spoke Fancy's name, it sounded like a cuss word.

"Got it."

With my parent's retirement/moving announcement came a ton of questions. When they said we had the ability to run the nursery on our own, what did that mean? Did it mean we would continue to run operations day to day, or was this a complete transfer of power? Over the past few years our parents stepped back considerably. There was a time when my father was in the nursery bright and early watering flowers, moving planters, and stocking accessories. Now he rarely made visits to the shop and when he did, it was usually because he needed supplies for his garden.

I was excited for the prospects, but Dial was moving faster than my liking. Icing Cyrus out wasn't going to fly with me. This was the family business and if he wanted, Cyrus would always have a place alongside Dial and me. As a kid I always imagined the three of us running the nursery together and teaching our kids to love this place as much as we did. Granted Cy wasn't interested in plants, customer service, our crunching numbers. He'd be good at it because he was good at everything, but he didn't have a passion for it like me and Dial.

After work, I headed home to take a quick shower before picking Fancy up. When I pulled up to my place, Fancy was already there sitting in one of the rocking chairs on the porch. My heart leapt in my chest. The sight of her was the best welcome home ever.

"Have you been waiting long?" I shouted. Her horse was roped to the porch banister on the shaded side of the house with a bucket of water next to her. Walking up to Fancy, it was clear from her sullen expression something was wrong. Moving her duffel bag to the side I knelt in front of her. "Is everything okay?"

She shook her head slowly.

Now that I was laying eyes on her, I could tell her face was ashen and stained with tears. "Talk to me."

"Darla was sleeping with Chap." She said the words in a matter-of-fact tone.

My eyes grew wide as her statement settled in. "How do you—"

"Moniece, my assistant caught them in the act months ago."

"And we believe Moniece?" Sometimes even the most well-intentioned individuals had a motive.

"She has no reason to lie. Trust me, I've searched my brain to come to a rational explanation, but Moniece is as trustworthy as they come."

Standing, I released a long sigh. "Tell me what you need right now? Do you want me to be honest or do you want me to provide a listening ear?"

"Honest." Her big brown eyes practically pleaded for clarity.

"Darla has always seen you as her competition for guys' attention or on stage. She's jealous of you and hides it behind fake smiles and unprovoked compliments. So, it doesn't surprise me she would do something like that to you."

Fancy jumped from her chair, practically ready to fight. "If that were true, if any of that were true, I would have seen it."

"Fancy you're not good at reading people, you never have been. You believed Darla was your best friend because that's what you were to her. I don't think you saw what I was able to see. The intense stares, the eye rolls, the smirks that never quite turned into a genuine smile."

"She always has a half smile, that's just her face."

"With you, yea. It's like she can't bring herself to be happy for you even when your success meant she got to tag along. You only see the best in people because that's what you offer to others but Darla—"

"Are you saying she's a snake in the grass?"

"I'm saying most of your mishaps can be traced back to her. Your mic not working at the start of a performance, your song journal going mysteriously missing for weeks. Who do you think smashed your guitar?"

"You're making her out to be an evil genius."

"Jealousy makes people do weird things."

"Jealous of what exactly? Darla is beautiful and talented in her own right."

"I don't think you grasp how difficult it is being dwarfed by your star power."

"So, she sleeps with my boyfriend … ex-boyfriend to get back at me? Maybe Chap is blackmailing her or he brainwashed her. Shit like that happens all the time. He got into her head and piece by piece broke her down. Trust me he's capable, he did it with me."

As if I needed another reason to hate this Chap fella. "Let me ask you this. If it wasn't for Whiskey Wild would you two still be friends?"

"She's my best friend." Her tone was incredulous.

"So was I and you didn't seem to have any problems with ghosting me." The moment I said it, I felt like an ass. I wasn't trying to make this about me. But witnessing her ride for Darla even after she stabbed her squarely in the back was pissing me off. For years I knew Whiskey Wild had an expiration date because eventually Darla would do some fuck shit and force Fancy to reconsider the strength of their relationship.

Fancy fired back. "I begged you to come with us, but you refused. So, who walked away from whom?" She stormed to the front door in an attempt to escape but it was locked. "Open the fucking door, Edison."

I walked over to her with her hands on her hips, looking defiant. "I understand you're upset, but let's not talk to one another like that." Leaning in closer, I whispered, "I'm sorry about what I said about you leaving. I wasn't trying to make this about me. We both made choices." I hoped my softer tone took a bit of the sting out of my previous words.

"I'm sorry too," she whispered back, burying her face in my chest. Her body shook in my arm as she silently sobbed. Sometimes you needed to cry it out before devising a plan of attack. When I received bad news, I usually sat in the dark listening to yacht music. Something about "Heaven Help Me" by Deon Estus centered me.

When she finally pulled away, I said, "It's going to be alright. And if you want to salvage a relationship with Darla we can figure it out."

"I don't know who I am without Whiskey Wild."

"You *are* Whiskey Wild. The music, the lyrics, the spirit. That was all you. Darla was just siphoning from your energy."

"It works because it's us."

"Nah, it works because it's you. It's in your blood. You are the heart and soul of this group."

"What am I supposed to do?"

"You don't have to have all the answers now. It's okay to take the time to process your feelings."

"I'm scared and I feel like my life is falling apart."

"That's fair."

"Maybe I should go. Home or back to LA. It's not fair to lay this all on you. You were expecting a good time and I'm just a Debbie Downer."

"I'm not going to tell you what to do. But I'm not asking you to leave."

"Why are you always there for me?"

I stared at my feet, kicking a thistle that had made its way onto the porch. The answer to Fancy's question was a simple one. Growing up whenever she needed me, I came running. She didn't have to ask. I eagerly volunteered to carry the load, brainstorm the problem, or quite literally kick someone's ass. Heat overtook my cheeks and ears as my gaze settled on her face and we locked eyes. I don't know who said it, but you miss all the shots you never take. So, I planted my feet and let a free throw fly. "Because … I love you Fancy."

After dinner, I led Cotton Candy to the barn, feeding her and the other animals. When I got back to the house, with my truck still parked out front, I remembered I had a surprise for Fancy. I moved the truck and collected the items from the back seat. In the house, Fancy was stretched out on the couch in a tank top showcasing her nipples and booty shorts that placed her curves on display.

"I come bearing gifts."

Fancy sat up. "You've come to the right place. I love gifts."

"First we have this." I placed a nondescript box in front of her.

"What's that?"

"This is a router for the internet I signed up for today."

Her face brightened. "You bought that for me?"

"Yeah. So now you don't have to run to town for service."

"This feels naughty, like I'm converting you to the dark side. Before we know it, you'll be fighting with strangers online who go by usernames like Macaulay Culkin's Left Butt Cheek."

My brows smashed together. "Is that supposed to be a real person?"

"Maybe, sometimes it can be a bot."

My expression was etched with confusion, probably because I mostly spent my time on the internet checking emails and searching recipes for thirty-minute meals.

"Awe it's like you're my grandma and I have to teach you how to work the group chat."

"I'm a part of several group chats, thank you very much. If you keep teasing me, I'll take my second gift back." I thrust a bouquet of wilted flowers in her face.

"Dead flowers?"

"They were a beautiful arrangement of flowers. But they've been sitting in my truck in the sun since five this evening, so now they are a representation of my good intentions."

"I love every parched petal."

"Don't worry I can probably bring it back to life by cutting the stems and dunking the entire thing in cold water."

"You don't have to buy me flowers."

"One, I didn't buy them because I own the nursery and two, yes the fuck I do."

Fancy hopped up and headed to the kitchen to unwrap the bouquet. Searching my drawers, she found a utility knife. "I didn't realize my boyfriend was so romantic."

My heart paused in my chest. *Did she just call me her boyfriend?* "Boyfriend?" I was in need of clarification before my head started spinning.

"Yeah, I mean I think that's the appropriate term when a guy and a gal are spending exclusive time together." Fancy's tone was casual as if she was sharing common knowledge.

She was offering everything I wanted, but it was hard to ignore the small voice in the back of my head telling me I was going to end up heartbroken. When the novelty of playing house with me on the farm wore thin, she would return to her real life. A life far more exciting than anything I could offer. All I could provide was a cluttered house and an orphan cat. How could that compete with touring and screaming fans calling her name?

Fancy just claimed me. Maybe she was ready for a change. Or maybe we could swing the long-distance thing. I didn't care a fuck about the logistics as long as I was with her.

While I filled a bucket with cold water, Fancy dutifully cut each stem. "During dinner, I kind of monopolized the conversation with my plots for revenge."

"It's fine. I enjoyed entertaining your murderous imaginings. My favorite was burying them in a shallow grave."

"Let's talk about something else, anything else. I know, let's pull out the yearbook and talk shit about the people we went to high school with."

"Can we start with Dial?" I took the flowers and submerged them into the bucket of water.

"Uh-oh, what did she do?"

"She's acting like we're in a game of Monopoly and is intent on grabbing up all the real estate. Dial suggested we buyout Cyrus's portion of Figs and Twine."

"Hmm." Fancy fluffed her curls while making her way back to the couch.

"What do you mean hum?"

"Cyrus hates the nursery."

I plopped down next to her. "Hate is a strong word."

"But it's one that he's used in the past. Now I've been out of the loop for a minute, so maybe his feelings have changed."

"You'd be fully okay if Oz iced you out of the ranch?"

"Well … no, because that's partially my inheritance. But I don't have any say in the day-to-day operations of Palmer Ranch. I defer to Daddy and when the time comes, I'll defer to Oz."

"Right so I'm just supposed to deny Cyrus his inheritance?"

"I thought you said Dial wanted to buy him out. Maybe Cyrus could use the money for his next campaign or to start his own business."

"So, you're siding with Dial."

"Whoa, slow down. I'm not siding with anyone. But if you and Dial are putting in all the work, maybe you should revisit the division of the pie. Instead of thirty percent each, Cyrus gets a little less. I mean I make more than my *former friend* because I write most of the songs."

"Something about that doesn't sit right with me."

"You need to remember Figs and Twine is a business first. That means doing what's best for the bottom line."

"How is me and Dial claiming the lion's share good for the bottom line?"

"I think you have to at least be open to having these conversations."

"Like damn, when is enough enough? Materialistically, I have everything I need. I couldn't really ask for more."

"You have an entire house to renovate."

"And I've already set aside money for that."

"Well okay Daddy Warbucks, I guess you have everything covered. But fair warning, once you get connected to the internet, you're going to have the urge to buy a cooling blanket or veggie peeler and it's just a gateway drug to more shit."

"And apparently I have a girlfriend now." I tried to act like everything was normal and she hadn't removed me from the dating pool with her declaration.

"Yep, one who's going through a quarterish life crisis."

"I prefer my women in the middle of a death spiral. It's easier for them to ignore my red flags."

"Smart man." Fancy ran her hand down my chest, stopping when it landed on my penis. It took very little encouragement for my dick to stiffen. "Should I put some music on?"

"No music. I only wanna hear you."

Fancy tugged on my pants, and I wasted no time stripping down to my birthday suit. Her mouth was warm and when she teased my tip with her tongue, I melted into the couch cushions. Watching her eagerly ease her mouth over my dick was my wildest dreams realized. She traversed the length of me, her slurpy moans of pleasure letting me know she was enjoying this as much as I was. Dick sucking was an art and Fancy was a fucking Basquiat.

Fancy's throat held the power to erase my mind, any stress or worries from the day dissipated as she stroked my shaft while circling her tongue over the tip. I gathered her hair in my hand to get a better view. Just the sight of her lips around my dick was enough to send me over the edge. Her big fuck me eyes settled on my features searching for confirmation her magic tongue had the intended effect. Tilting her head, she curled her tongue as she slid up and down.

"I think you're the sexiest when my dick is in your mouth," I groaned. Leaning over her, I whispered into her ear. "God, you are so good at this." Pulling off her shirt, I caressed her soft skin. Her moans shifted me into demon time. Standing, I looked down at her on her knees staring at me to make the next move. "Say ahh for me, darling."

Fancy complied and I slowly moved my hips back and forth, fucking her face. Collecting her hair once more, I guided her over my shaft. The sensation of her tongue running up and down my dick practically dropped me to my knees. "Take that dick, baby. Take all of it." She tried to accommodate more of me, earning an A for effort.

Her hand dropped to her crotch, and she worked her clit which made me jealous. I wanted to be the one pleasing her. Stepping back, I pulled her to her feet and in one fell swoop, hiked her upward until her thighs were on my shoulders, her feet near my head, and her pussy front and center. Fancy's squeal at the unexpected position change was followed by a deep moan as I dipped my tongue in her plump lips.

The sounds of her moans were my favorite tune. She released a series of melodic purrs before capturing my dick into her mouth. Her throat seemed to work overtime, reciprocating ever suckle, lick, and kiss of her clit with one of her own. The sensitive skin around my shaft goose pebbled as she teased me with her lips.

"Edison, I'm gonna come. Please —"

"Come with my dick in your mouth. I want your orgasm to echo through me."

Fancy bobbed for my shaft, sucking it back in. I slapped her ass, and she tumbled into ecstasy. Whimpering and humming against my dick. Her hands went limp, and I hugged her tighter to prevent her from falling. It took everything in me not to explode in her mouth. But I was greedy and wanted more. Releasing her, I gently laid her on the couch. Fancy's eyes were hooded still riding the wave of her sexual high. I lowered myself on top and was greeted by her wet and juicy center.

My eyes grew wide like I was experiencing sex with Fancy for the first time. Tonight, the act was slower and more intimate because I could see her face and kiss her lips when the mood struck. She didn't shy away, latching on to my curious gaze. I loved the way she absentmindedly massaged my body while we made love. Her hand kneading my thigh or caressing my arm with each thrust.

When I was a teenager, this is what I imagined a relationship would be like. Cozy dinners just us two. Silly dancing while the noodles boiled. Lazy days reading a book while music played as a soundtrack. And nights … nights were spent making love, your hips wobbling as you exchanged breaths. And the joy of knowing tomorrow you'd wake up and do it all over again.

While she rocked her hips, I pulled her further underneath me so my dick could sop up all her loving. Fancy pressed her lip to my ear and gave me a play-by-play of how my dick made her feel. How she'd never been this wet before and when I was in her vicinity it was difficult to think about anything else but fucking me. After each sentence, my breathing became more ragged, my hands tugging at her waist.

She nibbled on my ear and coaxed me. "That's it, baby. It's all yours. I'm all yours."

Shuddering over top of her I wedged my hand between us working her clit until she reached her edge and her eyes rolled to the back of her head as we grunted and groaned through our shared ecstasy.

Fancy wrapped her arms around me as her body twitched against mine. I licked the sweat from her neck and face because at this point, I was ready to consume this woman. Resting my face on her chest, I suckled her perfect breasts, sucking each nipple until it was taut. Fancy's hips were still floating underneath me, practically coercing my dick to come back to life. Grabbing my penis, she slipped me back inside for round two.

Yep, everything I needed was right here.

16

Fancy

IN THE MORNING, AFTER EDISON left, I decided to make use of the newly connected Wi-Fi. I contacted my agent, and she helped me craft a message to be shared with the label and included an offer to be available for a virtual meeting at any time. It was important that Chap wasn't the only voice they were hearing from. If he and Darla were attempting to cover me in dirt so the label and fans turned on me, I wasn't going to make it easier for them.

Edison's bedroom was large while being cozy at the same time. The bed was positioned so it overlooked his beautifully landscaped property. The house and surrounding land were like night and day. Outside was a sanctuary and the interior, aside from the primary bedroom, was very much a work in progress. I cataloged all the little finishes that would make Edison's place feel more like home.

Because that's what he was to me, home. It had been years and without missing a beat, he and I fell into our familiar cadence with sex as a bonus feature. Last night I let him know he was mine. Something in me was itching to make things official. *And before you start, this doesn't have anything to do with the fact that my life was a dumpster fire*. I didn't have shit figured out, but I knew who my heart belonged to.

Releasing a big yawn, I plotted out the rest of my day. I could help Edison by taking pictures of some of the items that needed to be posted online for sale. I'd also spied a guitar in one of the rooms, maybe I could work on tuning it. And then I had to get dinner sorted. A text message popped up, interrupting my restless scrolling.

Darla

When can we expect you back in LA?

I was taken aback by the intrusion. One minute you're looking at pesto chicken recipes and the next your conniving best friend is texting you like she didn't have a care in the world. *And did you catch the WE?* Who the fuck was we? Her and Chap? They were a collective now. Not Darla and Chap but WE. I was going to kick *their* asses, individually and as a fucking group. Everyone could get these hands.

Fancy

Did you sleep with Chap?

Darla

...

I secretly hoped she would type back "Eww, I could never." Or better yet she'd get mad at me and cuss me out for ever entertaining the thought she would betray our friendship. Edison asked if she and I would be friends if it weren't for Whiskey Wild. Darla had been in my life forever, not being friends never really felt like an option. I stared at my phone, watching those three little dots appear and disappear. She was a coward, and her lack of a response was all the confirmation I needed.

Fancy

> Just so you know. It's on sight when I see you.

Darla

> Fancy please.

Fancy

> ON FUCKING SIGHT.

I probably wasn't going to do shit, but I wanted her to think I was locked and loaded so she stayed far away from me. The most I'd do was probably unfollow her on social media and let the fans speculate over the reason why. Shit, Chap was claiming I was an addict, maybe I should show them bad press works both ways. Okay, who was I kidding. I wasn't going to do that either but imagining all the ways I could burn the happy couple was filling a void.

Downstairs I poured a cup of coffee and noticed the brown paper bag on the kitchen counter. Edison had forgotten his lunch. It was a little past nine, so I hopped in the shower, dressed, and then set off to make a special delivery.

When Cotton Candy and I pulled up to Figs and Twine, I secured her to a nearby pole. The parking lot was already littered with cars. Figs and Twine wasn't the only place in town that sold plants, but it was the biggest. It was situated on a huge plot of land with room to grow. It would be interesting to see what Edison and Dial would make of the place once their parents moved away.

Hume residents stopped me looking to say hello, most of whom had known me before I was even born. Ms. Upton gave me updates on her grandkids accompanied by a slideshow on her phone. Nathan, who was once the star football player informed me he now worked at the hardware store. I waved to a couple I'd never met but who seemed to know me, they must have moved to town after my departure.

At the front entrance, I found Dial outside watering some large potted plants. Dial was always no nonsense; she was a bit of a bookworm, and she'd only let her hair down if she felt comfortable with you. Because our families were close, I was fortunate enough to get a glimpse at the real Dial Birch. Growing up I remember admiring her independent spirit. Even though she was only a year older than me, I thought there's a woman who knows what she wants and she isn't going to let anyone stop her.

"Hey Dial, is Edison here?"

Dial turned to face me, almost spraying me with water from the hose. "No, he went to town."

I shook the bag in my hand. "He forgot his lunch, so I thought I'd run it to him."

Dial's forehead wrinkled. "His lunch?"

"Yeah, he forgot it on the kitchen counter when he left this morning."

Her eyes narrowed like she was processing new information. I guess Edison hadn't told her about us. "I'll make sure he gets it." She practically snatched the bag from my hand.

I wasn't sure what I'd done to warrant the attitude and frankly I was two seconds away from losing my shit. It was probably best I make a quick exit.

"Thanks, that would be great." The thing about me is I didn't like it when people played in my face. First Chap, then Darla, and now Dial. Was it so damn hard to be cordial? Not fake, not phony, just cordial. Was that too much to ask? I turned to leave, but the chilly reception was nagging at me, so I spun on my heels. "Did I do something to offend you?"

"What makes you think that?"

"You just seem … cold. I didn't expect you to roll out the red carpet upon my return, but I didn't anticipate this."

"Have you returned to Hume?"

I hopped a shoulder. "I'm back for a bit."

"Sure until Los Angeles starts calling." She turned her attention back to the plants. The spray from the hose made carrying on a conversation difficult. But I didn't back down.

"If you have something to say, stop gnawing on it and spit that shit out."

Dial released the handle, and the hum of the water ceased. Setting the hose at her feet, she wiped her hands on the legs of her overalls. "I've never had a problem saying what I mean."

"Well then shoot, because this passive aggressive stunt isn't working for me."

"The last time you left Hume, it took months for Edison to recover. I know you've been back since and I appreciate you keeping your distance. But I need you to remember you agreed to leave him alone."

"Yeah, because you bullied me into submission. And now I'm realizing that wasn't what Edison wanted, it's what you wanted." About a year or so after leaving Hume, I returned home with Darla. We were in town for a few days, and I had every intention of connecting with Edison, but I ran into Dial first. She informed me Edison was away at college. Then she asked me to keep my distance from him and claimed he went into a depressive state when I left. Dial made me believe I was bad for him.

"Because you're a taker Fancy. You just take and take until there's nothing left."

"That isn't true." Hearing Edison's words from a few nights ago regurgitated out of Dial's mouth caused me pause. Shit, maybe she'd gotten into his head too.

"You came back to town and needed an ego boost, and you knew just where to look."

"I didn't come back for Edison." I shrugged off her words.

"Do you think that makes it better or worse? Edison's feelings were never a consideration for you. You had one foot out of this town for years but still strung him along."

"He was my best friend."

"He was your lap dog," Dial spit out.

It was no secret there was no love lost between Dial and us Palmer siblings. She'd dated Oz and he broke her heart, or she broke his. I wasn't privy to the details, but ever since she'd had a hard on for me and him. She didn't have to like me, but she was trying to control my relationship with her brother and I was sick of it.

"I don't know what I did to make you so angry with me."

"You hurt my brother. That's all the cause I need."

"Edison and I are in a good place, a really good place. So you can pack up your cape."

"He's soft on you and willing to look past shit easier than me."

"And isn't that his right? Seeing how my relationship with Edison is between me and Edison."

Dial stood rod straight. Even though she was a few inches shorter than me, she had the power of intimidation on her side. I don't know if it was the slant of her mouth or the balled-up fist, but it was clear she wasn't looking to play games. "If you hurt him again, I will fly to LA and whoop your ass all across the golden state."

"I'd like to see you try." I squared my shoulders, never one to back down from a fight. Truthfully, Dial was stronger than me and could easily best me in a fight, but I was scrappy and wouldn't go down without connecting a few blows to her face and ribs. We stared at one another for a bit like those boxers do at weigh in before

I walked away in a huff. Getting into a fistfight with his sister would probably do me no favors with Edison.

"Go back to LA," Dial shouted, not caring who heard her. "No one wants you here."

"You better get used to this face Dial." I pointed right at my mug. "Because when you see Edison, you're going to see me standing right next to him holding his hand. Cry about it." I unhitched and mounted Candy before trotting away.

Back at Edison's spot, I obsessed over everything. The situation with Darla, my fight with Dial. Darla was a two-faced liar and she and I would cross paths soon enough and when we did, I don't know if I was interested in talking so much as whooping her ass. Chap cheating, I could get over. Fuck him, he was a dumb guy who took me for granted. A mistake he would regret for the remainder of his days. But Darla was my best friend. She knew everything about me, even the things I normally kept to myself. That kind of betrayal cuts deep. And it wasn't something I could easily move past. What that meant for the group I wasn't ready to think about.

Then there was Dial. It's funny how I came to Hume to escape my problems and just ended up picking up new ones. I didn't need us to be besties, but we had to find a common ground. One thing about Edison, he didn't play about his family; he loved his parents, and his siblings fiercely, so disliking Dial wasn't a route I was willing to take. If Edison and I were going to work, I needed to fix things as best as I could with her. Because if he was forced to choose, he wouldn't pick me.

Speaking of, where did all this protective, "Hurt my brother and I'll kill you" attitude come from? What exactly had Edison said about me to his sister because whatever it was appeared to make me out to be the bad guy. Which was absurd. But Edison didn't believe in shades of gray. There was only black and white. So, if he was the victim, that had to make me the villain.

I tried to keep busy, but I found myself stewing for the rest of the day. I checked on the animals, swept the porch, and cooked dinner, but all I could think about was Edison's perception of my leaving Hume all those years ago. It was never about him. I was doing what was best for me. When Edison entered the house, I met him at the door, my feelings turned up to ten.

"What did you tell your sister about me?"

"What do you mean?" He placed a shopping bag on the floor and removed his ball cap.

"Exactly that. What did you say to her because she has a real bad taste in her mouth whenever she says my name."

"Hello, my day was good. Thank you for asking."

"I'm glad to hear it." I tapped my foot, still waiting for an answer.

"It smells great in here." Edison approached me, looking for a welcome home kiss.

"Answer my question."

"I don't understand the question. What are you talking about? Our relationship?"

"No, I'm talking about when I initially left Hume for LA. What did you tell her about that? About us."

Edison shrugged. "You expect me to remember shit from ages ago?"

"Whatever you said stuck with your sister like a piece of popcorn caught in her molars."

"When you left, I was hurt, and she consoled me."

"She said you were depressed."

"Dial exaggerates. I was upset and I was a bit of a downer to be around for a few months."

"Does she know I asked you to come to LA before I left and after?"

"Yes, and to be fair that's probably one of the reasons she dislikes you. You were trying to steal away her little brother."

"She doesn't dislike me. People dislike pop music, the beach, black and white westerns. Your sister hates me."

"I disagree."

"She threatened to kick my ass."

"And I will talk to her about that." Edison's hand found my waist. "You know Dial, she's always putting twenty on ten."

I shook my head. "So, I tell you your sister threatened to beat me up and your response is cool story bro?"

"My response is it's Dial. And one thing she's going to do is hold a grudge."

"I should have never listened to her when she told me to stay away from you. I thought she was speaking on your behalf but—"

"What are you talking about?"

I was worked up and the words had just tumbled out. I fidgeted with my fingernails, hoping the sentiment flew over his head. "Nothing, never mind."

"When did we start lying to one another?"

I swallowed hard. I'd already said too much. The last thing I was looking to do was drive a wedge between Edison and his sister. "I don't feel comfortable talking about this. I think you should take it up with your sister."

Edison moved in close. "Did she say something to encourage you to stay away?"

My eyes pleaded for him to drop the subject. "Please don't ..."

I've probably seen Edison truly pissed a handful of times. And the glint in his eyes hinted he was ready to go to war. Through gritted teeth, he asked, "Will you be good alone for about an hour or so? I need to talk to my sister."

Wrapping my arms around him I said, "Stay with me. Your conversation with Dial can wait a day."

"It really can't."

I'd made the mistake before of coming into a conversation hot. And when I did, I said shit I didn't necessarily mean because emotionally I was fired up and ready to inflict damage. I needed Edison to take a beat. Him getting into a screaming match with Dial over me wouldn't do any of us any favors.

"It can and it will. Gives you a chance to choose your words. Plus, I already cooked dinner. Stay awhile, kick off your shoes, eat, and fuck me on the staircase."

His shoulders retreated from his ears. "You could have just led with fuck me on the staircase," he teased. And after eating my expertly prepared chicken, he did just that. Fucking me on the entryway stairs until every single thought that didn't involve me and him vacated our heads.

17

Edison

I'D BEEN SILENTLY FUMING ALL night, after Fancy hinted at Dial butting her nose where it didn't belong. When I returned from feeding the animals, Fancy tried to entice me with sex. Normally that would work, but I was too wound up to slow down and enjoy morning sex with her. I had to be soft in the head to turn her down, but I needed to clear things up with my sister.

The thing about me and Dial was, we've always been close. And she was super protective. This woman threatened my second-grade bully. Not because I couldn't protect myself, but because I was the one to turn the other cheek until my face was sore. She'd always taken on the protector role with both Cyrus and me. And we indulged her because it was coming from a genuinely good place.

I climbed the metal stairs to her office with views of the sales floor. Dial usually started her day going over the sales from the night before. She had a natural affinity for numbers even though she'd only completed a few classes at Hume Community College. Her brain was like a calculator constantly computing our bottom line.

"Morning," she said, her eyes focused on the computer screen.

"We need to talk." I closed the door and took a seat in one of the two chairs in front of the desk.

"Can it wait until I'm through?" She glanced at the paper ledger and then back to her screen.

"Nope."

Dial finally looked at me and probably sensed we were about to have it out. My sister knew me better than anybody. I didn't like it when things were out of place, and it was clear she and I were not on the same track. "Okay, shoot."

"It's about Fancy. She mentioned you two got into an argument yesterday."

Dial reached for her coffee, taking a thoughtful sip. "It didn't rise to the level of an argument."

"She said you threatened to kick her ass."

"First, it wasn't a threat. And second, when were you going to tell me?"

My brows slammed together. "Tell you what?"

"That you and Fancy were shacking up."

"What is this the seventies? We're not *shacking up*, she's my houseguest."

"A house guest who's sleeping in your bed." She pointed her finger at me. "I knew there was something off with you the last few days. You've been all chipper and that is not a word anyone has used to describe you. Walking through the aisle whistling and shit. Leaving at five o'clock on the dot like you had better things to do."

"Is that a bad thing?"

"It's peculiar ... with you traipsing through the shop like a Disney princess before she pricks her finger, eats the apple, or does some other stupid shit."

"I didn't tell you because I knew exactly how you would respond."

"We talked about this. You and Fancy aren't good for each other." Dial's tone made it sound like ancient law as if she was reading scripture from the good book. "An eye for an eye. He without sin cast the first stone. Edison and Fancy aren't good for each other."

With a long huff, I fidgeted with the brim of my baseball cap. "No, *you* talked about what *you* thought was best for me. I've asked you a thousand times to stop sticking your nose in my business. You did it with Willa and you're doing it again with Fancy."

"I'm looking out for you." Apologies were few and far between when it came to my sister.

"Dial, I am damn near thirty years old, I don't need you looking after me anymore."

"You're just too pussy whipped to see she's doing what she always does. She's going to hurt you."

"Fancy makes me happy, right now, in this moment. If I get hurt, I get hurt. But I'm not going to live scared. You don't have to like her. I'm not asking for you two to be friends, but you can't keep inserting yourself into my personal life like this."

"So, caring about you and your well-being is a crime now?"

"Damnit Dial, you just push and push. I have a lot of thoughts about you and Oz, and I've always bitten my tongue because I know you don't want to hear it. I'm asking you to do the same now. Bite your tongue and swallow the blood like I've been doing all these years."

"That's different." It was always different, or somebody else's fault.

"No it isn't … not really. What went on between you and Oz is your business. And what's happening with me and Fancy is mine."

"So, Fancy comes along and I have no say."

"You don't get a say," I shouted. "Not in how I live my life. Or about who I choose to love."

Dial sputtered out a laugh. "You love her now?"

"I've always loved her. It's always been her. You don't think I know she's going back to LA, and this is all going to be over? You don't think I fucking know that?"

"Then why put yourself through it when you know the outcome?"

"Because in this life you have to grab hold of what you can. Find joy in the simple moments. So yeah, I don't care if it's a week, a few days, or one second. I just want to be with her." Sometimes talking to my sister was like conversing with a brick wall. I was stubborn and set in my ways, but Dial was ten times worse because she was stubborn and judgmental. "And I know you don't get it because you prefer to push people away rather than be vulnerable."

My statement landed and I witnessed Dial's body language shift as she mentally checked out of the conversation. Her silence let me know we were at an impasse. We were not going to see this the same. Standing, I prepared to leave. if we kept at it like this, I was liable to say something that would be difficult to walk back.

"So that's it, you've picked your side?"

"I'm a circle. I don't have sides."

"I'm entitled to have concerns."

"Sure, but I'm not interested in them."

"You say that but a month from now when she's back on the road, you'll be looking to me to bandage your wounds. You can't tell me to mind my business, but then seek my shoulder to cry on."

"Noted," I called over my shoulder, leaving the office.

When Fancy and Darla left for Los Angeles. I was upset and conflicted, thinking maybe I should've gotten on that plane too. The thing is, Fancy and I were never a couple. Aside from one kiss when we were twelve, it was nothing. Did I want more, sure? Did she? I don't know. But when she left, I lost my best friend. And at the time it was the most painful thing to ever happen to me. Granted I was still too young to realize life was a mixture of joy and pain. And the longer you lived the harder it becomes to escape the sting of your existence.

So, I metaphorically cried on Dial's shoulder. And when Fancy stopped reaching out, I called her everything but a child of God. And Dial was there for that too. So, in a way I made Dial hate her because she saw I was in pain and the source of the pain appeared to be Fancy. My hurt feelings and sadness wasn't Fancy's fault, it was mine alone. I wanted something Fancy never promised.

After a long day of me and Dial scowling at one another when I wasn't completely trying to avoid her all together, I headed home. These past few days, going home held a new thrill for me. I wasn't returning home to an empty house and evening chores … well I still had chores. But now I had someone to do the chores with me. Fancy would sometimes tag along and help me feed the animals in the evening. She would talk my ear off telling me about her day and asking questions about mine.

Since Fancy was on vacation, her days consisted of working on new music, making jam with her mother, or catching up with an old friend for lunch. As we rode around the farm, I'd listen to the intricate jam making process and watch as her face lit up when she told me she'd brought me some strawberry jam to try. Before she arrived, I was content with nights alone tinkering in my garage but now having experienced what life could be with someone it would be hard to return to my normal routine.

When I exited the truck, Fancy was outside to greet me. Jumping into my arms from the top step of the porch. She almost bowled both of us over, but I managed to steady my feet.

"Welcome home." The way she greeted me made my dick throb. It was like she'd been anticipating my return all day and now that the boring workday was over, the fun could finally begin.

"Did you miss me?" I asked, desperate for confirmation this feeling wasn't all in my head.

Instead of words, her tongue invaded my mouth with a long, probing kiss, hinting at what the night had in store for us. When she finally released me, she claimed my hand and I followed her inside. Fancy had opened all the blinds, and the sunlight was beaming through the windows. My inherited collection of junk almost took on a mystical aura, transforming my place into one better suited for an antiquities dealer rather than a country boy.

"How'd things go with Dial?" she asked.

"It was like driving down a straight a way, hitting a dip in the road, careening through a cornfield and smashing into a tree."

She lowered the volume on Fleetwood Mac's "The Chain." "That bad, huh?"

"It's fine. We both just need time to cool off. Dial and I are really similar, but the majority of our disagreements are because of how we differ. I still love her. I'm just not real happy with her at the moment."

"I don't want you two fighting about me. If I have to, I will lock you both in a room and force you to talk it out."

I reached for her hand. "Listen, I owe you an apology."

"For what?"

"For Dial and how she came at you yesterday. She's mad at you because of me. Because when you left it felt like the world was ending. And as my big sister, she's protective of me. It's one of her best and worst qualities, the fierceness of her loyalty and love."

"So, she's mad at me because of the things you said."

Tossing my hands in the air, I did my best to explain. "I was unhappy for a host of reasons. After graduation I wasn't fully sure of my place in the world. I was taking classes at the community college because I was too scared to leave home. It was like everyone was moving on, pairing off, starting families, getting married. While I was over here trying to figure out my next move. Losing you was just added salt to the wound. It was a rough patch for sure. Dial was there for that—"

Tears threatened to spill down Fancy's face. "And now I'm back and she thinks my intentions aren't sincere and I'm going to hurt you again and she'll have to deal with the fallout."

"Pretty much."

"You're not the only one who had trouble finding their way. LA wasn't welcoming and more times than I liked to admit, I felt like I'd bitten off more than I could chew. I cried the entire plane ride to LA because you weren't with us. At some point I got mad. I was so mad at you. So, I stopped calling. Because what was so great about Hume that you'd choose it over me. We weren't even a couple, but I had this hole in my chest." She blew out a tight breath in between sniffles. "And I didn't know how to verbalize what I felt or the love I had for you, and it scared me.

"Eventually it became too late. The years passed and I just knew you'd moved on. I was waiting for my momma's weekly Hume reports to include news about you getting engaged or having a baby." Fancy tucked her curls behind her ears, her makeup smeared from crying. "I don't regret moving … I don't … but I do regret losing you. Because the truth is, I sort of love you Edison Birch."

It was difficult to catch my breath, and my heart was beating like it was looking for a way out of my chest cavity. I always knew she loved me as a friend. But now she was saying she loved me … loved me. She was telling me I was special in a way others weren't.

Her fondness for me wasn't because we'd known one another for years and were practically family. She just loved me and all the things that made me uniquely different from anyone else. In me she found a connection so deep it was scary, painful, and exhilarating simultaneously.

Fancy released a nervous chuckle. "Whoa, I think I need something stiff to drink."

In the kitchen, I poured us both a glass of bourbon. Fancy took the glass to the head and immediately regretted it, frowning at the nutty spicy flavor of the liquor. Opening the fridge, she selected a beer to wash away the taste of the bourbon. After a few sips, she eyed me curiously. "Are you not going to say it back? I mean you don't have to if you don't feel it … but …"

I drank the remainder of my bourbon before answering. I'd declared my love for her a few nights prior, nothing had changed. "First day of kindergarten you came in and your hair was in two twisted pigtails with big pink ribbons at the top. The ribbons were almost as big as your head. And I thought, wow. I was five and could barely spell my name, but knew my life was forever changed in that moment. So, I'm glad you're in love. Welcome to the party. I've been here waiting on you for a long fucking time."

She rested her hand on my cheek, her thumb stroking my face. "Well, I hope I was worth the wait."

"You were, you are, and you always will be."

18

Fancy

WHEN OZZIE ENTERED A ROOM, his presence was felt. From the porch he was banging on the door and beat boxing to some made up tune.

"Keep your pants on," I shouted from upstairs while I shrugged into a robe.

"Fancy, oh Fancy girl. Let me in."

I swung the front door open, irritation written all over my face. "What the fuck, Oz?"

"Don't tell me you were still sleeping. Not on a beautiful morning like this." He pushed past me.

"I like to ease into my day. Thank you very much."

"Whoa." Oz retreated, bumping into me. "Edison's a hoarder? I would've never guessed."

"He's not a hoarder. I mean sure this place has a lot of—"

"Shit. It's a crap load of shit."

"Edison bought the house as is. And he's sorting through the items at his own pace."

"A snail's pace. He's lived here for almost a year. You're dating a squirrel."

"What?"

"Have you ever come across a squirrel's stash house? Tons of acorns, mushrooms, and plants all stuffed to the gills."

"I'll have you know many of these items are sought after collector finds."

"One man's trash is another's treasure." His tone didn't match his words.

"Exactly."

"Like that two headed goat over there." He pointed to what I called the parlor of curiosities.

"It's not real."

"Ehh, are you sure about that?"

I wasn't sure. But I preferred my claim over the possibility of Mr. Castle beheading conjoined goats. "Do you want coffee?"

"Yep, you know how I like it." Ozzie followed me to the kitchen, sniffing the entire time. "Are you cooking?"

"No."

"Then why does it smell like cheese?"

It was too early for Oz to be picking at every single flaw in this sweet little house. "I don't know." I surrendered my arms in the air. I don't know what to tell you. The house smells like cheese. But it's just downstairs."

"Let me get this straight, Edison has your nose so wide open you are willing to shack up with him in his creepy old man house that smells like Limburger."

"Okay, first off who still calls it shacking up? And second, I happen to like this old smelly house."

"Whoa, lil Eddy got that thumpity thump thump."

"What?"

"That's the sound it makes when he drops trou. It's significant and heavy."

"We are not going to have a conversation about my boyfriend's penis." I added water to the coffee maker and selected a mug.

"You're right because we need to be talking about your possessive adjectives. How many boyfriends can one woman have?"

"I only have the one."

"What happened to Chap?"

"He got replaced."

"Is that what Edison is … a replacement?" His lips took on an unimpressed shape.

My eyes narrowed as I detected the bullshit. "Did Dial put you up to this?"

"She and I barely talk."

Stomping my foot like a child, I replied, "Don't lie to me."

"Dial may have mentioned something when I was dropping off Maple."

"She asked you to check on me?"

"No, she was venting. I listened and took it upon myself to check on you."

"Well, I'm fine." I did my best to add an air of finality to my words.

Oz took a long sip from his mug, any trace of humor fading. "Do you know what you're doing?" Serious Oz was almost as bad as life of the party Oz. In fact, I think serious Oz was harder to swallow because when Ozzie wasn't smiling he looked just like my father and now I felt like I was in trouble.

"Yes, kind of … sorta."

"Emm, Edison deserves for you to be all in."

"I am all in."

"Baby girl, I love you to bits. But you don't think things through. You never have. You ran off to LA and struggled for the good part of three years. Sleeping on people's couches and surviving on SpaghettiOs and the dollar menu at Taco Bell. You're impulsive and Edison is steady."

"I'm impulsive? Pot … kettle."

"I own that shit; us Palmer kids are like the wind. Now Edison, Dial, and Cy are more like the earth. Edison is a redwood tree. You know the kind with the massive trunk not easily moved. And you are like the Santa Ana Winds. It sweeps down from the desert and into California bringing with it smoke, dust, and the makings of wildfire."

"But I can also bring a nice breeze on a hot day."

"Breezes never stick around for long."

"So, Dial tells you to jump and you drive right over here and start stirring the pot."

"That's not what this is. You came to Hume to get away and in less than two weeks, you're in love."

"Just because it happened fast doesn't make it any less real."

"I don't think you've ever been single. You are what they call a serial monogamist."

"You say that like it's a bad thing."

"It is because it means you can't be alone. Why is that Fancy?"

I'd always been popular, and people gravitated toward me. Not trying to brag, just stating facts. So yes, when I lost one man, I usually had another one within three to five business days. What was happening with Edison and me wasn't planned but it was a sweet surprise. I was fully aware there were a ton of questions that needed to be answered. Primarily, was Edison interested in a long-distance relationship?

Normally I was a go with the flow type of woman, who often allowed fate to decide my next move. These are the things I know for certain; Edison loved me, and he was never going to leave Hume. Eventually we'd have to make decisions but right now I just wanted to fill his cup the same way he was filling mine.

"Thank you for your input. But if you want to help me, maybe start with suggesting how I can get on Dial's good side."

"Dial doesn't have a good side."

We both shared a laugh. She was a tough nut to crack, that was for sure. "I just want to reassure her that I have Edison's best interest at heart. What can I do to win her over?"

"You're asking the wrong person. I've been trying for years to get off Dial's shit list or at the very least get bumped down from the number one spot."

Tilting my head to the side, I examined his face. "What did you do to make her so mad?" I raised a silencing finger. "You know what don't tell me. Most men are fuckboys, and I do not have the heart to hear that my brother may be among the ranks."

"Listen, Dial is moved by actions not words. So, if you claim you're not going to hurt Edison, then don't. Now can you give me the penny tour because I'm nosy."

"Okay, but don't touch anything."

We'd driven to a big box store several hours away because I needed some essentials you just couldn't get at Welborn's Grocery Mart. I claimed I only needed a few things, but the cart Edison was pushing proved that was a lie. Inside the buggy was everything from body scrubs to a cute green vase.

"Ooo, I need a hot water bottle." It was that time of the month, and I didn't have any of my creature comforts, which is what prompted this trip. Edison navigated the store like a pro and led me to the appropriate aisle.

"Should I get the one with the pink fleece cover or go traditional?" I held up both bottles as if the fate of the world rested on him providing the right answer.

"Uhm, I'm not a heating bottle connoisseur."

"Pink fleece it is." I tossed it in the cart. "Now for the tea." He dutifully followed my directions and stood in silence while I debated over green or orange blossom tea. Back at the farm, all he had was black and I was craving something more exciting. I settled on the ginger-turmeric green tea. "Can we check out the board games?"

Edison's brows mashed together. "Board games?"

"Yeah, you don't have any games. You have one hundred vintage lighters, but not a single board game."

"I live alone?"

"How do you host game nights?"

"I don't."

"Your hermit lifestyle ends now."

In the games section, I tossed Scrabble, Pictionary, and Jenga into our cart. "What are your thoughts on Monopoly?"

"I hate that game. Not only is it outdated, it's boring. And when people think about board games, the first game they mention is Monopoly, which is embarrassing because the mechanics of Monopoly are the worst of any game. Candy Land is a more enjoyable experience. And don't get me started on the consumerism agenda."

"So no on Monopoly. Do you have any strong feelings about Taboo?"

"Taboo is acceptable."

We searched the shelves for other games vetoing suggestions we didn't agree on.

"How was your visit with your mom?" Edison's hand cradled my neck, occasionally massaging my muscles.

"It went well, we made more jam. I brought some home. Best apricot jam you will ever try."

"I hope she doesn't feel like I'm monopolizing your time."

"My mom loves you. With a capital L. She low key thinks you walk on water and are the nicest guy in all of Hume."

"Okay, I know your mom didn't say all that."

Leaning closer, I grabbed hold of his side, rubbing his rock-hard obliques. "She's not so silently rooting for the hometown boy."

"My mother has similar thoughts about you."

"Glad to hear someone in the Birch clan is pulling for me."

"My dad and Cy like you too." He said as if Dial hating me was just common practice … like breathing.

"How have things been with you and Dial?"

"We're giving one another a wide berth."

"You can't avoid her forever."

"I'm not avoiding her. I see her every day at work. I'm just not entertaining conversations about my personal life. I'm keeping it strictly professional."

"With your sister?"

Edison shrugged. "Dial and I have fallen out before and we always make amends … eventually."

"I really want us to fix this." My face brightened and I grabbed the Scrabble box. "What about a game night?"

"No."

"What, why not? Games, snacks, music."

"Sure, we'll just play Battleship and whoever's fleet gets sunk has to apologize."

"I mean—" I hopped a shoulder.

"No."

"I want to help."

"You help by staying out of it. I set clear boundaries with Dial, and she needs to respect them."

"Okay," I said before chucking Battleship into the cart, just in case he changed his mind.

Driving at night with Edison was peaceful because at night he preferred jazz or instrumentals, and his playlist was the perfect backdrop to the town whizzing by. I believed every human was allocated a certain number of perfect moments. And what that looked like was different for every individual. For me this drive home, with the stars puncturing the sky, the windows rolled down as a gentle breeze whispered through my curls, and Edison's hand absentmindedly stroking my thigh, was a perfect moment I'd recall in my final minutes on this earth.

I interrupted the serene silence after passing a billboard advertising Hume's upcoming fair. "I've been seeing flyers for Hume's festival."

"Yep, The Sweet Summer Jubilee is still going strong."

"When I was a kid that was my favorite thing about summer. Well, that and not having to go to school."

"And it's gotten bigger since you've left. If you can believe it."

"Is Ms. Irma still winning the cornbread cook off?"

Edison's face lit up. "Actually, Janette from high school is now the reigning cornbread queen."

"Shut up, I thought Ms. Irma would die wearing the crown."

"Janette uses a cold-water recipe, so her bread looks more like pancakes, but the taste is out of this world. She earned the fuck out of that title."

"Can't wait to try them."

He shot me a glance. "You want to go to the Jubilee?"

"Why not?"

"Because everyone in Hume will be there."

"Yeah, that sounds like fun."

Edison puckered his face with surprise. "I just assumed you'd want to keep it low key."

"Wait are you saying you don't want to be seen together at the fair?" I thought we were both all in.

"Going to the fair is a statement. People will ask questions and make assumptions."

"I mean yeah … that was kind of the point. I want everyone to know you're off the market." Edison tried his best to prevent a smile from curving his lips. "So, what do you say? Is it a date?"

"I'll be there with a bell on."

19

Edison

EACH SUMMER HUME COMMUNITY COUNCIL hosted the annual Sweet Summer Jubilee. It was a weekend-long event with crafts, petting zoos, cook-offs, and contests for the biggest squash or tomato. There was music, games, and food … tons of food. When I was a child, my family attended each year. Our parents would give us each twenty dollars and let us lose. The first thing I'd do was grab a turkey leg, because it's not a festival without meat on the bone.

Fancy and I walked around with a sample of Mr. Williams' collard greens. Another perk of this event was all the free samples. And even if they weren't free, if you stood around shooting the shit long enough, you'd be offered a sample. In my opinion the greens had way too much vinegar for my liking, but I was partial to my father's recipe.

"I forgot how crazy these things could get." Fancy discreetly chucking the rest of our uneaten greens in a nearby trash receptacle.

"I think each year the council dukes it out trying to find ways to top the prior year. Dial's a member and she doesn't tolerate mediocre. What was once balloon animals and the mayor's son performing his family friendly raps has morphed into massive bounce houses, carnival attractions, and hot-air balloon rides."

Her face lit up with recognition. "I remember the mayor's son and his God-awful raps. What was his stage name again?"

"Hines the Holy Roller."

"Yup, because he was rapping for the Lord. Is he still doing that?"

"No, he retired years ago, so now we get real local talent."

"Well, if Hines the Holy Roller has one fan, it's me and if he has zero fans it's because I've died."

"I think he still signs autographs. So, you just let me know and your Christmas gift is secured." I winked.

Fancy unleashed a hearty chuckle.

"Edison?" I turned to find Willa with Teddy Britell.

"Hey Willa, Ted." Wasn't there some kind of etiquette about the protocol when you run into your ex at the community event? Perhaps hightailing it in the opposite direction was an option.

Willa's lips curved into a half smile. "Francesca, I hoped you were still in town and we'd cross paths again at some point." Willa pulled Fancy into a hug.

"It's good to see you again. You look amazing. I love your dress." Fancy wasn't lying. Willa was a knockout.

"Thank you. I could say the same. Your boots are like art. Where can I find them?"

Fancy looked down at her sequined boots, which I could only imagine cost thousands of dollars. "Uhm, they're from a New York based designer. His name escapes me now, but I can text it to you."

The long uninterrupted stare as Willa drank the sight of me holding Fancy's hand was like tiny paper cuts all being inflicted at the same time. Willa finally turned her attention back to me and me alone. "I thought you hated these things?"

"Edison? He loves fairs, especially the turkey legs," Fancy chimed in.

Willa's gaze was carrying on a private conversation with me. Last year when she suggested we come to the festival together, I lied and said I hated the crowds and smell. "Hmm, so you two?" she asked.

Fancy pinged between me and Willa, sensing the building tension. "Teddy, do you think you could walk with me to get a lemonade? I'm parched, but I want to give Edison and Willa a chance to catch up."

I interjected. "Are you sure? I could—"

"I'm positive. Teddy doesn't mind." Fancy was right. Ted's smile grew three times bigger. Willa and I watched as they walked away.

"I'm not ready for a relationship. Those were your words. I guess the part about not wanting one with me was just silent."

"Can you keep your voice down?" I didn't like drama and rumors spread like wildfire in Hume.

"No, I will not. You picked Fancy over me?" She was shouting, and sweat was dotting my forehead.

"You're acting like this was some kind of competition. What happened between you and me has nothing to do with Fancy."

"Bullshit," Willa yelled. We were outside, but I really needed her to use her inside voice right now. "She comes to town and then you break up with me. How convenient."

"We were never a couple. And you seemed to have rebounded nicely with Teddy."

Willa pointed her finger in my face. "You're an asshole."

"I never … not once … lied to you about where we stood."

Willa moved closer so only I could hear. "No, you just fucked me until my knees were weak and held me while I fell asleep."

I'd already had two beers, so my filter was slipping. "Do you want me to apologize for making you come?"

Willa planted her hands on her hips. "Lose my number. Because when Fancy heads back to Hollywood, I don't want you even thinking about calling me."

"I respect that."

Willa's eyes grew misty. "How can you act like you never cared?"

"I did care, I really did. Just not as much as you." I didn't do well with endings, whether it was initiated by others or myself. And oftentimes to protect myself I could come off as cold, but I ended things with Willa for this exact reason. I didn't want to see her get hurt.

Willa shoulder checked me before walking away, sparing me from the tears threatening to fall from her eyes. All I could muster was a stuck on stupid stare silently analyzing our conversation and all the ways I could have communicated better. But in my defense, accosting me in public wasn't going to foster an honest discussion. I just wanted the yelling to cease and for passersby to stop staring and whispering.

Fancy came bounding back over, lemonade in hand. "How did it go?"

"Horribly. She's mad at me."

"Oh no, someone in Hume doesn't see you as the perfect gentleman." Fancy chuckled.

I flashed a hard, irritated expression. "No, I'm serious, she called me an asshole." I reached for Fancy's arm, turning her to face me. "Am I an asshole?"

"Probably."

My shoulders rounded into a heap.

Fancy cupped my face. "Edison, romantic relationships are complicated. And most men suck at it. Don't beat yourself up. No one is perfect. If I had a dollar for every heart I'd broken, I'd have forty-two dollars. You know what will make you feel better?"

"What?"

"A turkey leg."

"I mean it's kind of difficult to be upset when you're holding a medieval-sized turkey leg."

"That's the spirit. We can pretend to be pirates enjoying our smoked serving of meat."

We walked laps around MetCalf Park enjoying our food and people watching. In truth, people were watching us more than anything else. We couldn't walk but a few feet and someone new would come up to Fancy gushing about her music, asking her to sign their shirt, ball cap or take a picture. Picture taking usually fell to me and I was happy to do it. She deserved all the admiration and earnest words of affirmation.

Whiskey Wild was world famous, and this type of fan adoration wasn't just reserved to Hume. It made me wonder what the duo was going to do now. Dancing around and singing duets with someone who'd betrayed my trust would be a non-starter for me. Hard truth, the amounts of money Fancy and Darla were making wasn't easy to turn down. I wouldn't fault her if she decided to stay with the group. But how do you move past it?

One highlight of the festival was the musical acts. The west end of the park was home to the new amphitheater. It'd taken years to get approved and was only completed last year with Cyrus overseeing the ribbon cutting. Our amphitheater was probably the only state-of-the-art structure in Hume. Talent from all over came to perform at the festival and now, with a stage worthy of a show, bigger named acts were sure to follow.

Fancy and I weaved through the crowd to get as close as possible. Jace Montgomery was in the middle of his set, singing a slow ballad about the one that got away. Standing behind Fancy, I wrapped her in my arms, and we swayed back and forth. Reality washed over me, Fancy was all mine. Burying my face in her hair, I breathed deep. The hair products she'd selected during our shopping trip were worth it because she smelled like horchata, fresh salt water, and rum all mixed in one.

Jace's song ended, and he addressed the crowd. "This is a great night to forget your worries and just allow the music to move you. And there is no one better than moving a crowd than Fancy Palmer of Whiskey Wild." Jace pointed at Fancy and a spotlight landed on us. "I'm gonna ask a huge favor. Ms. Palmer would you grace us with a song?"

The crowd cheered while Fancy waved off the attention. She found my hand and squeezed it tight.

"Now Fancy we go way back, and you know I'm not above begging," Jace joked.

The crowd spurred her on with applause and hooting.

Fancy glanced up at me, uncertain whether to accept the offer. "I think you should do it. The people have spoken."

Nodding, she planted a quick peck to my lips before releasing my hand. The crowd was already electric by the time she strutted onto the stage, her white sequined boots emblazoned with pink flowers caught every flicker of light like a firework in motion. Fancy's smile lit up the night, a mix of genuine joy and unshakable confidence, and when she grabbed the microphone, it was as if the whole world tilted in her direction.

"You know I love it when you beg, Jace," she teased, a spark in her eyes. The crowd ate it up. Turning to the audience, which had grown bigger as word quickly spread, she said, "Hume, how y'all feeling?"

The response was resoundingly affirmative. When the hoots and hollers died down, Ozzie could be heard screaming, "That's my baby sister!"

Fancy turned to the band and whispered to the guitar player. She started with a few handclaps, the band kicking in with a fast-paced guitar riff for one of Whiskey Wild's biggest hits "Good Time Girls," and the crowd erupted, stomping and cheering as if their collective energy could lift her into the sky. From my spot in the center of the crowd, I felt like I was holding my breath, not wanting to miss a single beat of her magic.

She owned the stage, moving with a rhythm that matched the pulse of the music and the heartbeat of the audience. Fancy performed the perfect two-step while whining her hips, causing a blush to overtake my face at the thought of what those hips were capable of. Her voice was rich and twangy, soaring effortlessly through the lyrics of her chart-topping anthem about chasing men and raising hell along the way.

Fancy threw playful kisses at the crowd, twirling and stomping in perfect time, her curls bouncing like they had their own choreography. The hometown crowd sang back every word, their voices blending into a powerful wave of pride and love. She wasn't just a star; she was theirs. And for all her glitter and glow, you could see the girl who grew up here shining through, the one who used to sing in her church choir and this exact fair.

Darla who? I meant it when I said Whiskey Wild was nothing without Fancy. She was a superstar. Tooling around the farmhouse, it was easy to forget just how much of a powerhouse she was. Sure, this was Hume and everyone was going to love her because she was our hometown favorite. But she lived up to the hype. Fancy could put on a show and when she was on stage, it was like you were on a joyride in a stolen F-150.

At the final chorus, she grabbed a nearby banjo and began to play, inviting the audience to join in. The air was alive with sound, a sea of clapping hands and stomping feet shaking the ground. I caught her eye for a split second, and she winked at me, a moment so fleeting and intimate it felt like our secret in the middle of all this commotion. When the song ended, she threw her head back, laughing as if she couldn't believe this was her life. And watching her, I knew something she didn't, she wasn't just the star of the show tonight. She was our collective hopes and dreams, and I was the luckiest man alive to love her.

Fancy bounded off the stage and into my arms. "That was amazing," I gushed.

"Really? It's better with Darla next to me."

"I didn't notice, but maybe that's because I only have eyes for you."

"I will admit it was nice being on stage again. Performing was always my favorite part, feeding off of the energy from the crowd. Witnessing them sing along word for word. I've missed it."

"You were born for the stage." A lump the size of a grapefruit settled in my chest. It wasn't lost on me that annual festival performances in Hume weren't enough to fill the urge nestled in Francesca's core to entertain. Hume would never be enough. As much as she loved me ... I couldn't replicate the adrenaline rush her career provided.

Once the crowd of fans disbursed, we made a beeline for the beer garden. We ordered two beers each so we wouldn't have to wait in line a second time. I made quick work of my first one, and Fancy wasn't far behind. In the center of the tent was a makeshift dance floor and from the swing in her hips, I could tell she wanted to dance. I nodded my head in the direction of the dance floor, and she beamed in agreement.

Line dancing in Hume wasn't like most line dancing, maybe because the city was founded by Black folks and remained predominantly Black to this day. Our line dancing was a bit honky tonk with a whole lot of rhythm. We'd performed that soul filled line dance to Megan Moroney or Juvenile; it didn't really make a difference. And that shit was an art form. The basic steps were simple, but everyone had their own little spin on the parts in between. So, if it was one, two, dip, spin, shimmy, you were going to get fifty variations of the same move executed in sync.

Right now, Fancy was dipping her hips with each movement. Occasionally she'd back her ass up against me and we'd dance close, performing the moves like we were connected. We clinked our bottles, taking long gulps while rolling our bodies to the beat. Not going to lie, I felt like the big man on campus because everyone knew Francesca Palmer was here with me. And when Fancy claimed you, she acted like there was no one else in the room.

Francesca was a free spirit, and you could see it in the way her body moved across the dance floor. Arms in the air grooving side to side. I loved her adventurous nature the most, maybe because that was a quality I was lacking. When we were younger, Fancy talked me into skinny dipping in the lake. Truthfully, I opted to keep my boxers on. Now Fancy, was buck naked and didn't care. I stared for an unusually long time before averting my eyes. That woman kept me on my toes, and I relished every minute of it.

Life is short and long at the same time. And we remember our life in moments. Our memories like photographs sealed in time. You don't remember the mundane day-to-day tasks. Watering and feeding the animals, driving to and from work, Sunday dinner with the family. But we remember the special times. The days when we were really happy. Like the day my father bought me my first horse. I named him Turpentine because I thought the name sounded bad ass.

You also remember the days of immense sorrow like when our parents sat Cyrus, Dial, and me down and told us about Momma's cancer diagnosis. I remember breaking into tears at my big age because cancer sounded like a death sentence. Luckily our mother survived and was currently thriving. But fear of the possibility of life as you know it being over is scary as hell.

Right now, two stepping on the dance floor with the woman I loved was etching itself in my brain as a fond memory. The type of memory you call up when your head hits the pillow to help lull you to sleep. I was luckier than most because I had a healthy family, a town I could call home, and a woman who made me feel special even on the most ordinary days.

20

Fancy

I FELT HEADY, LIKE I was on a natural high the entire ride home. Edison's hand was intertwined with mine and I was stuck with a goofy smile that would not fade from my face. Shit if this was what love felt like, I've been doing it wrong all these years. I'd never been this content or at peace with Chap. Not ever. Maybe because he was always correcting me and trying to dull my shine. It's strange the time away was allowing me to clearly see things that should've been blatantly apparent.

They say love is blind but that shit with Chap wasn't love, it was codependency at best. I thought I needed him to fit into the country music industry. There weren't a lot of Black artists in the field. I stuck out like a sore thumb. Chap shielded me from all that. Or at least that's the lie I told myself to keep me with him. Plus, his stepmother was Billie Preston and the handful of times I met her she'd always been gracious, offering great advice. In the past I'd convinced myself if dating Chap meant I had access to a legend, I could grin and bear it.

I turned to Edison with puppy dog eyes and said, "I love you."

"Listen, I'm trying not to pinch myself because if this is a dream, I do not want to wake up."

I playfully pinched his arm. "This isn't a dream."

Edison's hand found my cheek. "I love you too, Fancy Face." In the low light from the moon, I could see the muscles in his jaw clench and circle.

"What's wrong?"

"Nothing."

"Edison, I've known you since you were five, and you've made that same pinched expression when you're nervous or worried."

He pulled off to the side of the road. Placing the truck in park. And I braced myself for what was to come. Because only bad news was delivered on the side of roads. "How is this going to work? You and me, I mean."

I unbuckled my seat belt and turned to fully face him. "I don't know. And I don't wanna try to figure it out tonight. Tonight was a good night."

"That's not going to work for me. This just can't all be vibes. You know me. I'm about things fitting in their place. I like details, I like a plan."

"Love isn't about logistics."

"I just need to know we're working toward the same thing."

"We are."

"Fancy, I want to marry you one day. I want to have a kid or two. I want to teach them how to grow vegetables and measure their height against a door frame. I want to dance around the kitchen at night while we clean up after dinner. I want us to renovate the farm so it's a safe and loving home for our family."

I cradled his face. "I'm onboard for all those things too. I don't know exactly what that looks like. But I want to build a life with you in it. It's probably not going to be as conventional as you outlined it, but if you're willing to think outside the box on some things, I think we can make this work. I really do."

"I hate to be that guy, but we need to iron this out."

"Okay. But does it have to be tonight when I'm feeling tipsy and just want to go home and fuck you?" My hand slipped to his lap. I was a bit of a coward because while I recognized we had tough choices to make, I wasn't ready to make them. If I could freeze time, I'd hide away with him forever. But I knew as well as he did I couldn't stay in Hume.

Edison removed my hand and placed it over his heart. He didn't say a word, just pressed on my hand so it was secure under the weight of his. Closing my eyes, the predictable beats of his heart vibrated against my palm. I could write a hundred love songs about this man. This had to work out because frankly, I'd never wanted something more in my entire life. I wanted Edison and the future he offered.

Edison would love me until his dying breath. I honestly didn't deserve a love like that, but I'd do my best to return his focused devotion every day until he had his full. He kissed my palm and then turned back onto the road. We drove in silence, not awkward or unnerving quiet like I experienced with Chap. It was an easy, content stillness because we both knew we were exactly where we were meant to be.

When we pulled up to the farmhouse, he leaned in to kiss me and the kissing spilled out of the truck onto the paved walkway and up the stairs. Discarded items of clothing scattered in the grass, flower bed, and dirt. We weren't making it inside. I pulled off my cowboy boots while Edison unbuckled his jeans, removing both his pants and boxers in one movement. Sitting on the oversized rocking chair, he pulled me onto his lap. Lowering myself onto his erect dick, I was eager for him to be inside.

As he entered me, we collectively exhaled a sigh of relief. Some people take hot yoga classes or meditate to relax. Me, I made love to Edison. With him I felt incredibly safe. I could turn my brain off and just let life happen because I knew when I was with him, he'd keep me protected. With Edison, I came first, and I meant that in every way possible.

The night air on my skin caused my flesh to pebble. Edison's mouth consumed my modest breast. His tongue circling my tightened nipple. Moaning, I rocked my hips over his length. I'd never craved another person as much as I craved him. Every part of my body ignited when he was inside me. He possessed the master key to secret places deep within. Unlocking a kaleidoscope of emotions. Awash in a pink, orange, purplish glow of love's first spark, the hue of a sunset kissing the horizon goodbye. My pussy literally salivating as I creamed on his impressive dick. Edison's steady frame grounded me as we worked in tandem up and down, in and out.

He gripped my ass and worked me over his length. Like a sorcerer he culled every moan, desperate gasp of air, and cries to a higher power out of me. Pressing my forehead into his, our eyes connected and in that charged silence, a thousand unspoken words passed between us. His gaze softened, lingering, tracing the contours of my face as if he was cataloging every detail. My gaze held steady, searching, a quiet invitation to go deeper.

A slow knowing smile flickered at the corner of his lips, answering the question shimmering in my eyes. *Was he all in?* Because I didn't have any more cards to play. In that moment there was no need for words, the longing in his kisses, and urgent thrust expressed a silent promise that I was not alone. This knowledge danced in the space between our gaze, speaking in a language only one's heart could understand.

Leaning back, my body coasted on air with Edison's hand at the base of my spine for support. Nature was an unexpected participant in my wave of ecstasy. My body unfolding like the night sky, an endless velvet tapestry, deep and mysterious. My eyes were stitched with countless stars shimmering like scattered diamonds. And Edison was the moon, his body slick with sweat, a silver guardian draped over me in a soft glow, casting dreams into my core.

Our love surged like constellations weaving their ancient tales across the heavens, guiding lovers to nirvana. When you are properly loved time slows, and the world breathes in the quiet magic of possibility. With Edison, it was possible to heal, forgive myself, and embrace the love I often questioned I deserved.

Since my return to Hume, I had the most restful sleep in years. Most nights I'd stare at the ceiling, trying to identify all the red flags. Not just with Chap but Darla too. Edison claimed Darla's duplicitous nature was always there, but I didn't buy it. Darla was my friend, but at some point our friendship became one-sided.

She teased me for being attached to Chap, saying who brings sand to the beach. We were famous and that meant having access to some of the hottest men in Hollywood. Darla thought it was silly for me to settle down so early. I'd never been a bar hopper, preferring to sit in my reserved booth at my favorite bar. And like Oz suggested, I didn't like being alone, bouncing from boyfriend to boyfriend with little lag time.

I'm not saying men were knocking down my door, but there was an active waiting area filled with eligible suitors. When one fucked up, I'd just call in the next. But I realized Edison wasn't someone you could easily replace. He was the guy who set the bar so high it became damn near impossible for others to measure up.

I gave my body a huge stretch and pulled the covers from my head. Edison's side of the bed was empty. Don't ask me how he managed to do it, but he was like a ninja each morning. Getting dressed in the dark and out the door to feed the animals all without waking me. I loved animals, but waking up at the crack of dawn to tend to them wasn't really my thing.

When Edison returned to the bedroom, he handed me a cup of coffee before stripping and jumping back into the bed. He positioned himself behind me so I could lean on his chest. I couldn't see him, but his face was buried in my mass of curls.

"Don't sniff my hair."

"I didn't."

"I heard you sniff."

"Your hair smells good."

"My hair smells like barbecue smoke and beer."

"Two of my favorite things." He squeezed my waist, causing me to spill coffee down my chest.

"You brat." I used the sheets to dry myself off. "How are the animals?"

"Fed, watered, and happy."

"Just like me." I smiled.

He kissed the top of my head.

Intertwining my fingers with his, I said, "I feel like we wasted so much time. If I knew loving you was going to feel like this, I'd of done it years ago."

"That's the thing, it's all about timing. A few years, shit a few extra days and this could have gone very differently."

"I guess you're right. I'm just thankful for right now." Shifting my body weight, I mounted his lap. "I'm ready to talk if you are." A flutter in my stomach filled me with dread. We were content in the impregnable bubble we'd curated for ourselves. In which our days were filled with laughter, music, and impromptu sex. Negotiating plans threatened to disrupt the peace we'd created.

Edison's body froze, and he examined my face. "One last kiss."

"Not the last."

His lips were soft against mine, not too eager, but filled with longing. Edison slid his hand down my naked back and my skin pebbled with goosebumps. I exhaled, melting into his frame, my hips slowly grinding because when he kissed me, I couldn't help myself. Moaning into my mouth, he abruptly pulled away. "We're supposed to be talking."

"Yeah, for sure I agree," I whispered breathlessly. "Where should we start?"

"How about location."

I was hoping to start with something less complicated like being granted use of a few drawers in his bureau. "Okay, you go first."

Before he could answer, the doorbell rang. Edison's doorbell sounded like a rooster crowing. The sound made me cringe. I'd never noticed before because he hadn't had any visitors during my stay.

"What the fuck is that?"

"I know, I ordered a new bell, it just hasn't arrived yet." He was stepping into his jeans.

"If I'm going to live here, I don't want to hear cock-a-doodle-doos every gotdamn time someone rings the bell."

Edison tossed a hesitant glance in my direction. "Live here?"

"Or not," I said. The rooster bell chimed loudly again, and Edison left the room, still pulling on his T-shirt. I sunk into the bed. Maybe suggesting me moving in was too soon. Realistically it hadn't even been three weeks. For me I'd fallen harder in these string of days with Edison than I ever had for any man. I wanted to invade his space, take up room in his thoughts, his home, and his future.

When I loved you, that was it. I didn't do half in and half out. I fell fast, but with Edison I knew I wanted to linger. This wasn't a passing fancy. I wasn't just visiting, I was ready to plant roots. And until just now it never occurred to me, maybe he didn't want the same. Maybe he'd considered the possibility and decided a long-term relationship would be difficult to maintain.

Maybe he'd had his fun fucking his dream woman and by this time next year, he'd be married to Willa and announcing the pending arrival of baby Birch. The thought made me want to crash out. Who the fuck did he think I was? I was prepared to live in his house of cheese, what right did he have to express reservations?

Edison's foot falls caused the stairs to creak as he ascended each one. When he stopped at the doorway, his face was ashen.

"What?" I shot straight up.

"It's Darla."

"What about her?"

"She's outside waiting to speak with you."

"Outside this house?"

"Yep."

I threw on the first articles of clothing I could find. A Funshine Care Bears graphic T-shirt and some sweatpants with Whiskey Wild emblazoned on the side. The joggers were part of the merch from our tours. As we made our way downstairs, the few sips of coffee in my stomach was churning. I never expected Darla to show her bitch ass in Hume. My hair was already piled on top of my head so at the first provocation I could get to scrapping.

Outside Darla was leaning on her mother's car. She looked well rested and was dressed like she was headed to The Grove and not the backroads of our hometown.

"Thanks Edison," she called.

"Yep." He kissed his teeth as if a piece of food was wedged in them.

"It's nice to see you again." Darla made another attempt to connect with him, but he was Team Fancy and wasn't impressed.

"I wish I could say the same." Darla placed her hand on her hip and offered that half smile Edison was convinced was fake. "Well, I'll leave y'all to it," he said, returning to the slightly cooler house.

"You look good," Darla called.

"I look a mess. I just woke up." I fluffed my curls.

"Your mom told me you were over at Edison's place. She had to give me directions. I didn't know he'd bought the Castle Farm."

I walked down the stairs, sticking close to the porch.

"Are you and Edison a thing now?"

"Why are you here?"

"I come bearing gifts." She opened her car door and Yeti Spaghetti bounded onto the grass, running toward me at top speed.

"Yeti, oh my God. I've missed you." I rubbed his belly and endured his wet kisses. "How have you been? Are you okay?"

"He's fine. I just thought you'd like to see him."

"How fucking kind. Well, that makes up for everything," I quipped.

"I thought it best if we talk face to face."

"Are you ready to answer the question I texted you and you ignored for days?"

Darla rolled her eyes. "Will you let me explain my side?"

I inched closer and Yeti moved in step with me. "I know you're not giving *me* attitude. I know the woman who fucked my boyfriend ain't popping off at the mouth. The fact that I didn't jump off the porch and whoop your tired ass—"

"Don't act like you're blameless in all this."

"If we are doling out blame, I'll take a portion for being a dizzy bitch. But the lion share goes to you and Chap."

"I didn't come here to fight."

"Well then you wasted a trip, cause all I have are these fists." I crept closer.

Surrendering hands in the air, she shouted, "It was a mistake."

"Which part? The part when you were sucking my man's dick. Or the part where you got caught?"

"I know you're mad about Chap."

"See that's the thing … I don't give a fuck about Chap. We're through. He cheated. I just never thought it would be with you."

"Fancy it was one time. We were drunk and it was the biggest mistake of my life." This is how we were going to play it? She flew all the way down here and put on her Sunday's best to tell lies.

"If you want to avoid this ass whooping you need to be honest. It wasn't a one and done. You two carried on an affair for months." Darla pulled out her phone like I was the one who showed up unannounced. I looked to the house, wondering how many punches I could get in before Edison pulled me off her. Snapping my fingers, I yelled, "Hey eyes front. Did you come to apologize or what?"

"I'm trying to. I'm sorry. In a moment of weakness, I made the wrong choice."

"Apologizing means nothing if you're not willing to lay out the whole truth. How do we move past this when you're still lying to me?"

"About what?"

"The full extent of your relationship with Chap. It wasn't one time. He probably claimed he loved you and what you two shared was special." The intensity of my glare was combustible. That man's words were hollow but effective because they'd kept me on the line for a few years.

"It was special, and he does love me," she spat back.

"No, he does not. He was saying the exact same shit to me. We got played Darla, the both of us. Chap was sleeping with you and then returning to the home he and I shared and sleeping with me.

We went ring shopping, he was going to ask me to marry him. Be fucking for real."

"It's not true. He was just with you because you were so fragile and needed guidance."

Guidance? I wrote all our songs, arranged the music and vocals, and helped produce every one of our albums. The name Whiskey Wild was my intellectual property. The cover art for our first record was a picture I took on my iPhone. Darla was intent on letting me lead, and I was cool with it because she had an undeniably great voice. To claim I was a drift with no direction was laughable. Maybe you can say that about my personal life, but when it came to music, I was as solid as they come.

"Honest question. Were we ever friends? Because I was willing to lay my life down for you and I thought you'd do the same. But now it's clear the danger isn't external; the call is coming from inside the house. That's what hurts the most."

"I'm sorry, I just fell in love. I tried to stop it but the heart kinda wants what it wants."

"And your heart wanted my sloppy seconds?"

"I love him, Fancy."

"Over me? Over Whiskey Wild? Over everything we built."

"We are still Whiskey Wild."

"No, the fuck we're not."

An unfamiliar car approached, slowing to a stop. Chap stepped out. Looks like Darla texted for backup. It was only fitting he'd show up to support the woman he chose. I hated him, but even I had to admit this man was gorgeous. Tall, tan, with brilliant blue eyes, and blond hair.

"Francesca, you look a mess." His eyes tripped over my disheveled outfit.

You'd think he would lead with an apology, but his first words were an insult. That pretty much summed him up. He was selfish and hurtful. And I took his verbal abuse because part of me felt like I deserved it. I suffered from major imposter syndrome. Don't get me wrong, I knew I was talented, but I often questioned whether I was deserving.

"Did you two come down here together thinking you could convince me of something different from what I already know?"

"No, I came here to tell you you're acting like a child. Not answering my calls and ignoring my messages isn't going to solve anything," Chap said.

"I'm not looking for solutions. I was hoping for closure, but at this point you can keep that too."

"We're a team. You, me, and Darla. We're Whiskey Wild." His smile was smug and unearned.

"Nope, Darla and I are Whiskey Wild ... and now we're nothing."

"I'm your manager. Whiskey Wild doesn't move unless I make it happen." He was so fucking entitled. I used to think it was attractive and claimed it was confidence. Now I could identify it as cocky bluffing to hide a lack of experience. Chap wasn't special, as our manager, all he did was what we paid him for.

"You're fired."

Darla's eyes grew wide like she was in the middle of a five-alarm fire. "Now wait a minute, he's my manager too. You just can't go and fire him."

"Bitch you're dead to me. You got your wish. You get to be with Chap. I hope he treats you just as well as he did me."

Chap shifted his tone from stern to light and airy. "Francesca ... sweetie be reasonable. There's still five months left on our current contract. Dumping me wouldn't be wise financially."

"I don't care. I'll write you a check for the remaining five months."

"What about the tour?" Darla protested. "We still have three months of tour dates. Whiskey Wild needs to get back on the road."

Fuck I wasn't expecting to have this conversation this morning. I could fire Chap, but walking away from the tour was complicated. We'd made commitments. Chucking the deuces on the tour would require us to pay back advances. Tickets had been purchased. The band and tour crew were secured and under contract. If I backed out of the tour, the record label would make sure I regretted it. A lot of people invested a lot of money into Whiskey Wild. I couldn't just shit on their efforts. Chap was right, Whiskey Wild was never just about Darla and me.

I jerked an uncertain shoulder. Making career decisions at seven in the morning was something I was ill-prepared for. "We finish the tour dates, but after that Whiskey Wild is over."

"Bullshit, you're not going to walk away from all that money." Chap squinted his eyes.

"I don't want to be paired with someone I can't trust. If she can actively attempt to steal my man, what's next … my money?"

"Fancy I get you're upset but think this through," Darla begged.

"I have. This tour will be Whiskey Wild's last."

Chap turned red and spit flew from his mouth as he screamed at me. "You stupid bitch."

He advanced quickly, closing the distance between us. Stumbling backward, I tried to retreat, tripping over my own feet and falling to the ground. I'd never seen him this angry, and I instinctually raised my hands in case I needed to protect myself. When the gunshot rang through the air, Darla and I screamed in unison.

Chap froze in his tracks and Edison was standing in front of me, the barrel of his rifle still smoking. "I'm gonna say this as respectfully as possible. Get the fuck off my property."

Neither Chap nor Darla protested, scampering to their respective vehicles. No doubt they noted the incensed glint in Edison's eyes. He aimed his rifle at Chap's SUV until it disappeared from view.

"Did you just shoot at my ex-boyfriend?"

Edison secured the safety lock on the gun. Helping me to my feet, he said, "I shot into the sky. But that joker is lucky I didn't aim it at his kneecap. He thinks he can come onto my property and threaten my girl. I bet his scary ass will think twice about that in the future." He claimed my hand, leading me to the porch. Setting the gun down, he turned his attention toward me. "Are you okay? He didn't hurt you, did he?" He brushed dust off the seat of my sweatpants.

"No, I'm just a little shook up."

"Your arm is bleeding." The way his face was marred with concern you would think my bone was exposed and my arm was hanging on by tendons.

"I must have skinned it when I fell."

"Fancy." He pressed his forehead into mine. When he pulled back, his eyes were misty with rage. "I'ma fucking kill him."

"No, you're not, because as far as I'm concerned, he's dead to me."

Edison stared into the vast, empty land, the muscles in his jaw ruminating. "I'm sorry if I scared you."

"I could never be scared of you." I slid closer in need of a hug, and he obliged. Wrapping me up in his strong arms.

Edison has always been my protector. When we were ten or eleven, we were walking down the road headed to a nearby stream and a dog came out of nowhere snarling and growling. Edison stepped in front of me and tried to shoo the dog away. But the animal attacked, latching onto his arm. He fell backward, pinning me under him. I was useless with fear, but Edison poked the dog in the eye until it released him and ran into the tall grass. Edison had to get a shitload of stitches and a faint scar remains behind.

"Whose dog is that?" Yeti ran off when the gunshot pierced the air, just now venturing out of his hiding spot.

"That's our dog. Yeti Spaghetti the II." Yeti ambled over to the porch, cautiously sniffing. Edison held out his palm, allowing Yeti to investigate. Climbing the steps, he settled in between Edison's legs, resting his head on his thigh.

"Good thing I'm not allergic." Edison scratched behind our dog's ears. "Are you hungry? Because I'm starving."

I nodded but wasn't quite ready to pull away. How was I going to leave this man for three months to finish up the tour?

21
Edison

JOSEPH AND SHELIA INSISTED I bring Fancy to Sunday dinner. I suspected Dial filled them in on my current relationship status and now they wanted to confirm it for themselves. The last time I'd brought a woman to dinner … shit … I couldn't tell you. But when I asked Fancy if she wanted to attend, she smiled that full effortless smile of hers and nodded, her big curls falling into her face.

Per usual Cyrus was absent but he gave his apologies in the group chat. I've had Cyrus's cooking, and it wasn't better than our parents. Why he chose to stay home or at work like he claimed was beyond me. And what mayor of a town this small couldn't clock out on a Sunday evening? He acted like he was putting out never-ending fires. Nothing ever happened in Hume and when it did it was still tame in comparison to larger cities.

Kids tagging stop signs, or a baby goat trotting around the Welborn's. Which in my opinion was a cute sight to witness as residents pulled out their phones to take pictures of the prancing goat. Cy wasn't saving the town, so why was he constantly declining family Sunday dinners?

Dial never missed a Sunday. Shit most Sundays she and I would show up early and just hangout. Being in your childhood home was earnest and humbling. No matter how grown, you were always your mother's baby. And Dial and I would fall into our teenage routine of cracking jokes, talking shit, and pestering one another. Now with my niece in the mix, I was able to teach her all my annoying habits, which pissed off my sister.

"I don't get it," my niece said.

"Get what, sweetie?" Fancy asked, grabbing an apricot from the snack board.

"How can you two be a couple if you're related?"

"We're not related," I said.

"But she's my aunt and you're my uncle."

"Yeah, we're related to you, but we're not related to each other. Because you're right, that would be weird." Fancy nodded.

Maple wrinkled her nose. She was the perfect blend of Dial and Ozzie. "But we're all family."

"In a sense, yes. But—"

"Are you two going to get married?"

"Dial," I shouted. "Dial, come get your child." Per usual Dial ignored my cry for help, just like she barely acknowledged Fancy and me when she came in. "Hey Maple, go tell your mommy Uncle Eddy said she's a gray sprinkle on a rainbow cupcake."

"What?"

"Just say it exactly like that. Gray sprinkle on a rainbow cupcake. Go, go, go."

Maple ran off to the kitchen.

"Why?" Fancy asked.

"Why not? She's acting like a loser. Plus, she has thick skin."

Maple came running back out of breath. "Mommy said, you're a pretzel that's unsalted and no one likes that."

"Oh yeah?" I tickled Maple and she giggled with glee. "You tell mommy Have a nice day, *somewhere else*. Say it just like that, start out nice and then go for the kill. Let me hear you."

"Have a nice day, somewhere else."

"Say *somewhere else*. Can you tell the difference? Maybe add a little attitude."

"Somewhere *else*."

"That's good enough. Go."

"Are you ten?" Fancy stared at me.

"What's the point of having a sister if you can't tease her every now and then?"

"Maybe we shouldn't poke the bear."

"We may be at a stalemate, but annoying my sister is my right as the baby of the family."

Dial entered the family room and gave us the once over. "Cute shirt Francesca. I mean I'm used to seeing your areolas, so this is a nice change."

Fancy gasped out a laugh.

"I think I liked it better when we weren't talking," I said.

"Hold on," Fancy raised a silencing finger. "I'm trying to imagine you with a personality."

Dial smirked. "Oh, is this the part of the night where we air out our grievances?"

"No, that usually comes after dinner," I corrected her.

"Can't wait." Dial turned on her heels and exited the room.

"Oh, she's big mad," I whispered to Fancy.

"Maybe this was a mistake."

"No, forget Dial. In this family dinners are always awkward. Someone is always mad at someone." I kissed her hand.

"I kind of feel like an outsider."

"Well, according to Maple we're kissing cousins." I tried to lighten the mood, and it worked. Fancy laughed and the death grip she had on my arm loosened.

"Fancy?" my mother called from the kitchen archway.

"Yes, ma'am." Her back was pin straight.

"Are you okay with eating on the back porch? It's a pleasant night but I know not everyone enjoys alfresco dining. Especially in Tennessee where the insects are as big as golf balls."

"I don't mind. Shoot I'd sit on the lawn if it meant getting to enjoy your home cooking."

"Alright, well dinner's ready."

My parents made some of my favorites, steak, au gratin potatoes, and Brussel sprouts with bacon and a honey drizzle. I would miss their home cooking if and when they actually moved away. If I was being honest, I didn't really believe it would happen. We'd lived in Hume forever. Our family helped found this town. My parents were members of the Hume City Council. The Birch name and Hume were practically synonymous.

It also didn't sit right with me them selling our family home. Almost every good memory I owned was connected to this house. Cyrus and Ozzie would have sleepovers as kids and sometimes they'd actually let me hang out with them. I'd listen to them talk and try emulating their style and swagger. We'd play hide and seek all over this property and when my mom wanted us to come home, she'd ring a huge bell that hung from the porch roof. She called it the kid wrangler because no matter where you were, you could hear echoes of the bell.

"I imagine it's been nice to take a break from work. You and Darla seem to be all over TV performing and collecting awards," my father said.

"Yes, it was unplanned, but it's been nice to slow down for a bit."

"Oh no. I hope everything is good with Whiskey Wild." Dial feigned concern.

"Uhm. Just going through a bit of a transition and I'm working with my lawyers about the future of the group."

"Are you two having trouble?" My mother's question was a mixture of genuine worry and her nosy nature.

"Just a difference of opinion. But nothing our lawyers can't work through."

"I remember you and Darla performing at all those fairs. I knew then you were going to be a star. Your mom can attest, I told her years ago you were special."

"Thank you for believing in me."

My dad added his thoughts, "It's hard work. And not everyone is willing to put in the time and energy. Whiskey Wild worked hard, and you've created a career for yourself and that's something to be proud of."

"I appreciate that."

My mother loved it when we brought our partners over. It gave her a chance to put on her detective hat and ask probing questions. "I heard you're going on tour."

"Yes, ma'am we are."

"How exciting," Dial chimed in.

My mother took a sip of her spiked iced tea. "Maybe we'll grab tickets to the Nashville show."

"I'm not taking your money. I'll get you some tickets. Just let me know how many you need."

"I like this. Edison, good job dating a superstar. Free tickets are a perk I could get used to," my father joked.

"So, are you two official?" My mother asked the question she'd been holding all evening.

"Umm …" I didn't want to put twenty on ten if Fancy wasn't in agreement.

"We haven't exactly figured it out, but I think we want to be together." She squeezed my hand. "I mean that's what you want right?"

Was she dense? "That's all I've ever wanted." When I stared into her mink eyes, the world blurred. It was just me and Fancy. Making goo goo eyes at a woman in front of my parents was uncharacteristic of me. I tended to play it cool no matter how infatuated I was. But with Fancy, being aloof wasn't an option. She made me giggle. Can you imagine that? A grown six-foot two Black man giggling like a child. With her, there was so much to be happy about, it left me reeling.

Dial cleared her throat, and the fog lifted. "And how exactly does that work when you're two thousand miles apart?

"Dial," my mother chided.

My sister turned to Maple and said, "Honey can you go and set up the ice cream bar? You know how we like it."

"All by myself?"

"Yep, you're a big girl and I think you're ready to be in charge of the ice cream station. You are now the Creamery Captain."

Maple was beaming as she pulled back from the table.

"Don't forget the sprinkles and napkins." We all watched Maple make her way into the house.

"I thought this was an open discussion. I'm just trying to comprehend the logistics." Dial propped her chin on her folded hands. "Didn't you just break up with your boyfriend two minutes ago and now you expect us to believe you love Edison?"

"Dial per usual, you're out of line," I said.

"For asking questions?"

"For being rude."

"I have to agree with Eddy. Francesca is our guest. This is a pleasant family dinner. No room for drama," my mother said.

"Momma, let's not pretend you don't have the same questions. Francesca will be going home soon, so where does that leave Edison and this *relationship?*"

"This really isn't the time or the place." I rolled my eyes.

"Maybe you're content to live in La La Land but someone needs to ask the grown-up questions."

"I don't really care what you believe. I don't owe you anything, Dial." Fancy wasn't a shrinking violet, and she wasn't going to be intimidated by my sister.

"That's my brother you're playing house with. So, I'm allowed to have an opinion."

"No one is asking for your opinion. Feel however you want to feel but keep the commentary to yourself," I huffed.

"Sounds like you don't want me asking questions because you're afraid of the answers."

My father banged his hand on the table. "Enough." His booming voice forced you to straighten your back. The gruff tone ended the conversation and was mom's cue to ask Fancy to help her with the dessert.

With Fancy and my mother inside the house, I turned to Dial. "Are you out of your freaking mind?" I didn't curse in front of my parents, and I never would.

"You two need to work your differences out." Our father stood. "No dessert until you do." He went into the house, leaving me and Dial at the porch dining table alone. We looked everywhere but at one another. The sun was starting to set and the heat of the day had burned off. I nursed my lemonade, not wanting to speak first but if

I waited for my sister, the sun would rise and set again before she uttered a word.

"What are we eight? No dessert for you," I mumbled.

"You're acting like a child."

"And you're being an idiot. I need for you to give this a rest. Fancy never led me anywhere I didn't willingly want to go."

Dial's arms were pinned across her chest. "When it comes to Francesca you make bad choices and then I have to be a one-woman clean-up crew."

"I turned to you for support one time. But you can't keep throwing one of the lowest points of my life in my face. I was nineteen Dial, I barely knew what love was. I just lost my best friend and the woman I thought was going to be my wife. So yeah, I cried and didn't shower for a week."

"For months you just went to work and home. I hardly recognized you. It was like Fancy took your joy with her to LA."

Dial was the type who liked to pretend nothing fazed her. When she and Oz ended things, there weren't any tears. I could tell she was hurting only because she was my sister. She was always so strong even when I reassured her she didn't have to be.

"I love you because even at my worst, you always showed up for me. This thing with Fancy is real and I need you to be okay with it."

"And what about LA? I'm not trying to find flaws; I just want you to use your head."

"Fancy and I have agreed to devise a plan that works for the both of us."

"So, what is it?"

"I don't know yet," I chuckled. "But I need you to trust that I've got this handled." I scooted my chair closer. "How can you stay mad at this face?" Sticking out my bottom lip, I flashed my puppy dog eyes. "It's me Eddy, your favorite baby brother."

For the first time tonight, her shoulders appeared to relax. "I'm an asshole because I care. You are the gentlest soul I've ever known, and you deserve all the good things. And you need to be loved by someone who makes you their number one priority because that's how much you love them. I'm not saying Fancy doesn't care because it's clear she does. My only question was can she love you in the way you need and deserve. I only pry because I love you."

"And I love you for it." Wrapping my arms around her, I pulled her close.

Dial didn't hug me back because that wasn't her way, but she did pat my arm. "Eww, Eddy, enough." I released her. "Can you believe dad threatened us with no dessert?"

"I'm surprised he didn't make us run laps or do pushups."

"Knees to chest. All the way down. You call that a pushup?" We shared a laugh.

Back in the house we were rewarded with a strawberry tart and ice cream. After several bites, Dial turned to Fancy and said, "Sorry for the static." For Dial that was a pretty good apology.

"Thank you." Fancy squeezed my knee before stuffing a huge strawberry into her mouth.

I showed up to our meeting with a laptop, notepad, sticky notes, and a tall glass of iced tea like we were negotiating a peace agreement. Fancy and I decided to sit down and have a comprehensive dialogue about our relationship. Was it romantic? No. Was it what I needed to be comfortable? Yes.

"Should we have hired a stenographer?" Fancy teased.

"I just like to be prepared." Setting my things on the antique dining table, I took a seat.

Fancy had already made herself comfortable with a red wine and Coke. I loved the way she looked at home in my space. She wore a tank top sans bra, which was her signature style, and her shorts were part of the gym uniform for Hume High School. I wasn't sure if they were the same pair from high school or a new one.

Fancy reached for her glass and took a long, thoughtful sip before folding her legs underneath herself. "So where should we start?"

"How about you tell me what your lawyer said." While I was at Figs and Twine Fancy was in conversations with her lawyers, agent, and personal assistant. Walking away from a multimillion-dollar country group was just as complicated as you'd imagine.

"What didn't she say? The only property Chap and I share is the condo. We contributed equally and so the sale of the unit would be divided fifty fifty. There is a chance he might want to purchase the place from me."

"How would that work?"

"We'd have the condo appraised, agree on a price, and he'd pay half of that."

"Have you considered buying it from him?"

"No, I don't want to give him any more of my money. Plus, I never really liked that place. Don't get me wrong, it's beautiful but it was never really my speed. I'm looking for a clean break. Fresh new start."

I scribed quick notes on my notepad. "Will he still be your manager?"

"No, he's been served with an intent to cancel letter ending his role as my manager. There is a hefty early termination fee, but I'm willing to pay it to be done with him. Luckily Darla and I signed our management agreements separately. If we hadn't, this could have ended up in a nasty legal battle."

"Do you really think she's going to keep him as her manager? At this point, she must be regretting choosing his side. And going forward, it's going to be difficult for you two to co-exist. Maybe the next album will just focus on betrayal and you both cussing one another out every other song."

"That's the thing …" Fancy raised her eyebrows. "After the tour, I don't ever want to lay eyes on her again."

"So, you don't think with time and a proper apology maybe you can move past it?"

"Not you offering Darla a Hail Mary."

"I just know what she means to you. Sometimes the people we love hurt us. But that doesn't mean we stop loving them."

Fancy pushed her curls from her eyes. "I'm going to love her from afar. I don't wish her any ill will."

The expression on my face made it clear that lies were detected.

"Okay I wish her a little ill will. I hope she steps on a Lego and her bra strap is constantly falling off her shoulder. I hope her edges never slick down, and her hair never curls over. Just limp, lifeless strands. And maybe just maybe if we live in a merciful world, she'll get scammed by a fake prince who steals all her money."

"So, you've given this some thought."

"Just a little."

"What does that mean for Whiskey Wild?"

"We're contractually obligated to produce one more album. But my agent thinks if we present another option they might bite."

My blank expression made it clear I wasn't following.

"A solo project … for me. My lawyer hinted I may be able to retain the group name. But I don't want to record under that moniker. Whiskey Wild was for Darla and me. If I go solo, I'll have to call myself something else."

"Fancy Palmer Solo Dolo."

"Single like a dollar bill." She dropped her eyes to the table, her shoulders slowly slumping. "Do you think it's a bad idea?"

"I already told you Whiskey Wild was more you than Darla. You don't need her, you never have."

"Yeah, but when you're a solo act, there's no one to share the blame when shit goes sideways."

"It's not going sideways, it's only going up from here."

"Maybe." She hopped a shoulder. "It would be exciting, sort of starting over."

"It'll make the success story all the more sweeter. You'll be like Lionel Richie, Diana Ross, Beyonce."

"No one is like Beyonce."

"I prefer Kelly Rowland myself. That woman could do ungodly things to me. I'm talking spanking, I would get on my knees and just—"

"Note to self, never allow you in the same room as Kelendria Rowland."

"Probably a good idea."

Fancy tossed a highlighter at me. "Seriously though, I have to finish the tour. I tried to get out of it, but my lawyer said I signed a contract and could be held liable if we miss any dates."

"How long?"

"Three months give or take." She worried her bottom lip. "More give than take."

Three months was a long time. In that time one or both of us could get cold feet. You know that saying, "Out of sight, out of mind," what if my absence made her heart grow frostier? "What happens after that?"

"I guess that's really up to you. I'm not looking to insert myself into your life if that's not what you want. I know you have a routine here and my presence can be disruptive. And shit maybe this is all moving too fast—"

"Take a breath."

"It's just so much change all at once. And I feel like I'm dragging all this baggage behind me. And it's not fair to expect you to deal with that."

"It's true I'm not a fan of change. But for you, I make exceptions."

"But that's the thing. You shouldn't have to settle. You deserve everything. The horse, the carriage, and the princess."

"In what world do you think being with you is me settling? I don't know how to break this to you … but I love you. I loved you before fans were screaming your name and begging for autographs. Fancy you have always been my endgame. These past few weeks have been some of the best of my life because I was able to love you. So, give me your baggage and I'll add it to my mommy issues and baby of the family syndrome."

"You're crazy for loving me, you know that?"

"Loving you is like breathing to me. It's just something I do."

Fancy wrapped her hand in mine, resting them on her lap. "After the tour I'll need to work on making an album, alone or with someone else, and that takes time. I could come back and we could spend the next few months or year together. The hustle has been unrelenting the past few years. Constant touring, interviews, photo shoots. The Whiskey Wild machine kind of took on a life of its own. I've gained all this success, and I haven't really had a moment to catch my breath and take stock of it all."

I raised my eyebrows.

"I think it would be nice to slow down. I'm not saying I'm gonna stop making music. I love writing and performing. I am saying that I'm ready to find a balance. And hopefully all the money I earned for the record label will allow me some input into the direction of my career."

"I don't want you giving up anything for me. I know how passionate you are about your music, and I don't want to hinder that in any way. I've been thinking too and maybe I move to Los Angeles for a bit, gives you time to renegotiate contracts or whatever it is the princess of country music has to do." Maybe Fancy was right. I had to be unwell to suggest moving.

"You would hate LA."

"Not if I was with you?"

"What about the farm?"

"I could hire someone to look after it while I was away?"

"What about Figs and Twine?"

"Dial can manage. Cyrus could pitch in. I could consult via video chats."

"Edison, I love you for suggesting that. But this isn't just about me. It's about us. You wouldn't be happy in LA. You're a family man and you're uncomplicated. And that's what I love the most about you. The joy you find in the simple things. I want that, I want that with you.

"I don't want the traffic or smog. I'm not interested in pretentious restaurants with tiny serving sizes. The last thing I want to do is attend another party where people are trying to figure out what I can do for them rather than looking for real connections. I prefer late night runs to the Gas Guzzle. And Friday nights at The Tipsy Owl. Lazy Saturdays in bed while we make love to the sound of rain on your tin roof. I've thought about this long and hard. And I've never been happier than I have these past few days. I truly believe it's all because of you and this town."

"So, you want to live in Hume … with me?"

"Yes, but if cohabitation isn't your thing, I could stay with my parents or find a small place."

I looked down at my notepad and reviewed the words written across it. Three-month tour. End of group. Music is important. Living together. Hume is home.

"Say something," she begged.

"I just feel kind of silly. I thought this conversation would be me trying to convince you to acknowledge Hume as a viable option. But here you are willing to make Hume your home."

"I want to be where you are. And I can write and record music from anywhere. Believe it or not I'm actually excited about the idea of letting grass grow around my feet. I could help you with the renovations. You can help me with melodies when I'm stuck. When I have to tour, maybe sometimes you could come with me. And when you can't, I'll be counting down the days until we're back together."

"I like that."

"Good. And you didn't even need your sticky notes." She stood and kissed me on the top of the head. "Oh I forgot, all my shit from LA should be arriving in the next day or two. I asked Moniece to pack up my belongings and ship them here. I hope that's okay?"

"I'll make space in the closet for you."

She caressed my chin. "Fair warning, I have a lot of clothes … and shoes."

"We'll make room."

"Ooo, we're gonna be shacking up." We both frowned at her wording. "Sorry Oz said that the other day and it just kind of wormed its way in my head."

And just like that Fancy grabbed her glass of wine and Coke and walked off toward the barn to visit with Cotton Candy. I couldn't contain myself and let out a loud yelp that was a mixture of relief and excitement. Yeti, who was resting on the floor in the sun, jumped and tossed me an irritated eye.

I was more than ready to start this next chapter with Fancy by my side. What was three months when we had forever together.

22

Fancy

MY LAST DAY IN HUME was filled with family. The hostess with the mostest, my mom, planned a big cookout and invited damn near everyone in town. It was reminiscent of when Darla and I first left Hume. With people wishing us well and telling us they'd be praying for us. At that point, I'd been in Hume for nineteen years and never felt more loved than when I was about to leave.

It was at that first farewell party where my mother pulled me aside and let me know I could always come back home. She said, "Fancy if it's not what you expected, if the dice aren't rolling in your favor, shit if you just need a hug, you can always come home. There's no shame in starting over or taking a break to catch your breath. Home will always be here waiting for you." Those words stayed with me and there were plenty of times over the past ten years I wanted to throw in the towel and come running back.

Chap cheating was the tipping point. I'd been unhappy for a while, silently pushing through thinking once the tour was over or the album recorded things would get better between him and I. But I didn't realize just how bad things were. Coming home was the best decision I could have made. Because in this month back I realized my happiness was more important than fitting in or being considered cool.

After a summer afternoon of good food, good conversation, and good friends, Edison pulled me aside and asked if he could take me somewhere else before heading home. My response without hesitation was yes. I would go anywhere with this man, do anything for him, and allow him to dick me down anytime and anyplace.

After saying our goodbyes, we headed west. Just the radio and his hand in mine. Edison offered no hints as to where we were going, but the further we drove, the more confused I became. There was nothing out here, except a few farms and a dairy factory. We turned left onto a dirt road as he hummed along to a Kane Brown song.

Edison parked his truck on a hill overlooking the town of Hume. "I thought we could share one last sunset together," he said.

"Not our last. I don't think I've ever been up here." We exited the truck, Edison lowered the tailgate and we took a seat, which provided the perfect view of the town below.

"Yeah, I love this spot. It's kind of outta the way and not many people make the trip. I mostly come here to think, this place is good for that."

"It's like a whole other perspective on home. Knowing everyone is down there living their lives while we look on from afar."

"Yep."

"Today was nice."

"It was."

"Tomorrow—"

Edison shook his head. "No not yet … I'm still appreciating what today has to offer."

Crossing my legs, I turned to face him. "Did you see our mothers in their little mom huddle conspiring?"

"They were probably planning our wedding."

"I think if we hadn't finally figured it out, they would've floated the idea of an arranged marriage."

Edison smiled through a chuckle. He had the most amazing smile. I could sit and stare at this man for hours. "Shit, maybe." His smile slowly faded and the muscles in his jaw protruded. He was mulling something over.

"This is the part where they say speak now or forever hold your peace."

"About what?"

"Concerns, second thoughts, doubts."

His eyes rested on my features. "You have doubts?"

My chest was heavy, and my heart felt lodged between my ribs. We had a plan. It was a good plan. But three months was a long time. Maybe once we were apart, this haze of cozy adoration would pass. Everything in my life was moving fast, including this. "Sometimes."

"Let me help alleviate them." He claimed my hand. "I am going to love you for the rest of your life and mine. Every day won't be perfect, but it will be better than any day without you. And our kids—"

"We're going to have kids?"

"Yes, if you want them."

"With you, yes. Tell me all about them."

"Our kids are going to be creative thinkers, free spirits, sometimes a little moody. And we're going to teach them to cultivate the land, sing happy songs, and appreciate sunsets. Don't ever doubt my love for you. Just come back." His thumb dusted my lips.

"I love you."

"I know it."

Whiskey Wild's song "Goodbye, Sweet Sunrise" played on the radio. And I laughed to tamp down the tears threatening to fall. The song was about leaving your hometown, saying goodbye to all you knew and the one person that was hardest to leave behind. I sang softly the words I'd written years ago, just as relevant today as any other.

> *Goodbye, sweet sunrise,*
> *Goodbye, your brown eyes.*
> *This small-town heart's gotta chase the sky.*
> *I'll carry you in every mile,*
> *Your memory in every smile.*
> *Goodbye, sweet sunrise, but not goodbye to you.*

Hume sunsets were like stepping into a painting. The sky a masterpiece of colors, with streaks of amber and gold melting into fiery oranges and soft pinks. As the sun dipped lower, its warm glow bathed the rolling hills and fields, casting long shadows that stretched lazily across the grass. Silhouettes of oak and cedar trees stood tall against the glowing horizon. Their leaves rustling in the faint evening breeze.

The air was sweet, a mix of honeysuckle and grass, with a hum of cicadas creating a soothing, rhythmic backdrop. Overhead, swallows darted and dove, their movements graceful against the deepening hues. As the sky transitioned to lavender and indigo, the first stars began to twinkle, and the faint glow of fireflies dotted the edges of the field, like nature's own string lights flickering to life.

It was the type of sunset that made you linger. We leaned into one another, savoring the beauty of this moment, one of our last. Leaving Hume had never been harder than it was tonight. I'd toured in over one hundred countries, sold out stadiums, screaming fans. I left Hume in search of something, only to return years later to find my whole world right here in my hometown. The sunset was a warm reminder of home, peace, and the quiet magic of Hume summers.

Exhaling a deep breath, I said, "I think I need to start writing some new songs for these new memories."

Back at home I walked around aimlessly, silently saying goodbye to all the things I'd miss. Goodbye rooster kitchen. Goodbye house of curiosities. While Edison was in the shower, Katt and I spent some quality time on the couch and the shy kitty tolerated my petting her. The house was silent apart from an unexpected rain that danced on the tin roof. My daddy was right, the sound was intoxicating.

Upstairs I passed Yeti who'd made a home in the corner of the hallway right outside Edison's bedroom. When I entered, he was already laying down in nothing but boxers. I jumped into bed, straddling myself over top of him.

"Please be easy. I ate way too many ribs," Edison half teased.

"No one was holding a gun to your head."

"You know I can't say no to your dad's ribs."

"County fair winner for best ribs seventeen consecutive years."

"And it's well deserved. Maybe a little rigged seeing how your mother is always one of the judges."

I gagged. "She's impartial."

"Is she?"

"Yes. The best ribs always win."

"And those ribs just happen to belong to your father?"

"Don't you start those nasty rumors." I playfully needled him in his chest.

"You're gonna miss the cook off next month."

"I am." The smile disappeared from my face. "I wish you were going with me."

"If I could, I would. But I can't leave Dial to run the nursery alone with no notice or preparation. Especially with my parents looking to move. We have a lot of knowledge transfer to cover in a short amount of time."

"I know. I totally understand. I'm just not prepared to miss you for months."

"I'm going to miss you too. I'm especially going to miss this ass." He grabbed a handful of my ass cheeks and gave a tight squeeze.

"Well seeing how it's our last night, we should make it one to remember." I needed the memory of him touching my skin seared in my brain for quick reference. Edison's dick hardened at my request. That thing had to be battery powered because with the slightest provocation, it would stand up and wobble like a patron at The Tipsy Owl.

The soft glow of the bedside lamp cast shadows over his face, that, mixed with the determined longing in his eyes for me, made him look even more devastatingly beautiful. I pressed my palm against his chest, the steady, reliable thump of his heart increased as I rocked over his dick. Outside the downpour thickened with each drop of rain a tiny percussion against the metal. An unpredictable melody would crest and fall, and our bodies worked in concert mimicking the rhythmic cadence of the storm, which blanketed everything beneath it into a peaceful, dreamlike state.

"I don't want to say goodbye," I whispered.

Edison caught my chin between his fingers, tilting my face up to his. His lips brushed mine, soft at first, then deeper, as if trying to fuse us together and make this moment stretch on forever. His hand slid down my back, pulling me closer until there was no space left between us. The warmth of his body seeping into my skin. I allowed myself to drown into him as his dick drowned in my pussy. Our strokes were paced out and slow in an effort to savor the pleasure and extend our time as far as it would go before reality pulled us apart. Every kiss, every touch, felt like a plea. His mouth traced a path down my neck and shoulder, sending shivers racing through me.

Our kisses were fierce and unrelenting, as if we were trying to defeat the time we would spend apart. The faint taste of his soapy skin lingered on my tongue blending with the warmth of his breath, his kisses were addictive. Edison's hands gripped my hips, his fingers pressing into my flesh, while my nails dragged lightly against the back of his neck. The sound of our breathing was ragged, echoing against the bedroom walls, punctured by the soft, wet sound of our bodies moving together in perfect, desperate harmony.

When we finally collapsed together, breathless and tangled, I pressed my forehead to his and closed my eyes. "How am I supposed to sleep without you?" I murmured, my fingers idly tracing patterns over his skin.

He took a long, thoughtful breath before sighing it out, his grasp tightening like he didn't want to let me go. "I'll meet you in your dreams." His lips ghosted over mine in a final lingering kiss. And I knew he was right. I'd dream of this, of him, until we were back in each other's arms.

23

Fancy

WHEN I RETURNED TO LA I only had days before we were set to hit the road with a prep list a mile long. There were fittings, photos shoots, and rehearsals. Meetings with my lawyer, agent, and new manager, Rochelle Givens. Rochelle was highly recommended, and I felt confident she'd be able to take my career sans Whiskey Wild to the next level. Moniece was a godsend; she was able to locate a realtor to begin the process of listing the condo. At the end of this tour, I wanted to be done with LA and this chaotic chapter of my life.

On top of all that, before the first show, our respective managers recommended a sit-down conversation with a professional therapist. Darla was still being managed by Chap; it made sense he would push for this. Neither of them believed I had the balls to truly walk away. I wanted to decline, but Rochelle was also pro therapy, suggesting hashing out our differences could help to make the touring experience less stressful.

In a home tucked away in Highland Park, we met with Dr. Alvin Sims, but he preferred to be called Dr. Al. I was only here because the label expressed concerns about our deteriorating relationship and the potential effect it could have on the brand. But I was a professional, I could hate your guts and still put on a show.

"So, what brings you two in today?" Dr. Al asked. Neither Darla nor I ventured to answer. We hadn't spoken to one another in weeks, and no one wanted to be the first to break the stalemate. "Okay, let me try this again. Francesca why are you here?"

"I'm here so I don't get fired, sued, or blackballed."

"Darla same question."

"Unlike Fancy, I genuinely want to work through our problems."

"She can say that because she wasn't the one who was betrayed."

"Grow up, Fancy."

"Shut up, Darla."

Dr. Al raised a hand signaling for silence. "So, there is clearly acrimony. What caused you two to end up in this place?"

"Do you want to tell him? Or are you going to continue to play the victim?"

"Fancy and her boyfriend broke up and now he and I are dating."

Dr. Al looked at me.

"What?"

"Do you have any thoughts on what Darla said?"

"Yeah, she's a liar. This is about cheating. She smiled in my face all the while plotting behind my back."

"Are you saying Darla cheated on you?"

"Pretty much, she crept around with my boyfriend at the time and never told me. I had to find out from someone else."

"It all happened really fast. We were going to tell you."

"It was months."

"You're just mad because Chap chose me."

"If that's what you really think maybe we were never truly friends. It's not about Chap, it's about you. Chap's a man, they're a dime a dozen. But you were supposed to be my best friend, ride or die, from the cradle to the casket."

"I still am. It's just complicated."

"No it's not, it's selfish. I would never have done that to you." I couldn't stand to look at her, instead focusing my attention on the massive chandelier overhead. The entire house, at least the parts I'd seen, were beautiful. I guess listening to people vent was big business. Everything in Los Angeles was more expensive, even mental health care. I'm sure I'd receive a hefty bill after this session. And for what, so I could sit next to Darla while she gaslit me.

"I just got tired of being in your shadow."

Her word brought me back to the present and lit me up like a match. "You were never in my shadow. You were right beside me. Every opportunity I garnered was also given to you. I'm tired of people feeling less than and blaming it on me. Because all I ever did was treat you like a sister."

Dr. Al scooched closer in his armchair. "This is good. Communication is good. Darla why do you think you gravitated toward Chap?"

I didn't give her a chance to respond. "Who cares? Who fucking cares Dr. Al. Because at this point, I just want to finish this tour and be done."

"You and Darla share a deep history. It would be nice to walk away with closure."

"That's the thing, I don't need closure. Actions speak louder than words. And Darla's actions told me everything I needed to know. I'm good off of her and I'm good off of Whiskey Wild."

"This tour is going to be difficult if we're at one another's throats," Darla shot back.

Fuck her comfort. She needed to be walking on eggshells anytime she approached me. "You're a good actress. Just fake it like you did with me all those months."

Dr. Al leaned closer. By the end of this meeting, he'd be sitting in my lap. "Fancy, are you saying you don't care about mending your relationship?"

"We just have to sing together. Work the crowd, play our songs, and sing."

I wasn't ready to forgive. Shit, Darla wasn't even remorseful. It was clear I was never a consideration. Darla made choices and now I was making mine. Some people would suggest I was being petty to break up Whiskey Wild over a man. But I can't stress enough that Darla was my best friend, and she hurt me to my core. I thought we'd be friends forever, but forever didn't last as long as I expected. I'm not saying never, but right now it was a hell no for me.

Twisting in her chair, for the first time this afternoon Darla's eyes met mine. "I don't want you to hate me, Fancy."

"Hate is a strong word. I just have an aversion to all things Darla. And the fact that you can't acknowledge you hurt me … hurts me. So, if it's all the same, let's just tell the label we're in a better place and looking forward to the start of the tour."

I wasn't interested in being the bigger person, letting water pass under the bridge. I was in my petty era. And Darla wouldn't get a smile, a head nod, or a handshake from me that wasn't performative. I was here for the fans, the money, and to say a final farewell to Whiskey Wild.

The US leg of the Girls Behaving Badly Tour kicked off on the East Coast in Boston. Everything was bigger than our last US tour two years ago. We had a solid catalog of songs and a dedicated fan base.

For the next three months Darla and I would be crossing the country to perform to sold-out crowds. I could still remember when we were the opening act. Playing in half empty arenas because people were only interested in the main event.

Despite the lack of a crowd, we would put on a show. Dancing and singing our hearts out. Soon the word got out that you didn't want to be late because if you did, you'd miss out on a great time. To come from that to fans chanting our name and singing along to all the words was hard to wrap my head around.

Unlike past tours, Darla and I were on separate buses and would look at anything but each other when we were in the same room. During the radio station visits and promo runs, we were all smiles, but once we were back in the SUV, we both pulled out our phones and pretended like the other didn't exist until the next stop. It was tense but when we hit the stage, it was like all the resentment was paused and we just rocked out.

Of course, all I could think about was Edison. It was difficult leaving him and being away for over three months sounded like torture. It's funny how a month ago Edison was a memory I chose not to linger on because of all the regret. And now I was staying up late talking to him on the phone and exchanging text messages. Any time my cell dinged or vibrated, I hoped it was him.

Day 5 of the Girls Behaving Badly tour

Edison

What city are you in?

Fancy

New Jersey.

Edison

How are things going with Darla?

Fancy

At this point we're not talking to each other. We ride on separate buses. She's in a bus with Chap. They're dating now.

Edison

Ouch.

Fancy

Not gonna lie it's kind of surreal. But they seem happy together.

Edison

Darla likes to pretend she's winning.

Fancy

I miss you. I didn't realize how hard it would be being away from you.

Edison

It makes sense, I mean I'm pretty amazing.

Day 12 of the Girls Behaving Badly tour

Edison

I have a beautiful blond in my bed right now.

Fancy

Do not play with me, Edison. I will hop on the next plane and scratch somebody's eyes out.

Edison

Well, Katt's claws are considerably sharper than yours and lately she doesn't play when it comes to me.

Fancy

I thought she was an outside cat.

Edison

It's been raining the last couple of days. I think she's looking for cover from the storm. But it's nice to have company. Yeti is also here and wants you to know I'm his favorite now.

Day 19 of the Girls Behaving Badly tour

Edison

Francesca?

Fancy

Whoa, are you mad at me?

Edison

Why would you ask that?

Fancy

Because you just called me by my government name. And that's rare.

Edison

My bad, I didn't notice. Not mad. Lonely, horny, and unmoisturized? Yes. But not mad.

Fancy

Why are you ashy?

Edison

Because when you left you took the fancy smell good lotion with you, and I've become accustomed to the finer things but I can't remember the name of the brand.

Fancy

I'll order you a jar, ASAP. I need you to stay pretty for me.

Edison

Thanks, if you could also slip a pair of your worn panties in the box I'd appreciate it.

Fancy

Eww ... but maybe.

Day 27 of the Girls Behaving Badly tour

Fancy

Look up at the sky. Is the moon as big in Tennessee as it is in North Dakota?

Edison

It practically takes up the entire sky.

Fancy

I like the thought that we're looking at the same moon even though we're miles apart. It gives me a sense of comfort. Is that weird?

Edison

I don't think it's weird. I like the thought of the moon as our compass. Anytime you look up at the sky you think of me and know that I'm doing the same.

Day 32 of the Girls Behaving Badly tour

Edison

That video you sent me was ...

Fancy

I wanted to remind you of what you're missing.

Edison

Not gonna lie I've probably jacked off to it more than I'm willing to admit.

Fancy

That was the plan. Every time you touch yourself, I want you to pretend it's me.

Edison

You keep sending images like that and I can guarantee you I will.

Fancy

Feel free to return the favor at any time.

Edison

You want me to make a single player porno?

Fancy

Ugh please don't call it porno, I hate that word.

Edison

What would you have me call it? Skin flick, X rated adult entertainment, a single subscriber Only Fans account. I mean if my dick's involved it's gonna be triple X rated.

Fancy

Video chat, now?

Edison

Yes.

Day 38 of the Girls Behaving Badly tour

Fancy

I don't know if I can continue to fake the funk like this.

Edison

What's wrong?

Fancy

I'm just tired and overwhelmed.

Edison

That's understandable, you're working really hard.

Fancy

Everyone thinks I'm making a mistake breaking up the group. And the label is offering up lots of money for another joint album.

Edison

…

Fancy

Do you think I'm making a mistake?

Edison

I don't think I'm the best person to ask. This decision has to be yours, but I'll support you no matter what.

Fancy

I'm scared.

Edison

Of what?

Fancy

Of fucking everything up.

Day 40 of the Girls Behaving Badly tour

Edison

Guess who just sold the rooster stools.

Fancy

No, I love those stools.

Edison

They were hideous.

Fancy

They were camp and fun.

Edison

So, you don't want me to sell the rooster stools?

Fancy

How much did you get for them?

Edison

Just under three thousand.

Fancy

For those ugly ass stools.

Edison

I thought they were fun and camp?

Fancy

That was before I knew some idiot was willing to spend close to three grand for them.

Day 45 of the Girls Behaving Badly tour

Fancy

What's the first thing you want to do when I get home?

Edison

Seriously?

Fancy

Yeah.

Edison

When you get here, I'm taking some days off. The fridge will be stocked, and the sheets will be fresh. And you will not be allowed to leave the house. Clothes will be forbidden. And our lips will be raw from all the kissing.

Fancy

So, you're going to make me your sex doll for a week?

Edison

Well, we have a lot of time to make up for.

Fancy

We sure do. I guess spending the day wrapped up in your arms will suffice.

Edison

Oh, I almost forgot. The shed was delivered today.

Fancy

Shed?

Edison

Yep, I got you a shed for your music. It looks basic right now but when me and Oz are through it'll be a temperature controlled cozy space to create. Right now, we're working on the electrical and plumbing. I'm gonna hold off on making any design decisions because I want you to have a say in the decor.

Fancy

Edison, you didn't have to go to all that trouble. I could have found a spot in the house.

Edison

No, you deserve a space all your own. I have the garage, and you'll have your she shed.

Fancy

She shed?

Edison

That's what they call it. Google it. There's a ton of inspiration. I've pinned a few interiors I think you might like. I'll text them to you.

Fancy

Sounds like you're really loving the Wi-Fi.

Edison

It comes in handy.

Fancy

Thank you. You didn't have to do that, but I appreciate it.

Edison

Baby, my home is your home, and I want you to love being there.

Fancy

No more purchases until I get back. Since when did you and Oz start hanging out again?

Edison

We're not hanging out. He's good with electrical wiring.

Fancy

Don't let Dial find out.

Edison

Rolling my eyes emoji.

Fancy

You know you could just use the actual emoji.

Day 51 of the Girls Behaving Badly tour

Edison

Are you still up?

Fancy

Unfortunately, yes, still on an adrenaline high from the show tonight.

Edison

Fans posted clips of the show. You and Darla look great up there.

Fancy

It's funny, we've spoken less than five words to each other but when we get on stage we lock in and it's like my best friend is back. Kind of a mind fuck.

Edison

Maybe there's still something there.

Fancy

If there is I'd have to sweep away a mountain of rubble to get to it.

Day 60 of the Girls Behaving Badly tour

Edison

This day just took a turn.

Fancy

What's wrong.

Edison

My parents put the house up for sale.

Fancy

Eddy, I know you were hoping
they'd change their minds.

Edison

I thought we had more time. It's not even
December. How could they just sell my
childhood home. I don't want strangers
roaming around in it.

Fancy

We could make an offer on it. And just
figure out the details later.

Edison

No. I'm not a do it for the plot type of guy.

Fancy

All in is it under a million?

Edison

Yeah.

Fancy

Let's buy a fucking house.

Edison

Fancy, whoa.

Fancy

I'm serious.

Edison

I know you are and that's what scares me.

Fancy

It could be an extra place for Maple or our future kids. Maybe Dial or Cyrus want to get in on this. It's a great investment.

Edison

You want to purchase and upkeep a home for the swimmers in my nut sack?

Fancy

Not just any home. Your home.

Edison

Decisions like this aren't made via text message.

Fancy

Then call me and I'll tell you the same damn thing.

Day 66 of the Girls Behaving Badly tour

Fancy

Whatcha doing?

Edison

Dial is over here making brisket and getting on my last nerve.

Fancy

Tell her I said hello.

Edison

...

Fancy

Did she say hi back?

Edison

Something like that.

Fancy

When I get back, I'm going to make it my mission to become her best friend.

Edison

Good luck with that.

Fancy

I'm talking about friendship bracelets, late night chats, and braiding one another's hair.

Edison

This is Dial. I don't like being touched.

Fancy

Okay we'll work on that because I'm a hugger.

Day 75 of the Girls Behaving Badly tour

Edison

When do we get to start the countdown.

Fancy

Countdown for what?

Edison

Counting down the days until you're
back in my arms.

Fancy

Wait let me pull up my calendar. I
count fifteen days.

Edison

Damn fifteen days? I need the number
to be in the single digits.

Fancy

You need to enjoy your last few weeks alone
because when I get back, I'm not letting you
out of my sight. You are going to be sick of me
after the first few days.

Edison

Not possible.

Day 86 of the Girls Behaving Badly tour

Fancy

Four days and a wake up.

Edison

I think I should warn you before you return. That I've dyed all my hair platinum blond.

Fancy

Whoa.

Edison

Yep. It was late one night, and I had one too many beers and dyed my hair, brows, and balls blond.

Fancy

Very funny.

Edison

It was funny at the time but now not so much.

Fancy

You're joking right?

Edison

You'll just have to wait and see. I tell you what when I go to The Tipsy Owl I no longer have to pay for my beers. Blonds do have more fun.

Day 88 of the Girls Behaving Badly tour

Edison

I miss you so much it hurts.

Fancy

We're so close. I feel like my entire body is tingling in anticipation.

Edison

Hmm ... you might want to get that checked out.

Fancy

Make sure you tell my mother no parties. I don't want a big fuss. I just want it to be me and you.

Edison

I can assure you there are no parties scheduled on your first day back. I can't attest to anything that may be planned after that.

Fancy

Ugh, that woman will find any reason to invite people over.

Edison

I'm nervous.

Fancy

Why?

Edison

I just feel like you're giving up a lot for me. And I don't want you to wake up one day and resent me for decisions you made so we could be together.

Fancy

I'm not stupid. I've thought about this long and hard. And I've waffled, but not because of you. I want everything you have to offer Edison Birch.

Edison

I love the fuck outta you, Francesca.

Our last performance was in Seattle, Washington. From my dressing room, I could already feel the kinetic energy from the crowd. Whiskey Wild's very first performance was at the Hume Sweet Summer Jubilee. Back then our stage name was Wildflowers because we were ten. It was chilly and I'd eaten an entire candy apple and was afraid I was going to barf. When we got on stage, and I strummed the starting notes on my guitar, a sense of calm fell over me. Granted, the crowd consisted of about fifty people, and we were currently selling out arenas and performing in front of thousands. But everyone has to start somewhere. And that small crowd in Hume with Edison standing in the very front cheering us on was how I got mine.

After our ten-minute set, I was hooked. You couldn't tell me Darla and I weren't going to be stars. I also believed we'd be friends forever. But Darla chose Chap's side, and I had to learn to let shit go. My lifelong friendship, the group I loved, and the fans we cultivated through an affection for folksy country music. I didn't think I'd be starting over at twenty-nine, but you know the saying when your plans fail, change the plan, not the goal.

Making my way to the side stage, I stood next to Darla. She looked beautiful in a long, sheer, fringed cover-up and bedazzled jeans. I wore ripped up sparkly jean shorts to show off my legs and a halter top. We were color coordinated but not matchy matchy. If you followed the group, you know we had our distinct styles. Darla was more refined. While I was the chick who kicked off her boots and danced around the stage barefoot.

"Can't believe this is our last show," Darla said.

"Neither can I." Staring straight ahead, I refused to look at her for fear I'd burst into tears. Yes, ending us was my decision, but I was still sad about it.

"I thought we'd be old and gray, with our tits sagging still cranking out hits."

"So did I. And I would've loved that for us."

Darla turned to face me and reached for my hand, giving it a soft squeeze. "I'm sorry Fancy, I really am."

"I know you are. And I still consider you my sister. I just need time and space."

"Moniece said you're going back to Hume after this."

"I am."

"So, you and Edison huh?"

My face cracked into a deep smile. "Yep, me and Edison."

Across the jumbo screens a montage of Darla and I through the years played. Whoops and hollers echoed through the crowd. The video highlighted the progression of our career with home video clips and of shows and backyard concerts. A picture of Darla and I at the age of four hugging each other tight was the last image. No doubt this was Chap's doing. This video hadn't played at our other shows; it was most likely his last ditch effort to change my mind about the group.

The three-minute retrospective of our lives left me misty eyed. We could've had it all, but a fucking man got in the way. If Darla had ditched Chap, I could've moved past it, eventually. I'm not saying it would've been easy but for Darla it would've been worth it. At the end of the day, I was devastated. Darla managed to do what no man ever could, break my fucking heart.

When we walked to the center stage, the crowd was pumped and from the first beat of the drums, it was like a whirlwind. Darla and I were in a zone feeding off the crowd and one another. One thing Whiskey Wild was good at was raising hell. I would miss this. I'd miss us. The news about our split had been kept top secret, with the label planning to release a statement at the conclusion of the tour.

Listening to Darla sing her verse, I was still in awe of her effortless voice. Good musical chemistry like ours was hard to find. Darla and I just fit. So, the fact she was willing to jeopardize that for a man who would end up as a footnote in her life was tough to accept. The lights were bright, the crowd was loud, and the harmonies were flowing. Hopefully lightning would strike twice, and I'd be able to gain this level of fame as a solo artist. But if this was it, then it was a hella of a way to say farewell.

During our last song, we danced with the crowd, performing a two-step across center stage while both hitting licks on the guitar. She and I bounced and gyrated like we were having the time of our lives. And maybe we were. I was always happiest when I was on a stage. The band ceased to play so Darla and I could finish the chorus together a cappella.

> *We're the good time girls, wild and free,*
> *Sun-kissed smiles and Tennessee breeze.*
> *Dancing on the bar like we own this town,*
> *Two-step spinning till the sun goes down.*
> *We ain't looking for forever, just a midnight whirl,*
> *Oh, we're the good time girls.*

When the last note fell silent, the crowd continued to roar. And as always, their love and appreciation was like a power bank filling my happiness meter. Darla and I took several bows while throwing kisses and waving at the crowd.

"You ain't gotta go home. But you do need to get the hell up outta here," I teased the crowd.

"Thanks for partying with us," Darla called out.

"We're Whiskey Wild and it's been a pleasure," I said, tossing my arm around Darla and walking off the stage.

The crowd cheered for an encore, not wanting it to end. There really was no other feeling like it, creating art and connecting with people who got it and saw you. I was grateful for the journey, even if the final destination was unfamiliar territory. Whiskey Wild was built from the ground up, and I could do it again. If that meant I had to start from scratch, I was willing to hit the fair and festival circuit to continue sharing my music with others.

Darla pointed to the stage with lights still flashing and our band riffing just in case we decided to play one last song. "Are you really willing to walk away from all this?"

It was a question I'd wrestled with for most of the tour. Being an adult was hard, especially when so much was riding on you getting it right. I didn't want to let anyone down, but I needed to stand on business.

"Yeah, I am." I removed my earpiece, secured my guitar to my shoulder and walked away. Moniece was right behind me, talking about flight arrangements for the next morning. This Whiskey Wild era had been amazing, but now it was time to conjure up new dreams and slay fiercer dragons.

24
Edison

CYRUS WAS THE LAST ONE to pull up to our parents' house even though he'd requested Dial and I meet him there. As mayor you'd think punctuality would be a mandatory job requirement. But Cyrus was only on time for things that were really valuable to him, and he knew Dial and I would grant him a fifteen-minute grace period. Our parents were in Gainsborough looking at properties. Which, along with the for-sale sign at the entrance road, made their move all the more real.

"Why are we here?" Dial didn't even wait for Cyrus to fully exit his car.

"Goddamn, does no one know how to say hello?" he asked.

"Hello, how are you? How's the family?" I joked.

"Why are we here? Edison and I left Figs and Twine early to meet you."

"Stop acting like you and Eddy are a two-man crew. You have staff who are more than capable of handling things while you're out."

"I believe the inclusive phrasing would be two-person crew. You should know that Mr. Mayor," Dial chided.

Cyrus ignored her, a determined look on his face. "I have a proposal."

Dial checked her phone, her interest already waning. "Shoot."

"I think we should buy the farm."

My antenna immediately started to rise. I wanted to save the farm too. But Cy wasn't sentimental, so his suggestion took me by surprise.

"No." Dial turned to head back to her car.

"I'm serious."

"You want to buy Mom and Dad's place?" I said. Fancy suggested I do something similar but at the time it seemed far-fetched. I opted not to broach the subject because I didn't want Cyrus and Dial teaming up to make fun of me for being mushy and idealistic.

"I've done my research. It's a great investment. We could rent it out for a few years. Maybe expand and add some tiny guest homes outback. Everyone says how beautiful this property is. We could host family reunions or weddings."

"Okay you've got my attention," Dial said.

"I've prepared portfolios for both of you. And I already have an investor." He handed off a substantial folder.

"Investor? Portfolio? Hosting events? This all sounds like a lot of work." I scanned through the documents.

"Who's the investor?" Dial asked.

"Anything worth having is worth working hard for."

"Nobody is coming to Hume on vacation," Dial said.

"As the mayor of this town, I'm privy to things you're not. People pay for experiences. If we offer a small-town country vibe, leave the hustle and bustle of the city behind. Disconnect get one with nature, ride a fucking horse, milk a cow. Eat real farm to table meals. Rich white people will flock in droves and Black folks will do it for the plot."

"So, this isn't about saving our childhood home and more about lining your pockets," I asked.

"Our pockets. The collective, the originals. The core four."

"Who the fuck is the core four?" Confusion lined Dial's forehead.

"You, me, Edison, and Francesca."

"You're losing me with the Francesca thing. How is she a part of this core four?"

"She's Edison's girlfriend. And she has deep pockets. She probably has a pool of money she jumps into each night. Let's not let the pretty brown eyes fool us. She's rich."

"I don't know if she'd go for this entrepreneurial endeavor. And I'm not really feeling you referring to my girlfriend as Scrooge McDuck."

"She's the big-name celebrity that is going to post aesthetically pleasing images on her social media site and get the word out."

"And what's my role?" I asked.

"You're good with a hammer and growing things."

"Wait, you're actually serious?" I didn't see this power move from Cy coming.

"Yes, at first, I just wanted to save our childhood home. But then I got to thinking and looking at comps on these other secluded vacation destinations. And I figured—"

Dial interrupted him. "You figured this would be a feather in your cap. Bringing tourism to Hume. Local businesses would profit. Your constituents would love you."

"Hold up," I interjected. "How much profit are we talking about?"

"I don't know. That's where Dial comes in. She's the numbers gal."

Dial paced back and forth. "There would be the initial investment. Your mystery investor could help absorb some of that cost. And then renovations to ensure the house can accommodate multiple guests. A build-out of several tiny guest houses. We'd need staff, housekeeping, a chef, and maintenance crew. Very rough estimate we're talking a couple million dollars. And that's just to start."

"Split five ways."

"A million dollars each?" I guffawed.

"We can reduce that considerably with sweat equity."

"Whose sweat exactly? Because I've never seen you swing a hammer, let alone build anything," I asked.

"We could take a loan against the house. Maybe Figs and Twine," Cy said.

"No, not Figs and Twine. I'm not sacrificing a sure thing to roll the dice on a maybe."

"I kind of agree with Edison. The money would have to come from outside of the nursery. Because if we lost that mom and dad would never let us forget it."

Cyrus raised his hands in the air. "Okay well you're the accountant so figure it out. We have this house and collectively we could take loans out on our individual properties. And if it all goes to shit, we can just move back into our childhood home. One big happy family."

"You joke, but that could be a real possibility."

"Don't act like you're not foaming at the mouth at the thought of us all under one roof, momma's boy."

"Hey—"

Dial interrupted my objection. "I need to crunch the numbers before we seriously consider this."

"That's all I'm asking." Cyrus rubbed the whiskers on his chin.

"This would be a heavy lift. We all have full-time jobs." I hoped to ground the conversation back in reality.

"I'm ready to be a weekend warrior if you are." Cyrus was a great salesman, but I suspected when it came time to roll up his sleeves he'd be MIA.

Dial had a familiar twinkle in her eyes similar to when she suggested we push Cyrus out of Figs and Twine. "It does sound exciting."

"And this could be something for Maple and future generations. Figs and Twine and this resort spot. That's major moves." Cyrus was adding the cherry to the sundae.

"We could just buy the place and do nothing," I suggested.

"Don't be a baby Eddy."

I looked to Dial for support.

"Is that a counterproposal?" she asked.

"Yes, it is."

"Okay let's hear it." Cyrus crossed his arms over his chest.

"Uhm …well. We could buy the house and consider it an investment property."

"How does that make us money?"

"It doesn't but it keeps the house in the family."

Dial cringed. "Sorry Eddy, I like Cy's idea better."

"I wasn't exactly prepared to present a comprehensive pitch."

"I think it's this or nothing. And we all get what we want. Dial gets a chance to expand the Birch empire. I get to boost Hume's economy. And Eddy gets to save his childhood home."

"Our childhood home."

"Sure buddy." He winked at me.

"What do you think Edison?" I could tell Dial liked this deal and after she ran the numbers, she'd probably love it.

"Maybe." I chose to be noncommittal. I wanted to save the house. But I already had so much shit on my plate I didn't think it was possible to add more. "I just need to read the proposal and do some Googles of my own. Talk to Fancy."

"Bonus selling point, it could be fun. The Birch kids working together again."

"Hmm …maybe."

"Okay well I've got to run. Because unlike you two crumb bums, I have important people waiting for me."

"No, you don't," Dial said with a straight face. He was the mayor of Hume, but he was also our brother so he would always get roasted.

Cyrus threw up two crisp middle fingers for me and Dial to share.

In the time Fancy had been away, I'd tried busying myself with projects that would keep my mind off missing her. I spent long days at Figs and Twine reorganizing the sales floor and greenhouse to make room for new plant arrivals. At home I focused on cataloging as many items as possible so I could sell them through online auctions. The living room would be almost unrecognizable when Fancy returned. Gone was the artwork depicting slices of farm life, the assortment of figurines and nesting dolls which were sold as a lot and earned me a pretty penny.

Why Mr. Castle collected so many candle holders I would never know, but I sold over twenty of them. I kept a few that were made of silver; after removing the tarnish I was able to appreciate their beauty. In the bedroom, I spent a great deal of time moving around clothes and shoes, making space for Fancy to spread out. On the property, I hired a crew to erect a three-stall stable. Cotton Candy would need a proper home and maybe a friend.

All this busy work made me anxious; the time wasn't ticking fast enough and the days, which normally fly by, now seemed to drag. Fancy and I talked or texted every day. When they performed in Nashville, I was in the front row cheering her on. In the middle of the show, surrounded by the crowd of screaming fans, I started to feel guilty. Hard to believe she would willingly walk away from all this.

Leaving Whiskey Wild had nothing to do with me. It was more about the deterioration of her relationship with Darla. But that night while we lay in the hotel bed, I let her know I would always support her and her dreams were my dreams. I don't think it needed to be said, but I could tell she appreciated hearing it.

In a few hours Fancy and I would be reunited. Last night I lay awake silently, willing the moon to disappear under the horizon. At the first signs of the sun, I was up and knocking out my chores. Today was similar to the first day of school. You'd pick out an outfit the night before and got a fresh haircut and you couldn't wait to get to school and walk the halls in your fresh new fit.

I'd offered to pick Fancy up from the airport, but she declined, stating she wanted our reunion to take place on the farm. So, although her plane landed an hour ago, I still had to wait for Oz and her to make the trek to Hume. I hoped time made her heart grow fonder and the distance wasn't giving her pause. I'd be lying if I said I was one hundred percent confident. More nights than I liked to admit, I sleeplessly analyzed our conversations, the hitch in her voice, the delay after I told her I loved her.

Love is terrifying. When you step back and think about it, it's a wonder people willingly open themselves up to it. I was a creature of habit and up until recently my life could be described as run of the mill. But Fancy swooped in and turned all that on its head. Now I spent my days distracted, thinking about our conversations from the night before. The funny stories she would share made me laugh until my belly ached. Or being able to stare into her chestnut brown eyes during our video chats, which often turned steamy. Love was all-consuming and it didn't leave room for much else.

When his souped-up truck pulled in front of the house, I nearly tripped over my feet trying to get to the door. I spotted my girl waving from the cab of the truck and I returned the gesture.

Both my wave and smile were big and exaggerated. Fuck playing it cool. I missed her and once the truck slowed to a stop, I accosted the passenger door, pulling her from the cab.

Her arms wrapped around me, clapping my back. God I'd missed her hugs. They were the best. Fancy's body was warm and soft and the fragrant scent of honeysuckle clung to her person. She'd been gone so long the house no longer smelled like her. All traces of her existence were eliminated. I tried to replicate the fragrance with fabric spray on my bed linens, but it wasn't the same.

When her lips touched down on mine, it was like a cosmic reset. All the time apart, all the lonely nights, all the doubt dissipated. It was just me, my favorite girl, and the country air with hints of bluebells, freshly mowed grass, and laundry drying on the line. Oz didn't even cut off the engine, he removed her two large pieces of luggage from the truck and just drove off. Fancy and I were too busy kissing to acknowledge his departure.

"Let me get a look at you." I pulled away and surveyed her frame, looking for even the minor of changes. At this point, I had Fancy's face mapped out like I'd majored in the science of perfection and all things Francesca Palmer in college. I could identify every dimple, freckle, and the flicks of amber in her eyes.

"I haven't changed."

"I think your ass got fatter." I gave her cheeks a playful smack.

Fancy preened, "Really? Because when I wasn't on stage, I was posted up in a hotel gym on the Stairmaster."

"Them steps did a body good."

"You look the same. But it's hard to improve on greatness."

The softness of her skin turned my heart into a wreck. "Is this real? Or are you just another one of my dreams?"

She leaned in close, kissing my neck. "Does this feel real?" Trailing her tongue up toward my ear, she gave it a nibble. "What about this?" Her lips dusted mine and she examined my crotch. "Your dick is practically busting through your jeans. I don't know but that feels very real."

"I'm gonna need more evidence than that. Like me inside of you."

"Yes, immediately yes."

I chased her into the house and up the stairs. The bags could wait. We needed to formally reintroduce ourselves. And for much of the afternoon we fucked one another dizzy. Being able to duck my head in between her perky breast and just breathe her in was damn near life affirming. Every thought, desire, and wish had Francesca at the center of it.

When we finally came up for air. Fancy smiled wide. "You changed the sign?"

"I did." Instead of saying Castle Farm. The sign to the entrance of my property now read Welcome to Whiskey Wild Farm. "I hope you're okay with me using the name? I don't want any static from your legal team."

"I love it. It's perfect and thoughtful." Fancy massaged the nape of my neck.

We hadn't stopped touching each other since her boots hit the dirt. I scooped her face in my hand and placed strategic kisses along her collarbone. "That's not the only changes I've made, but I can give you a tour tomorrow."

"Did you miss me?" she asked with uncertainty. The effect of being apart for three months.

"I damn near put you through this mattress, that's how much I missed you."

"You know what I need?"

I let out a goofy laugh. "I know what you need." My dick expanding, ready for round three.

"I was going to say food."

"Oh wow, embarrassing."

"Don't get me wrong, I'm not turning down the dick, never that."

By the time we made it out of the bedroom, the sun was hiding behind a thicket of trees. Hunger pangs were more persistent than my libido. In the kitchen I created two large salads with steak I'd grilled earlier while waiting for her return. This is what I'd missed, Fancy in nothing but a tank top and panties navigating the kitchen while occasionally caressing my chest or kissing my back. The thought of just this simple act sustained me over the past few months.

We sat on the porch and enjoyed our meal. Fancy hummed softly in between bites. Her feet propped up in my lap. I wasn't the guy who won the girl, but here I was with the woman of my dreams. A smile the size of Texas overtook my features, crinkling the corners of my eyes and pinching my cheeks.

"What?"

"I just love you. And it's dawning on me I am the luckiest man in all of Hume."

"Just Hume?"

"I can't say the entire world because there's a man out there married to Kelly Rowland."

"Yeah, I didn't miss your obsession with Kelly." We both shared a laugh.

Love is all about two people feeling the same thing at the same time. A rush of satisfaction washed over me. If there was more to be had in this world, I'd pass. All I needed was Fancy, this farm, and the life we'd make together.

"Are you happy, Fancy Palmer?" I had zero regrets and hoped she felt the same.

"I'm with you so happiness is guaranteed."

And that was music to my ears.

EPILOGUE

Fancy

THE SPOTLIGHT WAS FIXED ON me. Topsy Turvey was a popular Nashville nightclub. It was standing room. The space was sold out, filled to capacity with people all here to see me. Six months passed since the Whiskey Wild split, and I'd pretty much kept a low profile with Edison in Hume.

Living with Edison was quite different from my life in LA. For starters everything was simpler, the days didn't fly by, so you had a chance to appreciate every moment. Edison established routine became mine. Up with the sun, feeding and caring for the animals before getting ready for an honest day's work at Figs and Twine. While he was working, I'd write songs and have long conversations with my new manager. The record label agreed to sign me on as a solo artist. Which was both scary and exciting as hell.

On most days I'd hole myself up in the tricked out shed and try to write a hit. Humming softly, I'd jotted down lyrics about the carefree nature of love. Recently all I could pen were songs about immense love and longing. I think Edison was solely responsible for that. Every time I sat down to write, the only emotion I wanted to express was pure happiness. No one was going to want to listen to an album solely about the joys of love. Listeners always wanted a little heartbreak mixed in.

The label lined up a showcase at Topsy Turvy so I could perform some old hits and present some of the new songs I'd been working on. This was a first, I'd never performed alone, Darla had always been faithfully by my side. I can't tell you how many nights I fussed about this show and the set list like it was my first. Which I guess technically it was.

One of the things I loved the most about Edison was how supportive he was and when he critiqued my music, it was always coming from a place of genuine interest. Unlike Chap, his feedback was never laced with insults. When you know better you do better, and I learned I deserved more than scraps of affection. It took Edison's unique brand of love to help me realize it.

After singing a few well-known favorites, I performed a new song and to my relief, the crowd was fixated on me. My momma said I could sing the alphabet and people would line up for miles. Maybe she was right. The third time I sang the chorus on the mid-tempo tune, several in the audience were singing along, even though they were hearing this new song for the first time.

My heart swelled and my voice grew shaky as I tried to hold back tears. Stepping out of the shadow of Whiskey Wild was terrifying, but the crowd swaying side to side and all the flashing cameras made it less so.

Addressing the audience, I said, "I have time for one last song. And I'd like to bring out a special guest, if that's okay?"

The crowd whooped and hollered at my request. Pointing to the side of the stage, I signaled Edison to come out. His stride was timid as he stepped into the spotlight. The fact he was on this stage at all was a testament to his love for me.

"This is my boyfriend, Edison. So don't none of you get any ideas." Adjusting the microphone stand, I positioned one in front of him. "Since I'm in my home state. I thought I would bring out *my* hometown hero and my favorite music partner to accompany me." The crowd cheered. "Edison, this is just a few hundred of my closest friends."

"Hi." With a bashful wave, he slung his guitar across his shoulders.

I could make out our families in the front row. Even Dial showed up to support me.

"Friends this …" I pointed to Edison. "This is my heart and my soul and the love of my life."

The crowd yelled, "Hey Edison." Which I'm sure made him blush.

"We're going to play a stripped-down version of 'Back Road Trails.' Fun fact: I wrote this song with Edison years ago. We were fresh out of high school, and everything seemed possible. And for a long time, I stopped believing in the wonder of life. I got a bit caught up and it almost felt like I was living but I wasn't soaking anything in. I didn't linger in the special moments long enough to appreciate them.

"The Grammy's, the Country Music Awards, performing on Saturday Night Live. They were all pivotal, important milestones I neglected to savor. Because of Edison I learned to slow down and appreciate the moments that quickly turn into memories. So, I want to thank you for sharing this moment in time with me and Edison."

Edison counted us off starting the melodic intro to "Back Road Trails." And I couldn't help but stare. As his biggest fan, I knew I was lucky to be able to call him mine. I could wake up every day and love this man. For a long time I thought I wanted fireworks, a love that was big and obnoxious. Edison was more of a sparkler, he burned slowly and while doing so, he radiated a bright, fierce flame that flickered and popped.

I started to sing the first verse about second chances and finding something you didn't even know you were searching for. The song was about the things that made Hume special … family, friends, and that person who makes even the most mundane day a bit brighter. I'd sung this song a hundred times with Darla, but tonight it felt different because this song was always intended for Edison and me. This song was about our love for one another before we were able to admit it.

When I reached the chorus, Edison joined in, giving the song a rich and more complex tone. A small part of me wished Edison was a little less humble and interested in showing the world his talent. I would love the opportunity to perform alongside the man I love every night.

Our voices intermixed in a steady melody, the mid-tempo tune picking up speed. At the bridge we nixed the words, instead locking eyes and letting our guitars do the talking. My fingers strummed a fiery rhythm while Edison performed a sharp lick that ignited a ripple of cheers from the crowd. We playfully challenged one another, feeding off the energy from the crowd as they clapped along. The beat pulsed like a heartbeat as our instruments carried on a wild conversation. With a final slide up the neck of my guitar, we landed on the same chord. Ambling closer to Edison, we sang the final stanza into his microphone.

The crowd rewarded our efforts with loud applause. All the adulation forced Edison to duck his head. Praise embarrassed him, no matter how well deserved.

"Thank you so much for coming out. I'm Fancy Palmer and this fine fella is Edison Birch." We walked off the stage hand in hand.

"I hope I was able to hold my own out there," Edison said.

"Are you kidding me. Do you hear them?" I pointed to the stage and the crowd who were still giving us our flowers. "You were amazing."

"It's a lot harder than karaoke," he joked.

"Luckily, we make the perfect team." I draped my arms over his shoulder.

The stage was addictive. Who didn't want enthusiastic fans eating out of the palm of your hand? There was a time when all I wanted was to be on the road entertaining the masses. Hotel hopping, eating out of to-go containers. Never stopping long enough to catch my breath or collect my thoughts. But now I would gladly settle for my weekend concerts on the farm alongside Edison.

The sound of our goats demanding their breakfast. Katt stopping by to confirm we were still alive. And the warmth of the sun while we enjoyed our first cup of coffee on the porch. Wildflowers were lacing their vines through my toes as I contently settled in. Others raced through life hopping on the expressway to get to the next big thing. Edison and I were taking the scenic route, stopping to skinny dip in lakes, picking flowers in fields, and appreciating the open road ahead.

Just the two of us.

BONUS CHAPTER

Fancy

IT WAS TEN O'CLOCK IN the evening, well after business hours, but I'd agreed to ride with Edison to Figs & Twine so he could fetch catalogs he was hoping to review for an upcoming order. He didn't have to do much convincing because I'd grown accustomed to his presence and the thought of even fifteen minutes without him didn't sit right with me. Plus, I loved being a passenger princess tooling down the road with country music playing and Edison's hand firmly clutching my thigh. And when I was feeling naughty, I'd open my legs and let his hands wander. How he managed to keep the car on the road while fingering my sweet spot, I'd never understand.

Ozzie had taken to calling me Edison's shadow because where that man went, I wasn't far behind. And who could blame me? I loved everything about him. Who knew the love of my life was right here in Hume where I'd left him all those years ago? When I said my prayers at night, I thanked the good Lord for saving this man for me. Shit, I was even grateful for the heartbreak that forced me home, because without that I wouldn't know how it felt to be truly loved. Edison Birch fucking *adored* me, and I wasn't going to waste time trying to figure out why.

"Did you like college?"

"Where did that question come from?" Edison rolled the windows down, preferring the cool night air over AC.

"I just want to be well versed on all things Edison Birch." I stroked the back of his neck.

"Starting with my college years?"

"Yes."

"It took me a minute to acclimate, but once I did, I had a good time."

"Was it a big adjustment?"

"I'd imagine anyone who leaves Hume for a major city goes through growing pains."

I nodded. "I sure did."

"Yeah, how so?"

"I think the biggest lesson was that you couldn't rely on years of familiarity. Your families didn't go back decades. Everyone was a stranger, and I learned, eventually, that people had their own agenda, sometimes befriending me for access to something or someone else. I suppose you encounter people like that wherever you go, but it was my first time dealing with fakes and phonies. In Hume it's hard to pretend you're somebody you're not when everyone's quick to remind you they know you better than you know yourself."

"I'd imagine that would make building relationships in L.A. difficult. The fakes and phonies, I mean."

"Yeah, I was sleeping next to a snake for years, completely oblivious, so I guess you could say I was easily fooled. In L.A. it was all about who you knew. And if you didn't know anyone, you had to be pretty or funny enough to be admitted entry."

"You had the pretty part down pat."

"I'm also very funny."

"No, no you're not." He gave my thigh a squeeze.

"Do you think I don't know what you're doing?"

"Meaning?"

"I ask you a question about yourself and then you flip it on me. We're you popular in college?"

"I had a circle of friends who appreciated me."

"Were you in a fraternity?"

Edison's eyes slammed into me, telling me *hell no*. I hadn't planned on the twenty questions, and I was sure he regretted extending the offer for me to tag along. But when I was in love, I wanted to hear every story, anecdote, and embarrassing moment. The person who stuck their tongue in your ass shouldn't feel like a stranger. And although Edison was far from that, there was still close to ten years to catch up on.

"Did you have a girlfriend?"

"I did."

"Were you in love?" I teased.

"I was."

My brows inch upward in surprise. The thought of him loving someone who wasn't me was hard to comprehend. And I don't mean to imply he wasn't allowed—of course he'd lived a life before me. We weren't even together back then. But knowing *how* he loved made me jealous of a woman I'd never met.

"What happened?"

"Graduation. My plan was always to return to Hume after, and she couldn't see herself fitting into life here."

"I'm sorry."

"Shit happens for a reason."

I pinched at the spaces in between my fingers. "Was she, like, the love of your life?"

"No, that title is reserved for you."

I smiled at the reassurance. "When you came back to Hume, were things different?"

"It was exactly the same. Same people, doing the same shit. Is it weird for you being back here?"

"Yeah, it's like so much has changed but everything still feels the same. And I'm not sure if that's a good thing or a bad thing."

"Maybe it's neutral."

"I love this town, I do, but it feels like it stifles dreams. Like the people are almost in a coma."

Edison's gaze was disapproving. "Or maybe for some people, Hume *is* the dream."

"I didn't mean it like that."

"Then how did you mean it?"

Any talk of Hume being anything other than a utopia was met with resistance by Edison. I shared his heart with the town. He wouldn't tolerate any disparaging remarks about Hume, the people, or its politics. Everything he loved was within the city's limits, his quaint childhood memories of swimming in the river, enjoying fireworks in the park, and eating Popsicles in the yard after running through the sprinklers for hours. So much of Hume was woven into Edison that there was no separating the two.

"This is my hometown too. I critique it because I love it. Look, I've lived in L.A. for years and it's never felt like home. It's hard to build community when there isn't a support system. I'm not saying it's impossible—it just requires more work. Even though people live right on top of each other, you often don't know your neighbor's name. It's very individualistic in that way. Which is the opposite of Hume, which is community based and frowns on individualism. In L.A. being unique or eclectic is celebrated, while here it's a cause for concern."

"I hear you. Hume isn't perfect. But no place is. And I'd like to think we're getting better at the inclusion part."

"Erm…"

"Baby steps are still forward motion."

"Maybe things will be better for our kids."

"Ours, collectively?"

"Ours, generally."

"Do you wish you'd gone to college?"

"Sometimes I do. I think I would've crushed higher education. Mind you, I'm talking about the 'making friends and partying' part, not the academics."

"Yeah, because you were a horrible student."

"I'm sorry if I didn't find the molecular structure of this, that, and the third interesting. I excelled in the classes that mattered— English, music, and PE."

"Well, I'll admit it was a solid plan, because look at you now."

At night, Figs & Twine nursery twinkled against the sky, the effect of the dimmed lights in the main building and the twinkle lights strung from poles and columns throughout the property. Edison parked his truck, and we entered through a side door leading to the greenhouse. This space was even more stunning at night in the low light and with the hum of sprinklers. I could see glimpses of him throughout the space, his green thumb encouraging things to grow.

They say you should talk to your plants to stimulate growth, and I was overtaken by a sudden bout of envy at the thought that these plants had had the pleasure of Edison whispering sweet nothings into their leaves. "Do you talk to them?"

"The plants?"

"Yeah?"

"I do chat them up. I give them names." Edison canvassed the space, checking in on various flowers and plants even though he'd left them just a few hours ago.

"Names?"

"Yeah, not all of them." He dropped his voice to a whisper. "But the special ones."

"I need introductions."

"Fair warning, some of the names are silly and were never meant to be shared."

"Noted."

He pointed to the plant directly across from me. "I call this one Apple Twist because she reminds me of the Apple Jacks cereal I used to eat when I was a kid."

"When you said names, I thought you meant Sally or Leon."

"There's a few of those too." He motioned toward Apple Twist again. "Don't be rude, Fancy, go on and say hi."

"To the plant?"

"It's more like my coworker. These plants keep me sane and grounded."

I stepped up to the plant whose leaves were chartreuse yellow and apple green. "Hello, nice to meet you. I'm Francesca, but everyone calls me Fancy." I pushed out a frustrated breath, turning back to Edison. "I feel stupid."

"It's just like talking to yourself. Plus, they're amazing listeners. I've told them all about you and they've never complained."

I knew he was just joking, but it still caused butterflies to flutter in my stomach. "Have you and Dial given any more thought into the improvements you want to make to this place?"

"Nah—you know, before our parents' announcement we'd randomly have conversations about what we'd do if we were in charge. And now that retirement is no longer an *if* but a *when*, all I can think about is not fucking this up. The nursery has been in my family for generations. What if Dial and I fail?"

"You two are practically running the place already."

"Yes, but with guardrails. Major changes have to be run by my parents. They're an excellent sounding board, and oftentimes they consider things Dial and I missed."

"I understand this is going to be a big transition, but you need to trust that your parents provided you and Dial with the tools and education you need to be successful. You've been working at this nursery since you could form complete sentences. Joseph and Shelia are entrusting you with this because they know their legacy is in good hands."

"I just don't want to disappoint them."

"Then make them proud by putting your unique stamp on Figs & Twine. I think your ideas for this place are amazing, and who doesn't want a fine-ass horticulturist teaching them about fertilizer and soil?"

"'Figs & Twine—let's get dirty one plant at a time.'" We shared a laugh.

"That slogan next to a picture of you would increase business twenty-five percent. Shit, people from the neighboring town would make the trip to see you."

"That was a joke. We will not be doing a 'planting after dark' series."

"That's fair, but a cute little coffee shop would be instantly successful. And I vote for making that happen first."

"It's something Dial and I have wanted to do for a long time."

"As the boss you can do that and so much more."

Edison planted a kiss into the mass of curls on the top of my head. "I'll be right back. I think I left the catalogs in Dial's office." He walked through the greenhouse to the main building.

I remembered coming to Figs & Twine as a kid with my mom. And while she shopped, Edison and I would laugh and tell secrets while zigzagging through the aisles. Even back then I found myself wanting to be near him. He was still so much like that little boy, so grounded and thoughtful. The little boy who'd held doors open for my momma had become the man who held them open for me.

I'm not going to say it was always Edison, because that would be a lie. Young Fancy didn't appreciate all he had to offer; I was too busy chasing the star athlete or the neighborhood bad boy to seriously consider Edison in a romantic way. Thank God for growth, because now Edison made sense. He was the guy you settled down with, not the guy you settled for.

A few weeks ago, Edison was but a memory, and today I couldn't imagine living my life without him. And I wanted to know *everything*—his secrets, his dreams. The things he was too scared to say. Standing here with Apple Twist and all his other botanical friends, I felt the urge to immerse myself in his life. There was so much I still didn't know, and to properly love him, I needed to dive deep.

"I got 'em." He returned to the greenhouse with a stack of catalogs in his hand. "You ready to go?"

"Teach me something."

"About what?"

"About the flora. I wanna love what you love. And see things through your eyes."

"Seriously?"

"Like I'm laid out in a casket, fresh-to-death serious."

His smile ruined me every time. And I imagined that twenty years from now it would still cause my knees to wobble and my heart to race. I'd known Edison damn year my entire life, and after the last few weeks I was determined to love him until my dying day.

He dropped the catalogs to the ground and joined me in scanning the aisles. Claiming my hand, he led me to the far end of the greenhouse. "This is an Oakleaf hydrangea nicknamed Ruby Slipper."

"That's a silly name for a plant."

"Not so silly when you realize what it can do. You see these large, deep pink blooms?" He cradled one of them in his hand like he was holding a newborn baby.

"Yeah." I moved closer.

"They start out as white, and then each summer they burst into this bright, deep *ruby* hue."

"Hence the moniker Ruby Slipper."

"Exactly, and they're strong, Fancy. It could be raining cats and dogs and these sturdy bushes ain't going nowhere. A little water and occasional grooming and this plant will last several generations."

There was an excitement in his tone that only these plants could elicit. Plants for Edison were like music for me. It was my reason. When all else failed, I could pick up my guitar and write a song. And I imagined for Edison, caring for his plants—watering, trimming, sticking his hands deep into the soil—brought him that same peace.

"Why are you looking at me like that?" he asked.

"Because I love hearing about the things you're passionate about."

"I'm not boring you?"

"No, sir, I want more. Pick another one, your favorite."

Edison took a deep breath and slowly made his way down the aisle, occasionally stopping and staring at a plant before moving on. We traversed several aisles until we settled in front of a large rosebush. The color reminded me of the inside of a pomelo fruit.

"Okay, this is the peach drift rose. They're highly fragrant." He stepped aside so I could take a whiff.

"I'm picking up a honey scent."

"Yep, it's pleasant but not overpowering, which is nice."

"Are these the same flowers you brought home the other night?"

"Yes, this is my go-to flower. If I'm putting together a bouquet, these bad boys are making an appearance."

"What makes it your favorite?"

"First, they're low maintenance, which makes it a great starter plant. Customers love the idea of rosebushes but fear they'll wilt and end up as an eyesore. Second, huge color payoff—look how *vibrant* that is. You can't see this rose and not appreciate the majesty of Mother Nature. And lastly, we have this big bloom. Some roses never fully blossom. But not so with the peach drift. You see how beautifully it opens up?"

A wicked smile tweaked the corners of my mouth. "Hopefully, you'll be saying that about me later."

Edison leaned in, dusting his lips over mine. "Oh, you always open up real nice." He gave my ass a gentle slap.

Unfortunately, this greenhouse was all concrete floors. Because *baby*, if there was a soft place to land, I'd be on my knees gagging as we speak.

"Do you want me to show you which plant reminds me of you?" he asked.

"Yes, I wanna meet my plant doppelgänger."

He grabbed hold of my hand and escorted me to a section of the greenhouse that almost felt hidden. The aisles back here were narrower, so we had to walk in single file. But my hand never left his.

"This is a clematis, which is a flowering vine," Edison said.

"Meaning?"

"They call her the queen of the climbers, similar to ivy."

"Did you pick this particular plant because I've always got my nose in everybody's business?"

"No, I did not. This climber is called Sweet Summer Love."

"You're redeeming yourself. I like it already."

We came to a stop in front of a flower wrapped around a wooden post with hundreds of violet blooms, deep purple in the middle fading into a cranberry red. The sweetly scented plant was a sensory overload, and I wanted to bury my face in the leaves and inhale deeply. The fact that Edison was reminded of me when he passed by this vibrant and beautiful flower left me speechless.

"I picked this because it's kinda how you make me feel inside. Like you've invaded my heart and now you're blossoming everywhere, just taking up space. And I'd like to think you're thriving because I'm giving you what you need."

"And what does a plant like me need?"

"You need food."

"I can't live without your steak. I'm addicted."

"You need attention. Not in a needy way, but in a way that's equally all-consuming. At the same time, you need space because you're still figuring shit out. And finally, you need love because I think that's something you've missed out on. And that lack of love has made you scared and unsure of yourself. So every day I try to give you a little bit of all those things."

"I do have a few things figured out—chiefly among them that I love you," I replied. "And not just because of the way you love me. I've been to Hume and back, and I've never met a man who was so self-assured and comfortable in his own skin, and that makes me feel safe, safe with my heart and my dreams because I know they're in good hands. I just love you to bits, Edison. And that night back in the California desert turned out to be the best night of my life, because it led me back home and here with you."

Edison cupped the sides of my face. "I love you too, Fancy, more than you could know."

I stood on tiptoes and Edison did the rest, capturing my lips with his. He dipped his tongue into my mouth cautiously, but when mine circled his, he moaned, pulling me closer. I tossed off his baseball cap and scratched his head. I'd recently learned his scalp was one of his erogenous zones and been rewarded with his folding me like fresh laundry. Hopefully I'd get a repeat of that tonight.

"Have you ever fucked anyone in this greenhouse?" I was already stepping out of my panties.

"No, ma'am."

"Let's remedy that."

Edison pulled off his shirt, nodding eagerly.

We quickly ditched the rest of our clothes and Edison latched on to my nipple, rolling his tongue over my skin until it was perky and hard. He backed me into a pallet loaded with bags of soil and draped me over them. Dropping to his knees, he tasted me to confirm I was ready. What was intended to be a sample turned into a meal as he ravished my plump folds. I loved the way he fucked my lips like he was on death row and my pussy was his last meal. His audible moans let me know he would die a happy man.

Standing, he flipped me onto my stomach. The bags of soil were piled so high that my feet didn't touch the floor. Edison wasted no time giving me exactly what I wanted, easing his dick inside. We'd probably fucked nearly a hundred times, and my breath still hitched when he filled me up. Edison's thrusts left me tongue-tied as I clawed at the plastic bags filled with earth.

He rubbed my thighs and ass as his whispered grunts and groans made me dizzy with desire. "I need to see you, kiss you," I breathed. My wish was his command, and Edison pulled out, flipped me over, and slid back in before I could finish screaming his name. Wrapping my legs around his waist, I leaned forward, sucking his lower lip into my mouth.

"You feel so good," I moaned.

"You like that?"

"Now, sir, you know good and goddamn well I like what you're doing."

He smiled over my mouth. "Just checking."

"Tell me it's mine," I demanded.

"It's all yours, my one and only." He brushed my hair from my face. "Every inch." The series of thrusts preceding his words were diabolical, knocking the air from my lungs. It was like Edison was mining for gold in my honeypot, and after digging me out he was rewarded with precious resources as I creamed onto his dick. We both stared in awe as he thrust in and out. Our skin glistened as the moonlight cast a haunted glow over our surroundings.

When I said it was on sight, I meant it. It didn't matter where we were—henhouse, outhouse, or jailhouse—I would shift my panties to the side to get this good dick. Edison positioned my legs over his shoulders, and the pleasure was so intense that all I could do was scream. "Edison, my God. Fuck me. Take this puss—"

My body was racked with a ripple than threatened to send me over. I dug my nails into one of the bags on the pallet and soil poured to the ground. Edison didn't flinch, just continued to drive deeper. It was disrespectful, as my legs quaked and my mouth hung open, but it was also intentional, as he rocked his hips and propped up his leg so no cranny was missed. I would be feeling his dick well into the morning, a sweet reminder that Edison had been here.

Wrapping my arms around his shoulders, I hoped to gain control of my impending orgasm. Edison grabbed hold of my ass and worked me up and down. My nipples rubbed against his hard chest. The feel of his skin against mine was my favorite part. Nibbling his ear, I whispered, "You've got me dripping wet, baby."

"It feels so fucking good. I'm so lucky to have you." Each word was punctuated by an ardent thrust.

That was the spark that lit the fire in my core. No one was luckier than me as my pussy convulsed over his dick. The walls of the greenhouse disappeared, and it was just us and this all-consuming pleasure. When Edison groaned, I relished in the shared moment as we climaxed, shaking in unison as he gripped my waist, filling me up with his desire.

When our movements finally stalled, Edison pulled out and my feet touched the ground. He brushed my big curls from my face. "You good?" He planted kisses along my collarbone.

"You might have to carry me to the car," I teased, because my legs felt like rubber.

He handed me my dress. "Listen, I know Hume isn't L.A. or New York, but I hope you still see the good in this town."

"L.A. and New York are great cities, but they lack one thing."

He stepped into his boxers. "Oh yeah, what's that?"

"You, Edison. And as long as Hume, Tennessee has an Edison Birch, it's my favorite spot on the map."

FALLING BACK TO YOU

PREVIEW

1

Dial

"CAN YOU MOVE THOSE NEW planters to the north side with the rest?" I asked Luke one, of our staff, while walking through the nursery. Slowing to a stop I checked out the new cacti plants. They were some of my favorites because I could relate to being prickly but beautiful to look at at the same time. My daddy called me Prickly Pear on account of my fetching visage but thorny demeanor. I'd been like that my whole life and the people closest to me were often left picking spines from their asses.

This nursey was like my safe haven and now my second home. Since our parents retired it demanded much of my time. I've always been a workaholic. In early and staying late. Starting at my laptop screen until my eyes blurred. My momma always said, "The only thing that out beats hard luck is hard work". The Birch family didn't need luck because we were smart and resourceful. And that trumped the luck of the draw any day.

Take this nursery for instance, which has been in my family for generations. The only reason it hadn't shuttered like other businesses was from working smart. Not being reactionary or chasing trends. Listening to our customers and offering up expert advice about flora and fauna.

Figs and Twine was now the largest nursery in town the only rival was them big box stores in Nashville.

It put a smile on my face knowing I'd played a small part in that success. Shit, I was being modest and that wasn't really my style. I worked my ass off and it was satisfying knowing I had a significant hand in keeping our legacy alive. For the longest time I thought giving one hundred and ten percent to the nursery, with it's never ending demands, was one of my best qualities but now I wasn't so sure. You know the saying all work and no play makes Dial a dull girl. Well, my personal life was unremarkable in every way.

My life consisted of three things. Maple, my beautiful seven-year-old daughter, work, and family, which other than Maple included my two brothers Cyrus and Edison. Those three things kept me busy but of late it wasn't keeping me content. And I wasn't all too sure what I needed to do to fix that. But I did know I couldn't keep ignoring the nagging itch for something new and exciting. Which was silly really because there was never anything new or exciting in Hume. Life here was predictable, that was kind of the point of living in a small town.

As you can suspect, dating in Hume was like trying to hit the moon with a dart. First, I was a hard nut to crack. And second, men were … stupid. I can't remember the last time I'd met a guy that piqued my curiosity. Maybe I was interested in what was in their pants but their heads and hearts I couldn't care less. Plus, relationships were just as much work as a full-time job. I didn't have room in my busy schedule to cultivate a meaningful connection. Sure, I'd considered lighting the vacancy sign just to see if I still had it. Thoughts like that were short lived when men tried to flirt with me while I loaded bags of fertilizer into their truck or helped them pick out the best bushes for the yard.

Climbing the steps leading to my office I was greeted by Edison, my baby brother and joint owner of Figs and Twine, coming from the other direction.

"Not you being early for a meeting?" I joked.

"Fancy brought us coffee and some pastries." He handed me a cup as we entered my office.

"I know she's bored to tears if she's going on coffee runs." Fancy was Edison's girlfriend and a big-time country music star. Something was in the water because unassuming Edison, who recoiled from the spotlight, ended up with a woman who was chased by paparazzi and the cover girl on magazines. Like literally, I peeped her preening on the cover of Elle while getting gas and jerky at The Gas Guzzle.

"She was taking a smooches break." He flashed a goofy smile.

I rolled my eyes flopping into my chair. "Ugh gross."

"The concept of love or—"

"You two and your googly eyed kissy face sessions."

"Dial Birch ladies and gentlemen, the only woman who detest human connection."

"I'm fine with the human connection but the emoji filled text messages and you two handing hands like one of you might get lost is getting old."

"Aren't you tired of being a hater?"

"No, I actually delight in it. It's one of my best qualities."

"Uhm … no." Eddy too a sip from his cup. "You know I could get you in on this action."

"What action are you referring too?"

"Dating."

"I'm not interested."

"Fancy and I were in town the other day and Shelton asked about you."

"Why would he so that?"

"I thank he has a crush."

"Shelton Krause was … he was attractive. Tall, handsome, with all his teeth. You'd be surprised how that wasn't always the case. We'd gone to school together and I knew he had a crush but at the time I was dating Ozzie Palmer on and off. And when we were off men were too afraid to approach me because they knew if word got back to Oz there would be a fight. I'd been single for a long time, but I think guys were still traumatized from the fear of 6'5" three hundred- and thirty-pound Oz coming around looking to tussle.

"What did he say?" I wasn't good at acting disinterested. Dating Shelton was a no for me but a girl could live vicariously in delusion.

"He asked how you were and if he came calling would another man answer the door."

"Hmm."

"I told him you were hopelessly single with zero dates and few options."

"Fucker, you better be joking."

"Nah, I told him he should shoot his shot."

"You are setting that man up for failure."

"What's wrong with Shelton? Fancy said he was cute."

"He is … cute. But I don't do cute."

"Yeah, I know who you do." Edison teased.

"That was a long time ago."

"Erm, tell Oz that," Edison whispered.

"What now?"

"Nothing."

"Is Cyrus coming?" I asked. Cyrus was the eldest of the Birch clan. Just like Edison and I he was an equal owner of the nursery, but he didn't lift a finger to help.

"You know the drill. He'll come up with some lame excuse for why he missed it."

"He called this meeting. You know, it must be nice to do absolutely nothing and reap a third of the profits."

"In his defense he is busy running Hume."

"Hume? Population 4,853. Hume runs itself."

While Cyrus was kissing babies and pardoning turkeys Edison and I were here at Figs and Twine busting our asses. Our parents recently retired and handed us full reins. The thought of which still caused my breath to catch in my lungs. Edison and I knew eventually we'd run the show, but we never anticipated eventually would come so quickly. Cyrus was the mayor of Hume, but his loyalty should lay with his family first. Edison, Figs and Twine, and me.

Honestly, I should be lucky Edison showed up. We were both usually off on Sundays but now that we were responsible for Figs and Twine, our sixty-hour work weeks were closer to eighty. The business and ways to improve it consumed my thoughts every second of the day. It was the first thing that crossed my mind each morning. I kept a notepad on my nightstand in case I woke up in the middle of the night and needed to capture a thought or sketch a display layout.

"While we wait—"

"For nothing. He's going to be a no show per usual. I'm just gonna say it I think we may have made a mistake jumping on this bed and breakfast project. If Cyrus can't show up to this then who's to say he'll show up when it's time to swing hammers."

"I hear you. But this was his idea."

"Maybe his plan is to have us do all the work while he reaps the benefits."

"He doesn't move like that."

"With those two left feet? He doesn't move at all."

"Can you be nice?"

"Have we fucking met?

"It's a good thing he's late because I've been meaning to talk to you. It might be time to hire a few more people." My face crumpled as if the vent were releasing toxic gas. "We're busy. And with the new classes and increased demand, that isn't going to stop any time soon."

"I hear you, but we just hired three new people for the horticulture classes and cafe."

"Yeah, and our staff is stretched thin."

"Maybe your girlfriend could help."

Edison rolled his eyes. "You said you were going to try."

"I have been. But she is kind of sitting on her ass all day."

"She's writing songs for her first solo album."

Did I like Francessca Palmer? Not really. But I was really trying hard to find common ground. But she and I were like night and day. I'd struck out with all the Palmer offsprings. They came off as entitled and self-important. I think it was the Hollywood upbringing. The Palmers were horse trainers with a sprawling ranch that sat atop a hill looking down on us regular folk. Our families were close but like much of life adulthood changes things. And I wasn't interested in entertaining fake friendships.

"Just something to considered."

I handled the finances and HR task while Edison was the plant expert. We made a good team. "I'll see what I can do. But we may have to pitch in for the time being."

"With what hours? We're both here all the damn time and now we're gonna start work on the B&B. I don't know about you but I need like six hours of sleep minimum to function."

"Maybe we can hire some interns, pay them in lattes and experience."

"Ain't nobody trying to provide free labor."

"I'll reach out to the 4H club maybe we can barter a trade."

4H's local chapter leader was Ozzie but I planned to bypass him and go through Clarice, the secretary instead. She and I went way back and were on good terms. Maybe I'd invite her out for drinks. Can't even remember the last time I'd gone out for fun. I'd been neglecting my friends and had some making up to do.

I'm afraid the years had taken the shine off the apple. At thirty I was a single mother with very little to show for myself. I guess that's why I was so fiercely protective of Figs and Twine. Eventually Maple would grow up and search for her place in the world outside of me. I understand she only seven but life comes at you fast. Two blinks ago she could fit in the crook of my arm and now it was getting harder to carry her. The nursery was the one thing I could shape into my own and it would never leave me, or be disappointed, or secretly think I wasn't enough.

The clanging of the stairs let us know someone was approaching. "Happy Sunday family," Cyrus sang out.

"I know you fucking lying."

"We were just about to count you out," Edison said.

"I'm the one who called the meeting so way wouldn't I be here."

"Who's thirty minutes late for a meeting they called?" I huffed.

"I'm just busy."

"That is the lamest excuse I've ever heard. We are all busy Cy. And it's Sunday we'd rather be home."

"Well then, I'll keep it brief. The permits were approved."

"It took long enough," Edison said.

"As our mayor couldn't you have helped expedite the process?"

"No, because that would be favoritism. Which is borderline corrupt." Cyrus talked in a cadence that made me want to smack him in the face.

"Well, what the fucks the point of having a brother who's the mayor if he can't make shit shake for you?"

"Can you focus?" He pointed at one of the unclaimed coffee cups. "Is that mine."

"Knock yourself out," Edison said.

Cyrus leaned on the window ledge that looked out into the nursery. "Now that we have the permits, we can start moving forward with the build out for the bed and breakfast."

Our parents left Hume and us kids pooled our resources to purchase our childhood home. For the past few months since closing its sat untouched because we needed permits from the city before we could start knocking shit down and erecting structures. But now we finally had the green light. Yet another project I'd have to make time for.

"This is going to be an all hands-on deck type of project. Edison, I expect Fancy to be there too."

"She's busy writing music." I teased."

"Fancy is more excited than I am for this project," Edison said.

"Great, Dial I thought you and Fancy could start in the house. Taking an inventory on what our folks left behind and what we'll still need. You know plates, silverware, towels, sheets, pillows, that kind of stuff."

"When do I get to demo something?" Counting spoons and forks wasn't really my jam. I wanted to knock down walls.

"Don't worry you'll get your hands dirty."

"You expect the four of us to knock all this work out?" Edison asked.

"When the time comes we'll hire some additional bodies. But right now, we need to focus on the stuff we can do on our own to cut cost."

"When do we get to meet this mystery investor and what promises have you made to them."

"Our first day on sight will be this Saturday and my guy will be there."

"It's not Ozzie, right?" Ozzie was Cyrus's best friend and he'd been very tight lip when it came to who was partnering with us.

"No, if it was Oz, I would've told you."

I searched his face for falsehoods. Either Cyrus was telling the truth, or he was a good liar. "Okay."

I was in love with my two-story ranch house. It was the first independent purchase I made over four years ago. The home search took months because I was shopping for a forever home for me and Maple and when I crossed the threshold, I knew I'd found it. It was older and surrounded by massive trees. Each night I pulled up to my place, all the worries from the day instantly washed away.

I'd been living with my parents before moving here which had its perks because they could help me with Maple. And I needed all the help I could get because I didn't know shit about babies and being a mom. My mother made it look so easy with three little ones under foot, but motherhood didn't come naturally for me which was difficult to accept because I was typically good at everything.

In the kitchen I performed my closing shift. Which was essentially wiping down countertops and loading the dishwasher. Since Maple was at her father's place for the week, closing shift had been a breeze. There were no little fingerprints on the fridge or random spills that required elbow grease to lift up. I missed her when she was gone but cosplaying as a child free person every other week wasn't too shabby.

Most of the week consisted of girl dinners of my choice. My favorite being caramel popcorn out of one of those vintage tin canisters. I also watched a lot of television while updating the website for Fig and Twine or signing off on onboarding documents. Even when I was off, I never fully got a break. Edison was always preaching the virtues of work life balance, but I didn't come with a chill button.

Heavy footfalls on the porch, let me know my solitude was coming to an end. Ozzie Palmer knocked on the screen door but didn't wait to be invited in. I rounded the corner into the hallway with a huge smile ready to greet my precious girl. When I realized she was dead asleep in her father's arms the smile slipped from my face. Ozzie didn't deserve smiles. Smiles were reserved for the people I loved. Instead, he received my resting bitch face.

"Barely started the engine before she was knocked out in the truck."

"I got her." I reached for her knowing good and damn well she was getting too heavy for me to carry.

"Nope, no need to disturb her. I'll tuck her in. She's already in her PJs. And before you ask, yes she'd bathed, brushed, and groomed." Ozzie pushed past me taking the stairs like he belonged here.

After seven years of shared custody, we kind of had this co-parenting thing on auto pilot. We alternated weeks with Maple. During his weeks, Ozzie picked her up from school on Monday and dropped her off on Sunday. Fortunately, Hume was a small town and Ozzie and I lived less than twenty minutes apart. It made things less hectic, and I think Maple appreciated the routine of always knowing what to expect.

Our scheduled drop-offs were the only times we saw one another. Mostly because I avoided any place Ozzie might frequent. The Tipsy Owl was my favorite bar, but Ozzie was there every other Friday, so I kept clear of it. I rarely made runs into town because Ozzie was always hanging around with Cyrus, his best friend. Yes, the father of my child was my brother's best friend. And if I had a time machine, I would've warned younger me of the headache that would cause. Ozzie was invited to every BBQ, camping trip, and birthday party like he was family because for a long time he was.

I returned to the kitchen in the hopes cleaning would convey I was unbothered by Ozzie's presence. When he descended the steps, I grabbed a hand towel and pretended to fold it.

"It smells good in here." Ozzie settled into the doorway of the kitchen, his burly frame blocking the light from the hall. His style hadn't changed since we'd dated. He was still sporting a neutral-colored T-shirt, dark wash denim, and a Carhartt jacket. To be fair the look worked on him so there wasn't much need for an update.

"They're having a classroom party at Maple's school tomorrow, so I made some cupcakes."

"What kind did you make?"

"Carrot, I just need to frost them."

"I didn't know kids liked carrot cupcakes."

"Maple likes them."

"So, you're basing your cupcake selection on a child who just a year ago was eating dirt."

"It was a one-time thing and she was curious." I would not accept any Maple slander.

Ozzie entered the kitchen, his head on a swivel. "Can I help you?" I inched further into the kitchen and away from him.

"I'm just admiring the place. I like the backsplash." He pointed to the blue tiles which had been up for over a year. I could always tell when he wanted something because he'd make small talk. *Strange weather we're having. Did you hear about the Abbott's mare?*

"What do you want?"

"Why do I have to want anything? Can't a guy just catch up."

"If it doesn't pertain to Maple, you and I have nothing to catch up about."

Ozzie seeped in breath of air. "Maple's dead to the world."

"I know it I watched you carry her to bed."

"Every week you play this same game like we both don't know where it's going to lead."

"Hopefully with the door closing behind you."

"Why are you so difficult?" He reached for one of my locs and I smacked his hand away.

"Why are you so easy and predictable?" Ozzie rounded the corner of the kitchen table and thoroughly invaded my personal space. "I told you it was never happening again."

"You've been saying that for weeks. But every Sunday night you end up getting stretched out by me."

My face flushed. I hated this man. Ozzie Palmer was like an upset stomach on a long flight. A bee sting that when scratched only got worse. Like walking up a steep hill only to realize you forgot your basket when you reached the top. He was also the father of my child. If you saw him from across a crowded bar after a few drinks it would make sense. He was tall and with me clocking in at five feet seven inches and all muscle he made me feel dainty. And he could carry my weight, I'm talking upstairs, into trucks, and over his dick. But if you spent any time talking to him you'd question my judgment. In my defense I was lonely and each time he fucked me it felt like physical therapy. He'd crack my back and have me walking funny for days after. His dick and how he wielded it was my weakness. No one made me feel as good as Ozzie did … or as bad.

My hand landed on his silver belt buckle, and I aggressively unlatched it. I didn't have to look at his face to know he was staring down at me with indignation. I'd been lying for weeks, each time promising it was the last time only for him to bend me over the kitchen table, the couch, the stair rails. When I unzipped his pants and pushed my hand into his boxer briefs, I was greeted by the thickest fucking dick I'd ever had the pleasure of sucking.

"Look how hard you've got me."

"Don't talk, you cocky son of a bitch."

"If I go mute, how am I going to tell you how good you feel while I'm inside you?"

A shiver trilled up my spine. I wanted that so bad. To hear how good it was and for him to call me his talented girl. Ozzie leaned forward like he was going in for a kiss on the lips. I immediately halted his advance with a stiff arm to the chest.

"Don't worry, Suga. I remember the drill. No kissing on the lips."

I was weak but I had standards. Kissing in my opinion was far more intimate than bumping uglies. When we kissed, we were granting the receiver access to our soul. Kissing on the mouth was strictly forbidden.

Ozzie kicked off his boots, removed his jacket, and stripped naked from the waist down. His dick wobbled like it was tipsy. Fishing a condom from his jeans he suited up. I shimmed out of my panties. After getting home and showering I purposely picked a flowy dress Ozzie could easily pull up for quick fucking.

His overgrown hand wrapped around my neck, and he used it to guide me toward the fridge. Hooking my leg with his arm I was lifted off the floor and before I could catch my bearings he was sliding inside. Ozzie grunted out a breath as he slipped into place. "Who's my beautiful girl?"

"I am." Ozzie knew how to make me feel soft. As the middle child of two brothers, I'd always had to be tough. Some perceived me as what you might call a bitch. But that was only because I spoke the truth without the accompaniment of any sugar additive. I was good in my role at the nursery, and no one could tell me what to do. Except Ozzie when he was quite literally rearranging my guts.

With my back pressed against the fridge and my legs wrapped around his waist. I allowed him to lead. Ozzie's face was buried in my chest. Since he couldn't kiss my lips, he'd always pay close attention to my breast. Suckling and teasing until I begged for release. His tongue circled the surface of my tit before devouring it whole.

"Take it for me, I know you can." Ozzie grabbed hold of my ass so he could control the intensity each time I moved up and down his shaft. He was fucking me so hard the contents in the fridge where jiggling. Clutching the top of the fridge I tried to center myself. My internal wiring was overheated, and it felt like my core was going to explode. Ozzie knew an orgasm was imminent, so he pulled out. When he backed away, I slowly melted onto the floor. "Stay with me sweetheart. You're not getting off that easy."

"You really think you snapped with that don't you?"

Ozzie bent down. His hard dick inches from my face. Did I want to suck it? I did. But I managed to muster restraint. "You are literally dripping all over the kitchen floor. I'd say I've done a whole hell of a lot." His thumb landed on my clit. The pressure from his touch had the desired effect. I ground my hips working my clit against his stationary thumb. The internal battle that raged inside me. I wanted to come but I hated it was him that was making it happen.

"Good, now a little faster." he whispered, staring intently into my eyes. Everything about Ozzie was over the top. The way he talked with that slow southern drawl. His walk, that was almost comical until you realized he was serious. It was more of a peacock strut. And his big as a circus tent personality was present in the way he fucked. It was like he was trying to drain me of all of my resources until there was nothing left.

And like a dumb fuck I handed over every moan, every leg quiver, and every cry of ecstasy. Right now, I was babbling on the floor when an orgasm overtook me. Ozzie's smirk was one of satisfaction. He could no longer have a say on what I did. But he still knew ways to wield authority over me. Pulling my legs open he slid back into my pulsating honey pot.

"Stop looking at me like that." I eeked out.

"Like what?"

"You know." Like a few well-timed dick strokes could mend my broken heart.

He hid his face in the crook of my neck fucking me on the kitchen floor. There wasn't a square foot on the first floor that wasn't laced with a memory of him. I clawed at his arm to let him know I was close and just like everything in our lives we orgasmed in unison. A well-rehearsed routine. Pick up Maple, ignore one other for much of the week, drop off Maple, get to hunching on the travertine tile.

Ozzie pulled out and made his way to the half bath downstairs. When he returned, I was dressed and in full control of my facilities. "We're never doing this again. I mean that on everything I hold dear".

"Okay." He winked.

ACKNOWLEDGMENTS

To the bookish community, readers, reviewers, romance lovers who I grown to love and respect. When I joined social media as an aspiring author in 2020, I didn't know what I was doing. I didn't even have a completed first draft. But I gained friends who eventually also became readers. If you ever sent me a thoughtful DM or shared your love for my books, I want you to know just how important that was to me. It was your words of encouragement that gave me the motivation to keep telling stories and improving my craft. Specifically, I want to thank Natashia Crawford, (@thebookish_wife). Nat, you've always checked in, cheered me on, and reminded me I could do this, even on the hard days.

Heartfelt thanks to Keisha, and Honey Blossom Press for taking this leap with me and giving Edison, Fancy, and my small-town romance series a home.

To my editor, Courtney Driver at Whoproofedit. Thank you for providing editing services on several of my books including the original release of Love You a Litte Bit. As always, I appreciate working with you and know my books are in good hands under your watchful red pen.

To my husband, who never, for one moment, doubted me when out of the blue I told you I was going to write a book. You supported me and kept my spirit steady through every chapter of this journey.

To my son, I have many book babies but you are the most important character in my life. It has been an honor raising you and I'm so proud of the independent and thoughtful man you've become.

Finally, to my mother, Beverly and my sister Twana, I am so lucky to have your love, guidance, and support.

ALSO BY KASHA THOMPSON

Working Through It
Figure of Speech
Holding Back the Years
Last Night a DJ Saved My Life
Sight Unseen
Jamaal the IT Guy
Christmas with Kris Kringle

The Las Vegas Ramblers Series
Defensive Stance
Jump Ball

www.ingramcontent.com/pod-product-compliance
Lightning Source LLC
Chambersburg PA
CBHW021133310726

48971CB00002B/300